in the

context

of

Love

in the context of Love

by

Linda K. Sienkiewicz

Buddhapuss Ink LLC • Edison NJ

Published in the United States by Buddhapuss Ink, LLC, Edison, New Jersey.

Cover Photo by Dominik Martin
Author Photo by Danielle Sienkiewicz
Cover and Book Layout/Design by The Book Team
Editor, MaryChris Bradley
Copyeditor, Andrea H. Curley
Library of Congress Control Number: 2015932884
ISBN 978-1-941523-04-9 (Paperback Original)
First Edition September 2015

PUBLISHER'S NOTE
This is a work of fiction. Names, characters, places, and incidents are either the product of the author's imagination or are used fictitiously and any resemblance to an actual person, living or dead, business establishments, events, or locales is entirely coincidental.

The publisher has no control over, and does not assume any responsibility for authors, the authors' websites, or for third-party websites or their content.

To contact the author or learn more about her work, go to:
http://lindaksienkiewicz.com.

Buddhapuss Ink LLC and our logos are trademarks of Buddhapuss Ink LLC. Learn more about our books at: www.buddhapussink.com.

To my loving family

Chapter One

I had convinced myself I could stomach seeing Gavin since social services told me it was in the children's best interest to see their father. Despite his trespasses, I knew they missed him. They needed to see for themselves where he was and that he was in one piece, but I certainly didn't need or want any such assurances. The closer we got to the Madison Correctional Center, the sicker I felt. I knew it wasn't going to be a picnic, but I'm not sure I can convey how awful it was.

Michelle, age ten, remained glued to my side, chewing her lip. Jude fidgeted like a typical eight-year-old. I'd brought games and books for them to share with Gavin, which, as it turned out, we had to leave in the car. They shuffled nervously into the visiting room, eyeballing the prisoners. Many of them looked like any man you might see working behind the counter at the post office, stocking soup cans at the supermarket, or delivering a package to your front door. Some flinched oddly. Others had bristled jaws or tattoos on their necks. I studied their hands, wondering if they'd forced a woman to her knees, pulled a trigger, or simply written a batch of bad checks.

Gavin's face looked etched with lines, and his clothes hung on his wire-hanger frame. The four of us sat at a metal table, falling into the same seating arrangement we used to take at the dinner table. He seemed unable to look us in the eyes. I was glad he'd ditched his typical smugness. There was no way he could clown his way out of this one—the damage he'd caused was as clear and tangible as the waxed floor and steel bars. In a weaker moment I might have pitied him, but mostly my heart ached for our kids. I was fuming that we had to be here at all.

"Hey. Thanks for coming," he said quietly, sitting rigidly, shoulders clenched, kneading his hands in his lap.

I glared at him for a few seconds, then smiled. "Gee. Thanks for having us."

He exhaled hard, as if it were my job to make this easier for him. He scuffed his feet around under the table, then said, "So, yeah, this is where I'll be holed up for a while, but I'm okay. It's not so bad. I get to watch TV and play cards and work out. The food is lousy, but I can't complain."

I lifted my chin and scowled at him. Why couldn't he say he was sorry? Was he? Did he even wonder what I'd told the kids about where he was, and why?

The two of us hadn't spoken to each other since our blow-up in the kitchen, and that was before his arrest and sentencing. I was angry at myself for sugar-coating things when I should have been blunt with the children.

Jude looked up, a mix of nervousness and innocent concern on his face as he picked at the dried blood from a scab on his elbow. "Dad?"

"What, big buddy? Go on. Ask me anything."

He wanted to know if they slid Gavin's meals under the bars in his cell, if his bathroom had a door, if he slept with a pillow and blanket and wore leg chains when he went outside. Michelle asked if he had a roommate and his own television. I imagine they had expected to see him wearing a black-and-white striped uniform, like in old movies, and his state-issued blue pants and shirt disappointed them; but at least they found something to talk about.

Gavin loosened up and soon had them laughing. I was amazed that he found something to joke about. Was it a gift, the way he always made the best of things, or was he in denial?

"Yeah, so don't worry about me. Just remember, I'm still

your father," he said, his eyes catching mine when visiting time was over. He needn't have worried we would forget. "You guys be good, you hear? Love you both." It wasn't unexpected that his love no longer included me, but hearing it smarted.

Rules stipulated that inmates couldn't hug or touch visitors. Michelle started to cry. The guard said he couldn't give us extra time. Red-eyed, Gavin turned his head and coughed into his fist. Michelle pushed my hands away when I tried to comfort her on the walk out.

Once outside, she hollered at Jude that he had asked dopey questions. He punched her in the back and told her to "get real." He asked me in his high-pitched, boy voice, "Can we put Dad inside a big box and sneak him out next time we visit?"

I shut my eyes and took a deep breath, having no idea what was going to happen to us. This was something I couldn't fix.

"Sorry, kiddo. It doesn't work that way."

"You're such a dope, Jude," Michelle said. She looked up at me. "It's your fault, you know."

I stopped walking and grabbed her arm. "Sweetie, what are you talking about?"

Lips tight, she just shrugged. I made her look at me while I explained that her father was the one who broke the law, and he did that all on his own. "Even Daddy doesn't blame anyone but himself. Do you understand?"

Michelle was too young for her brows to be pinched together the way they were, so much like mine. "Do we have to come here again? It sucks. I hate it."

"No. Not if you don't want to. What about you, Jude?"

He was standing off by himself, scratching his elbow. "I don't know. Won't he be mad if we don't visit?"

"Don't worry about him being mad. You know what? You should be mad at him."

I tried not to rage in despair as I drove home. Michelle's hands were clenched in her lap, her forehead pressed against the glass of the front passenger door. She grunted and pulled away when I reached across the seat to touch her. Jude, in the backseat, sliced his hands through the air while making terrible noises, like screaming jet fighters, machine guns, and scudding bombs. I'd prepared a list of questions to help them process the visit, such as What did you like? What didn't you like? What made you feel better? But now it sounded like psychobabble. The entire trip had been hell.

For whatever reason, I thought of you again, and how different my life might have been had we still been together. I brought up my right hand, as if fixing my hair so Michelle wouldn't see my angry tears. Where were you? Why was everything so hard? I wanted to scream. Honestly, I hated you almost as much as I hated Gavin at that moment. You had become the scapegoat for everything that had gone wrong in the last fifteen years, even though I was certain I still loved you.

Filing for divorce when your spouse is in prison is no different from when he's not, and since Gavin didn't contest, there were no lawyers or lengthy mediations. I got the house and everything in it, the station wagon, our savings, the credit card debt I hadn't known about, and a spongy backyard full of moles. His chauffeuring business was dissolved. I sold his wrecked '86 Cadillac Seville for parts.

Despite everything, I missed him. It made no sense—after all, he had been gone more than he was at home. It was only his likeness that had slithered like a cold snake in and out of our bed for such a long time. I cried like a baby in the middle of the night while craving a fifth of Chivas Regal. I developed an irrational fear of sharp things. The idea that my flesh could be torn open by broken window glass, a tin can, or the edge of an innocuous piece of paper sent me into shivers. Anything could catch me unaware, cut and bleed me. Nights were shadowy and deep with no stars, and I felt disoriented and exhausted in the morning as if I'd been pushing my way through drifts of snow to get to the other side of something. The same old fears that began in high school, after you disappeared as cleanly as if you'd been tied to an engine block and dumped in Lake Erie, came back. Sheathed in blue ice, I had no more substance than the frosted air that eked from my lungs.

Late at night, when the children were in bed, I would turn to your old tattered notebook, tucked safely in a box in the back of my closet. Reading your poems was one of the few things that gave me solace:

> You cannot pass from child to adult
> without falling into holes of doubt,
> broken wheels of trust
> and traps of betrayal.

In what ways had you been betrayed? What holes of doubt did you have? I was certain you and I felt the same sadnesses, even though our childhoods were vastly different. This thought made me feel close to you, as if, even in your absence you understood all I'd been through: my horrible secret, my mother's pain, my family's betrayal, my husband's disloyalty, and my own unfaithfulness.

◀▲▶

CHAPTER TWO

How quickly you sidestepped when I backed my chair into you in the high school cafeteria, how your chop suey, white rice, chocolate cake, and flatware slid across your lunch tray. Do you remember? It was the eighth of November 1974. You shook the shaggy dark hair from your eyes and frowned at me as I apologized for not having eyes in the back of my head, but I recall a spark of interest as you eyed my rolled-up skirt and bare thighs. At least, you gave me a brief smile and told me it was okay.

After you had walked away, Lizzy howled. "Smooth move, Ex-Lax. That's Joe Vadas, you know."

Oh, I knew who you were. Jozsef Vadas, Hungarian heart-throb, the Gypsy King, whether your immigrant parents were actual Gypsies or not. The kind of thick lashes that girls wished Mother Nature had bestowed on them framed your black-coffee eyes, your lips were lush, and your skin was a lucent olive.

"Oh, Mamma, he's a stone fox," Becca said, and noisily sucked milk up her straw.

"My sister graduated with his brother Fabian. He tried to get in the pants of every girl in their class," Paige said.

"His brother Adam was a horn dog, too," Becca said, slurping again, sounding like a human wet vac, to which Lizzy said, "Do you have to do that? There can't possibly be one more drop of milk in that carton."

"You guys know what happened to Adam, don't you?" Paige

asked. We were such insufferable gossips.

"He knocked up Bobbi Koski."

"Shotgun wedding."

"Didn't she drop out?"

"My mother swore she'd strangle me with her bare hands if I were stupid enough to let something like that happen to me."

I didn't want to entertain thoughts of what Mom would do if I were to get pregnant. "How many brothers are there?" I asked as my finger traced the words *suck me* someone had gouged into the laminated tabletop.

"At least five. He's the youngest," Becca said. They tried to name all your brothers, and agreed the oldest was János, and then Larry or Lance or something that began with an *L*, Fabian, Adam, and you. Becca insisted there was an older sister, but no one knew for sure. As an only child, I couldn't imagine a family with six children. The freshmen chatter at the other end of the cafeteria rose like a wave. Someone stood and lobbed French fries across the tables.

"Don't look now, but he's looking at you," Paige said to me. My heart was thumping wildly, though I pretended otherwise as I concentrated hard on not looking. I prayed you didn't notice.

"He's fast. Too fast for you," Lizzy said.

"Is not." What did fast mean, anyway? Trying everything before you're too old to enjoy it? I really didn't see anything wrong with that.

A few days after I'd launched myself into your path, I was craning my neck to watch you weave through the maze of lunch tables, carrying a tray with three hamburgers. You glanced in my direction, so I turned away to stare through the long windows at the snow-covered field and bare trees until the washed-out landscape turned into a sea of white—snow and sky blended as one—as blank and numb as my existence.

I feared my longing could be read like a billboard.

By my friends' standards, I was "cute," but cursed with mouse-brown hair that frizzed when I wanted it to lay smooth. I also hated being 4 feet 11 inches. Mom once told me I was a mesomorphic, something that sounded more fitting for a rock formation than a girl. For so long I'd prayed that someone like you would pluck me from the mass of tall, slender, silken-haired princesses; that somehow, maybe, through osmosis, or a fortune in your cookie that said surprises come in small packages, you'd intuit how smart I was, how much love I had to give, what a blast I could be…when I was out from under Mom's watchful eyes. Joe Vadas, Joe Vadas, Joe Vadas—I repeated your name in my head like a mantra.

Paige poked me. "Are you even listening to me? What's with you?" She followed the direction of my starstruck gaze, then smirked. "Don't be a turkey. You got to do something about this. It's not healthy. Want me to talk to him for you?"

I told her I'd soak myself in kerosene and ask her for a light before I'd ask her to play matchmaker. Lizzy, as subtle as polka dots and plaid, asked loudly, "What? Vadas? She's still gaga over Vadas?"

Did you hear your name? I was staring right at you when you looked our way. Actually, all of us were staring, but I don't think you noticed the others. You seemed to zoom in on me with one brow raised in surprise or curiosity. Were you sizing me up? Mentally undressing me? Waiting for me to foam at the mouth? You smiled, and I felt trippy.

Paige told me to quit drooling and make a move, "Unless you want 'Here Lies Miss Prude, Dead from What She Never Did' written on your tombstone."

"In your face," I told her. The bell rang, and we streamed from the lunchroom into the halls. My Spanish class was in the other direction, so I told Paige I'd catch her later and headed toward the open lobby, where the sun warmed the south hall. In the winter when the sun was low, the glare would be so bright we had to shade our eyes. I thought the light was playing tricks, but there you were, leaning against the wall by the drinking fountain, feet crossed at the ankles, hands in your pockets, watching me pass. I gave you a modest smile. You smiled back and lifted your chin in a single hello-nod before walking down the opposite hall, boots clopping. The coolest boys wore boots, never tie shoes.

The rest of my day was charged with electricity. Sex buzzed in the air, it was chalked on the blackboards, it danced seductively between the lines in textbooks and tumbled from the lips of teachers and friends. A hundred times over I recounted those exquisite seconds when you nodded at me, and each time, the significance of your sly smile magnified, making my heart pirouette. I was certain my life was going to change.

It did change, but in ways no one could have predicted. By spring you would be gone, and the way I viewed myself and the world around me would be permanently altered, clearing the path for a man like Gavin.

That's the part of the story you don't know.

◄▲►

CHAPTER THREE

After school, Paige and I carefully picked our way along the edge of the road because sections of the sidewalks were slick with ice. Clouds had disturbed the November sky, and the wind reddened our cheeks and noses. I was detailing for her, again, exactly how you had looked at me in the hallway that afternoon when a car—a sleek arrow, long, low, and turquoise blue like a parakeet's chest—rumbled up alongside us. You swung open the passenger door, and your deeply melodious voice vibrated hot inside me when you said those four fateful words: "Hi. Want a lift?"

"You go. I'll walk. My house is just up the block," Paige said to me, grinning like a conspirator, her eyes begging me to call her later and tell everything.

Your car looked like a swimming pool on wheels, with the same blue in the interior. I settled in with my sociology book and binder between us on the seat. I hoped you didn't notice that I blushed when I saw the woman's garter dangling from your rearview mirror. In my eyes, it made you seem worldly and mature.

"So…you're Angelica Lowsley, the pretty girl who tried to make me dump my lunch," you said. Not to downplay the fact that you'd called me pretty, I was pleased you weren't one of the many classmates who called me Angelica *Lousy*, which, in my mind, confirmed your intelligence. You propped your bent arm on the back of the seat so your hand dangled over my books and steered with your left, looking laid-back and cool. I was at a complete loss because, in another minute, we'd be at my house, and my short life in your beautiful, floating car would be over.

"My house…there," I said, and pointed, and watched, open-mouthed, as you sailed on past.

"You mean here?" You slowed in front of a brick bungalow with red awnings. "Or there?"

"No, back there!" I was baffled. You turned onto Greenwood and nodded at a blue clapboard house with a snow-capped deer in the yard, asking, "Here? Or here?" Then you admitted you knew where I lived, but you wanted to take the long way there. So I asked, "What if I don't want to go that way?"

You took your foot off the gas to look at me. A Coke bottle rolled out from under the seat and hit my foot. "Then I'll take you home, if that's what you want."

I kicked the bottle back, glad I had a choice. "The long way is fine." Too fine, until I remembered the standing rule: I was to come straight home from school unless I informed Mom, whose need to know where I was every single second of my life was unbearable. What could I do? Ask you to pull over at the next phone booth so I could call my mother? No, I was not going to spoil this, even if I had to pay for it.

You turned south on Brecksville Road; the car rumbled as if it wanted to go faster. In a strange, duck-like voice, you began a tour guide spiel I would never forget. "To your left, the building with the neon sign shaped like Italy is Manny's Pizzeria. There's Lenny's Auto Shop. Coming up, the offices of Doctors Sinister, Lobotomy, and Yankyerteeth. Houses. More houses…obviously, a residential zone. The house that looks like a dumpster is where Louie Moorhead lives with his dumbass sister. Oh, I didn't mean to say that. Sorry." You coughed into your fist. "She has a nice smile. Ahead, the Spanish Tavern. They serve surf and turf. All I can afford is burp and barf. Maybe I'll save some bucks instead of blowing it all on my wheels and take you there sometime."

I was entranced. Still talking, you took Chippewa Creek

Drive into the Brecksville Metropark. Towering red and white oaks canopied the parkway, although, on that day, they were nude silhouettes against a sinus-gray sky. Heavy snow was in the forecast. You parked at the Oak Grove picnic area and turned to face me as if there were no destination other than getting to know me. You brought up your knee to rest near my books, and I noticed the start of a frayed hole in your jeans. I thought about offering to patch it for you if it wore through. The possibility of your bare skin showing through was enough to make my breath quicken, to hold your jeans in my hands was to go to heaven.

The backseat of your car was littered with shirts, shoes, cassette tapes, a blanket, and library books. I didn't know any boys who willingly read library books, so I asked if you were going to college. I was applying to five. I had big plans, back then.

"No. Even if I had the bread, my old man doesn't think I have the smarts. Like he's got any," you said. The muscles in your face tightened as your raked your hand through your raven hair as if to distract me, and you laughed the laugh of someone who pretended not to care.

"Come on, it can't be that bad," I said, and you gave me such a wild look.

You said you didn't care about grades or school. "I just want my diploma to make my mother happy. She deserves that much."

I wondered if she was unhappy. "What are you going to do then?"

"I think I'll drive this rust bucket all the way to California and sleep on rooftops in Venice and write songs, like Jim Morrison." It sounded romantic. I imagined myself as your muse. The heater fan clanked like a rodent running on a wheel, and you leaned forward to fiddle with the lever. "Damn thing. Are you warm enough?" You seemed so gallant.

"Yeah. I'm good. Is this your car?"

You nodded and stretched your hand toward me across the back of the seat, making the nape of my neck tingle, the fine hairs lifting with electricity. "Yep. 1966 Chevy Bel Air."

"Then you must have a job?"

"Been working at Hillside Market since I was fifteen." You sighed so dramatically. "Stocking shelves, packing bags, smashing little old ladies' loaves of bread, swabbing floors, killing rats. You wouldn't believe how many rats we find in the storeroom. Fun stuff. I love my job." I was horrified to think of rats roaming in the store where Mom bought our groceries.

I was embarrassed to admit the only work I'd ever done outside of my home was to babysit. We talked about our families, your many siblings, my lack of. The snow-covered pavilion in front of us was ice covered, and the wind blew powdery snow in upward spirals that looked like rising ghosts.

You stroked the orange rabbit-foot on your key chain. I imagined your fingers stroking mine. Then I noticed the dashboard clock—we'd been talking for more than an hour. Mom would be frantic. Your gaze never left me, and now that I'd inserted her into the picture, my stomach tensed. I thought about your fast reputation, your brothers trying to get into the pants of girls and impregnating them. The sky had darkened to a threat. Your eyes glowed like 150 watt bulbs.

That's why I told you I should get home. "I swear, my mother thinks someone's going to kidnap me." My tinny-sounding laugh was an embarrassing cover, but you said you didn't blame her. We fell silent as you drove me home, and I saw everything coming to an end. I was going to return to the same sparkless existence I'd known before, as if this had never happened, never mind that I was in deep trouble. I stared at your hand, your angular knuckles and the length of your fingers, wrapped around the steering wheel. I replayed our conversation, looked for clues that told me you'd enjoyed talking to me, recounted your smiles, nods, and laughs.

You had no idea what a wreck I was.

My heart leaped when you asked me out to see *Butch Cassidy and the Sundance Kid* on Saturday. That was the once-monthly Dollar Night, aka cheap date night, but I didn't mind being a cheap date. I quickly said yes, afraid you might change your mind if I dithered around. I didn't know how I was going to manage to get out of the house.

Mom was standing at the window of the door, holding the curtain aside so she could peer out. She must have heard the rumble of your car. Her face morphed from panicked worry to relief to outrage in the few seconds it took me to walk to the door. If only you could have seen her.

She opened the door and yanked me into the breezeway. "Angelica Marie! Where were you? Do you know what time it is?" Her round face was flushed and damp, and wisps of loose hair from her bun were curlicues around her temples and neck. The house was filled with yellow light and the thick scent of beef stew with allspice, but it didn't mask the tension radiating from her body. My seventy-eight-year-old grandmother was bent like a comma at the kitchen table, toiling over a crossword puzzle. Two pairs of eyeglasses, prescription lenses and bifocals, perched on her nose.

I steamrolled over Mom with a hastily made excuse, something I'd learned to excel in. If I told her that a boy I barely knew had picked me up off the street and taken me for a ride, she might never have recovered from the shock. I reasoned occasional lying was justified. "I am so sorry. I was at the library working on a group presentation on American Indians in the Civil War. I had to go. It was the last day we could get together before it's due. The work took longer than I expected. I couldn't call because the pay phone was broken."

"There's more than one phone in that library." She checked the burner on the stove before searching through the bottom cupboard for something, her polyester-clad rear swaying as she bent from the waist.

"But I had to help my group, not run around looking for a phone. Anyway, I figured the sooner we got the work done, the sooner I'd be home."

She straightened up, holding a jar of pickled beets in her hand. "I was sick with worry. I called Paige's house, and there was no answer. I was about to ring your father." Her voice sounded thick and tangled as if dragging something heavy through the dirt, a duffel bag of bad dreams. "You can't imagine the things that go through a mother's mind. Remember that young woman whose body was found in the city park last year? Strangled and…and no clothes from the waist down?" She couldn't even say the word *naked*.

"Well, I'm home now, so you can relax. Smells good," I said, nodding my chin toward the stove. Her glare told me she saw through that ruse. "I'm sorry. It won't happen again."

"It better not. And yes, I'll relax now that you're home… until the next time." She rapped the jar of beets on the edge of the counter before trying to twist off the lid. Her plump elbows jutted to the sides as she wrestled with it. I let out a slow breath of relief that she hadn't asked me to show evidence of my fictional history project. "This lid is impossible. Who brought you home?"

I decided to be honest. I reasoned that, on our first date, you would come to the house and meet my parents, the way it happened in the house of every other teenage girl I knew. Positive thinking, I thought I could will it to happen. I should have snapped a clothespin on my tongue every time I thought such things. "One of the boys has a car. He did most of the research, too. He's real smart and—"

"What's a seven letter word for *messenger*? Starts with *C*," Grandma said.

"And he asked me to the movies on Saturday. Everyone on

the school project is going to meet up. Can I go? I'll be home by eleven."

"*Courier*," Mom said to Grandma. Jaw set, tendons in her neck taut, she banged the beet jar on the counter so hard I thought the glass would break and then twisted the lid with a grunt. It opened with a startling pop. "Goodness."

Glad she was distracted, I kept talking. "So I told him I could. The whole group will be going. You can meet him when he picks me up. I think you'll like him." I started to edge my way out toward the hallway. Getting permission might be easier than I'd thought.

"Wait. Who's picking you up for what?"

"Joe Vadas. I told you I'm going to the movies with him on Saturday. You said yes."

Things really started cooking. Mom's brows scrunched together. "Vadas? You said *Vadas?* Good Lord, Angelica. Everyone in Cuyahoga County knows that family. They live in the sticks. His father is a drunk. The man's got at least a dozen sons, and probably another litter no one knows about. Hungarian thugs, they are."

I was shocked. "Where did you hear that? Val's Beauty Salon?" I envisioned a row of nodding women, their heads under silver hair dryers, yakking loudly enough to be heard over the hum.

Her voice rose; her face reddened. "His father practically lives at Rendell's Tavern. The police get calls from there all the time."

Grandma took the rubber-tipped bobby pin she'd been sucking on from her mouth. "Crazy DP Hunkies, they dance like *dummköpfe* to that violin music. It turns them wild." She moved the pin like a bowstring across a miniature instrument, making the white flesh of her upper arm flap. I knew *DP* meant "displaced person," an immigrant who came to America as a political refugee; but, from the way Grandma used it, you'd think it meant "dumb person."

I reminded her that Grandpa was a shoe slapper. Grandma's great-grandfather, Otto Grundhoffer, came to America from the Rhineland and settled in a German neighborhood in Cleveland to open a tailor shop. One of Otto's sons shortened his name to Grund, which caused a rift among the old Grundhoffers that resulted in us having relatives we've never met. Grund and his wife had three girls: Harriet, Ruth, and Gertrude. Gertrude was my cantankerous grandmother. The *Schuhplattler*, or shoe slapper, was Frederick Bauer, a third generation German American who apparently charmed Grandma at a beer festival. If you've never seen *Schuhplattlers* perform, it's quite a sight. Imagine a troop of men gussied up in shorts and suspenders, knee socks and caps, smacking their knees, thighs, and soles as if battling an infestation of red ants. I doubt that German shoe slappers had more finesse or intelligence than Hungarian dancers.

Grandma ignored my comment. "They should stay down there by St. Emeric's on the west side, not come where they don't belong. They bought a church on Thirty-Second from the Germans in 1908 and turned it into the Hungarian Reformed." She fiddled with the bobby pin.

"So?"

Her dowager's hump rose majestically as she sat straighter in the chair. "Never you mind. The world would get along better if everyone stuck to their own kind." The pin sprung from her fingers and sailed past Mom's ear.

"You're not going anywhere with a *Vadas*," Mom spit. Gripping the wooden spoon, she stirred the stew pot with determination as if to make me feel her wrath inside, long after I ate. "His father is a no-account good-for-nothing whose boys leave bastard babies all over town." Mom threw a handful of salt into the pot as if to say *So there*.

Grandma lifted her knotted finger. "Hungarians pierce their

daughters' ears when they're still babies. Newborns! With ear-rings."

I gaped. "What does that mean?"

"It means they'll be popping out babies by the time they're thirteen."

"He's not the kind of boy I want you associating with," Mom said. There you have it.

I snatched my books from the table and gripped them protectively. I put up with her crazy rules because I loved her, and I felt loved, but I wasn't going to pass up a chance to find the kind of love that made my insides flip like a Ferris wheel. "The son of a no-account good-for-nothing asked me to the movies on Saturday and I'm going." I hurried out of the kitchen, not waiting to hear her reply. You would have been proud.

"That's not happening, Angelica. Angelica Marie! You hear me?" she called, but the sound of her voice was deflected, like a sparrow hitting a window, by my back.

Dad wasn't a philosophical man who dispensed polished gems of wisdom for me to tuck away for later use, but he let me know when I needed to carry an umbrella, and his steady aim at the Home Day Fair ball toss had won me teddy bears and floppy-eared dogs, never mind that they leaked sawdust. To his credit, he was patient with my mother's octopus imagi-nation. Once in a while he would attempt to talk some sense into her so I didn't have to stretch the truth to get out of the house on my own, but mostly he told me, "Well, you best do what your mother says."

To date you, I figured my best bet would be to pit my parents against each other.

Several inches of Lake Effect snow had fallen overnight. I love the mean arctic wind that picks up moisture from Lake Erie and dumps it on Cleveland and its suburbs. Dad and I flung shovelfuls of snow to the side of the driveway, making diamond chips sparkle in the sun, as I argued my case. "I just want to go to the movies. Mom hasn't even met him, and already she's painted him as a thug. What's the worst that can happen? He's not the Zodiac Killer."

The only sound was the scrape of metal on cement and the swoosh of talcum-light snow flying through the air. It was so cold, the inside of my nose pinched when I breathed. He finally stopped to rest his hands on the shovel and said, "You know how she gets."

"Yeah, I know how she gets. He's coming to pick me up tomorrow. What am I supposed to do? Tell him at the door my mother says no? If that gets out, the whole school will be laughing at me. Do you know what that will be like?"

"I'm sure that won't happen."

"It will. Honestly, Dad, this isn't one of those 'everyone else is jumping off the bridge, so why can't I' things I'm asking for. I'm a senior. I just want to go a date. If she had her way, she'd keep me locked in my room until I turned twenty-one. You can't tell me that's right."

"It's her nerves. She can't help it."

"No, she gets herself worked up. Why punish me by making me friendless? Dad, you have to help me. Please. She's ruining everything."

"All right. All right. I'll see what I can do," he said, squinting in the flashbulb glare of sun and snow. "Maybe we can work out some concession that will make her feel comfortable."

I was horrified. "You and Mom cannot come to the same show!"

"That's not what I meant." He laughed, then cleared his throat. His eyes bounced around as if searching for uncomplicated, glossing words. "But if I let you go, you know what we expect of you. No drive-in movie. No parking. No hanging out. Make sure this boy understands it's hands off, right from the start. Catch my drift?" He lifted his shovel and tossed a poof of snow toward me.

I assured him that I did.

It was the start of what eventually tore my parents apart.

◄▲►

CHAPTER FOUR

Saturday morning Mom bustled with frenetic energy in the kitchen, blurting random warnings. "You better keep your wits about you. Otherwise you'll be melting in his lap, you with your fancy notions about romance. Love isn't like it is in the movies. There are no ringing bells or violins when you kiss. And if you think a kiss means you're special, you got another thing coming." She put a box of cornflakes away in the refrigerator.

"You can count on me when it comes to wits." I leaned on the counter to watch the coils in the buzzing toaster glow as I waited for my bread to pop up. I was to come home immediately after the movie and show her the ticket stub to prove that's where I'd been. If I didn't, I would never see daylight again.

I still have that ticket stub.

Grandma got up from the table, set her empty cereal bowl in the sink, and then took the false teeth from her mouth to rinse them under the faucet. "When your grandfather kissed me, I didn't hear bells ringing. I didn't feel love either." She popped the bridge back into her mouth. It clacked into place. "I felt his hands pawing me. He was drunk, so I popped him in the nose. That's when he fell in love with me. Then he threw up."

I'd often wondered how my grandparents' courtship went, after the shoe slapping.

"You'll be alone in a car with him. I don't know why I agreed to this. Why can't you go on a double date?" Mom leaned against the counter and began to pinch the loose skin on her throat. This was not a good sign. "That's what you should do. Make it a double date."

"How am I supposed to do that now?" Annoyed, I wished she had a job or a hobby other than knitting to occupy her agitated mind. "You worry too much. Just because his brother got a girl in trouble doesn't mean he's the same way." Bringing that up was a mistake.

Mom limply fanned herself with a pot holder. "Double date or no date. Call Paige and Becca. They like the movies."

"I can't just invite my girlfriends along with us. I'll be fine."

Dad overheard us from the living room and said, "Do you want me to follow them? Is that what you want? We already told her she could go. You can't change the rules now." Times like this, I adored him.

"Oh, you'd let her swim in shark-infested waters if she wanted to." Mom pressed her fingertips to her forehead with a huge, shaky sigh. "Since you're so determined, you go ahead. You'll see what happens. When he makes you cry, don't come running to me. Run to your father. Let him handle it." Then she bustled out and up the stairs, presumably to lie down with a cool rag on her forehead.

Would it help you understand if I explained what my life was like before we met?

At the age of twelve, hormones exploded from my pituitary glands like a pipe bomb. My first period started at school. The streak of blood panicked me, but then I felt full of pride and somehow wise. I wondered if anyone could tell if I carried an odor or walked differently. I wanted others to know and I didn't.

I grew breasts overnight. I wasn't sure how to carry those new accessories, two tender burdens to protect from boys' stares and elbows in the hallways. Adolescent girls are envious of anything they don't have, and rumors that I stuffed my bra with tissues or I was "asking for it" floated around the middle school. It was always about sex. Every girl was judged by her walk, her talk, the way she chewed her gum, the color of her lipstick, the length of her skirt, how dirty or clean her hair was, the way she sat—trying to keep it straight was exhausting. A girl could end up with a bad reputation for no other reason than her body developed faster than the others.

I don't recall how my friends and I got our clammy hands on *The Sensuous Woman,* a paperback so explicit that the author didn't disclose her real name, but the text was far more enlightening than the dime-store romances we paged through for the sex scenes ("Ashton crushed Millicent's white bosom to his bare chest in a brutal embrace.") We passed it around more than a few times. I stayed up late studying "how to please your man," although some maneuvers, such as the Hoover, made me squeamish. Back then the thought of putting a boy's dick in my mouth was nasty enough, much less sucking it. Understanding how a woman faked an orgasm wasn't clear either. If I didn't know what it was like, how could I fake one? And why would I?

By the time I was thirteen, men were turning their heads to watch me pass. I'll never forget the day Mom and I were walking to the library when a group of boys whistled and hooted at me as they drove past. You'd have thought they were firing a shotgun out the window of their car by the way she jumped. She gripped me by the elbow and hurried me along. "Don't walk that way," she said, uncharacteristic sternness in her voice as if I had done something wrong.

Mom changed from nurturing to neurotic. Suddenly, my shorts were too short, my shirts were too snug, the night was too dark, and men were too hungry. She insisted I wear anklets or knee socks because fishnet stockings were obscene. Shoes with any kind of a heel were out of the question, despite my lack of height. She had fits over the tight hip-huggers and miniskirts I begged her to buy. She didn't like me walking anywhere on my own, not even three blocks to the corner store to get an ice cream. A friend, and that meant female, had to accompany me, and Mom actually had to see that friend—it wasn't enough to say I was meeting her.

She lectured me. "Don't ever go anywhere or do anything with a boy you don't know. Do you understand me? Only stupid girls go on dates with boys who haven't been properly introduced. Then they're never seen or heard from again. Who knows what ditches or fields their bodies are dumped in."

Instead of gaining freedom as I moved into my teens, I was losing it. She insisted that either she or Dad drive my friends and me to the movies or shopping. Parties, dances at the community center, sleepovers, and bonfires got an automatic no. Boys? Forget it. Before I left the house I had to recite an itinerary of where I was going, who I would be with, and what time I would be home. She wanted to meet everyone I went anywhere with and insisted on having their phone numbers, too. If I was more than five minutes late, she started making calls. Every minute late earned five in a lecture.

I was bound to be the only girl in Huggs High who couldn't date unless her mother came with her. By the time I backed my chair into you in the cafeteria, I didn't want her shadowing me anymore. I wanted to morph into something sultry and sinful, the complete opposite of my mother. This was the self I wanted to present to you.

I was still a far cry from the hardened woman who met Gavin.

Our dog, Cookie, barked wildly at the sound of your rumbling muffler the moment you pulled into the drive. Your aftershave wafted into the room with its own hello when I opened the door to let you in. I recognized the scent of tropical flowers, woods, and spice but couldn't remember the name of the aftershave. Dad's smile was tight across his horsey yellow teeth. Mom's hello came grudgingly from a closed mouth as she struggled to hold the dog back.

You may not have noticed Mom examine you as if you were a fistful of dirt—your worn jeans and the belt with that heavy brass buckle, your unzipped Army jacket and tattered scarf, your crooked bottom teeth and unshorn hair, and the soft plumps of snow that dropped from your scuffed boots onto the throw rug. As for me, I wasn't sure if I wanted her to like you or loathe you.

She would examine Gavin in much the same way when she met him, except I was long past teenage rebelliousness then and wanted her approval.

Dad asked you about your car, and the teenage boy in him whistled when you said it was a 427. Mom started plucking at her throat, breathing rapidly, undoubtedly calculating the risks in letting me go unsupervised into the unknown with this messy boy and his muscle car. She'd sooner drop me down a mine shaft. At last Dad said, "Well, you kids have a good time. Drive carefully. I hear more snow is on the way. See you at eleven."

Mom was wringing her hands. "Wait. I'd feel more comfortable if, just in case something should happen, I had your parents' phone number."

Dying inside, I implored Dad with my eyes to tell you it wasn't necessary, but without a second thought, you gave her the phone number, and we were finally on our way.

Your car smelled as if it had been doused with aftershave, too. I remembered it was Brut because I'd bought a bottle for Dad one Christmas. He thanked me as if it was just what he'd wanted, but he only used it once. I heard Mom say she didn't like him smelling like a hooker. I bet she hadn't liked the way you smelled either.

There we were in the theater, in the dark, and close enough to touch but sandwiched in a mass of coughing, throat-clearing, nose-picking strangers. I was quivering inside. At that moment Mom was probably pacing in the kitchen or feverishly knitting a scarf while a blunt-edged fear I didn't yet understand punched holes in her bruised heart.

Butch Cassidy and the Sundance Kid transported me into a celluloid vision of the Wild West. The bedroom scene where a man holds a gun on Etta Place, played by Katharine Ross, frightened me. Only his hand and the weapon are visible as he orders her to take off her clothes, piece by piece. Trembling, doe eyes wide, she complies. Then the camera pulls back to reveal the gunman as Sundance, her boyfriend, played by the affable Robert Redford, with that proud meringue of hair. Obviously Etta and Sundance enjoy this game, because she smiles. I squirmed uncomfortably in the theater seat, wondering what it was like to have your boyfriend point a weapon at you and make you strip. I imagined you with a gun trained on me, and found it alarming and thrilling, but didn't understand why.

By the time I met Gavin I understood.

You and I flew out of the theater when the credits started. Huge white flakes were falling madly from a blue-black sky. Tiny specks grew to the size of bombs by the time they hit my lashes, nose, and lips. The dazzling illusion made me dizzy. You stared up, too, and I was sure you thought this moment was as beautiful and perfect as I did. I had the feeling we understood each other so well that we wouldn't ever need to speak.

You opened the car door for me, jogged around, got in, and started the motor, then reached across the mile-long vinyl seat to pull me close. Icy air blasted from the clattering heater. The scent of buttered popcorn, Clearasil, and Brut aftershave flooded my senses when you kissed me. I no longer felt my body inside my coat, my feet inside my shoes, or my hands in their mittens—everything took place right where your lips moved against mine. I closed my eyes and saw myself falling. We parted for a moment and then pressed our lips together again as if now that they'd met, they couldn't bear to be alone.

Warm air finally started to blow from the heater.

As we kissed, the parked cars around us came to life, shook the snow off their backs, and lumbered out on crunching tires. You drove me home with your arm draped around my shoulder. The windshield wipers battled the white onslaught, the beat measured a silence between us that was too precious to disturb. You cut the lights when you pulled into my drive and kissed me again before we kicked our way through the snow to the door.

Your kisses tasted like freedom.

◄▲►

CHAPTER FIVE

Do you know how your parents met? Mine met over a plantar wart.

I spent many nights trying to understand what the attraction between them was. Since they both were cold fish, perhaps they saw through each other's shyness to the possibility of something warmer, but I concluded they married each other because there was no one else.

Dad's only brother, Keith, drowned as an adult in a sudden squall on Lake Erie, along with four other sports fishermen. Then his father, Henry, died in an automobile accident a few years after that. Mom told me Henry had been driving south on Route 21 when a motorboat came unhitched from a north-bound car, flew across the center lane into oncoming traffic, and blasted through his Oldsmobile like a missile. It grazed the ear of Henry's wife, Astrid, but decapitated him. Astrid was crippled with grief and refused to leave the house, fearing danger could come flying at her from any direction at any moment. Dad took care of her until she passed away, which must have put a stranglehold on his social life.

Marta Bauer, my mother, had two brothers. Carl had married, Tim was in the Coast Guard, and Marta was living at home with her parents. After she had graduated high school, she worked as a ticket taker at the Superior Theater in downtown Cleveland. I can only assume it must've been hellish to live under Grandma's thumb, but Mom didn't talk about what her life had been like.

Then the wart. Marta tried everything—vinegar soaks, hot

match tips, and duct tape—to avoid having to see a doctor for the cauliflower-like growth on the bottom of her left heel. Soon the tenacious thing had her hobbling in pain. Someone in the neighborhood recommended a podiatrist named Dr. Lowsley. I imagine Mom's pocket-size body in his oceanic examining chair as he held her naked and tender foot in his hands. It can take months to get a plantar wart under control, plenty of time for them to get to know each other.

But what was the spark when they met? An underlying abhorrence of men seemed imprinted in Mom's brain. I wouldn't have called my parents' union loveless, but other than an occasional peck, I don't remember any kissing or cuddling. There was never any goosing—and no coy giggling behind closed doors unless I'd blocked it out, which is entirely possible. Mom probably closed her eyes and separated herself from her body when they had *relations*, her detached self gliding in a basket along the Sky Lift at Cedar Point, eyes closed while she hovered above, untouched, as pure and white as a bridal veil. Most likely she put up with it until she got pregnant with me and so loathed the act that she couldn't bear to do it again.

An exciting night out for my folks was going to Manner's Big Boy for burgers. Most evenings, Dad read *TIME*, licking his thumb as he flicked pages, or he watched *The Six Million Dollar Man* or *Baretta*. Mom read dime-store mysteries or knitted. Dad might say, "Alice Bloom came in today with nail fungus. Her big toe was the size of a—" Mom would interrupt him, wincing painfully, and say, "Ed! What makes you think I want to hear a thing like that?" He'd rustle his magazine and softly say, "Well, anyway, she said to tell you hello."

She turned into someone who could have starred in a Valium commercial as the before patient when I was in my teens. Dad talked her into seeing a doctor for her "nervous condition," but she was too nervous about the side effects to take any medication. Sometimes I felt I was the one who could have benefited from prescription drugs.

When I was seventeen, I didn't plan to spend my days knitting or battling ring-around-the-collar or vacuuming under couch cushions, where my biggest thrill would be to find a few coins to fill my apron pockets like Mom. I wanted more out of life than a kitchen with no-wax linoleum, avocado-green appliances, and a husband who muscled a lawn mower back and forth across the grass as his sweat darkened the shirt that I'd later wash and hang on a clothesline in the backyard for that fresh-air scent. I had plans for college and a career, and then a husband, someone like you, and children. I didn't want to lose my identity like Mrs. Edgar Lowsley, whose idea of a good time was to meet with her knitting club.

Over the years I'd learned many interesting things when the knitters met at our house. Needles and jaws would clack rowdily as anywhere from four to seven women sat in the living room with baskets of yarn at their feet. They discussed how to cope with early menopause, prevent their husbands from succumbing to a midlife crisis, and keep a cat from littering outside the box. I heard that mixing an expectant woman's urine with Drano was supposedly a good way to determine the baby's sex based on the resulting color, although there was no consensus on what color indicated which sex.

On the afternoon you called me for the first time, I was helping Mom serve snacks to the knitters. I carried a tray of deviled ham and egg salad petit sandwiches to set on the coffee table and overheard Ruth tell Mom, in what she thought was a quiet voice, "She actually thinks cranberry juice will fix it. Don't quote me, but it's caused by shenanigans in the bedroom." Mom looked appalled.

Grandma grabbed my hand as I set a bowl of mint wafers on the table; she gestured toward the other end where she thought they should go, so that's where I put them. When I returned to the table with a plate of cookies, Mom was moving the bowl to where I had put them to start. As soon as she turned her back, Grandma picked it up and set it elsewhere. I was tempted to move it again, just for fun, maybe to another table altogether, but the telephone in the kitchen trilled.

I heard your voice and felt a pang, like a secret wish between my legs, and had to sit down. You said something that sounded like "Tomato baby head," but the magpie chatter was too loud. I asked you to hold on, set down the phone, and slunk through the dining and living rooms to the front of the house, and then ran upstairs to my parents' room to use their extension. I picked up the phone and asked you again to hold. Then I rushed downstairs to hang up the kitchen phone, hoping and praying you'd hang on. Mom's eyes followed me like angry bees as I went back upstairs.

"I'm calling from Skip Kincora's. It's the only place I get any peace," you said. "Skip's old man blew town last year, and his mother lets his band practice in the basement." When I got to know Skip better, it seemed to me that she let him do pretty much whatever he wanted.

I was impressed when you told me you wrote song lyrics and even more impressed when you sang for me, in such a supple growl, "Twenty pills south of the Alabama line, she waits for death to ease her pain…" I pictured you onstage, a microphone in your hand, with the band behind you. I put myself in the front row as the hand-waving girl you penned love songs for.

The sound of your voice pouring over me made me woozier than a stolen beer. You talked about lyrics, the difference between rock and pop, and how disco caused brain damage. You said Skip's band was named Blue Bus, from the Doors' song "The End," and you sang something about doing a rock on the back of a blue bus, whatever that meant.

I was sure you had made up those lines. "I never heard such a song."

"It doesn't get played on the radio because it's obscene. Morrison based the lyrics on *Oedipus Rex*. I doubt if he wanted to fuck his mother, though. My theory is he just wanted to kill his old man." You paused before adding, "I can relate."

I sat up, startled as if you'd thrown a glass of cold water at me, and asked, "You want to kill your father?" I don't think you ever answered me. You cleared your throat and said you could loan me the album, but I didn't need Mom overhearing such a song.

"So, what are you doing today?" you asked.

"My mother is torturing me. Can girls have an Oedipal complex?"

I was glad you laughed at my joke.

"Beats me. I only took one semester of psych, and McAllister skipped over Freud. I think he was embarrassed by the whole penis envy thing, you know, and considering he's got no balls…" You guffawed. I thought you were the funniest, smartest boy I'd ever talked to. "What method of torture does your mother employ? Bamboo shoots under your fingernails? Palmolive in your eyes?"

"She invited a pack of housewives waving knitting needles like swords into the house."

My heart tap-danced to know you'd considered stopping by to visit me or, better yet, that you wanted to rescue me from my torturous afternoon, like a knight in a shining Chevy. The smile in your voice made me feel warm and liquidy. I considered grabbing my coat and running out the door, but Mom called me. I said, "Maybe later," although I knew it wasn't likely to happen. After we had hung up, I rolled onto my stomach, swathed in Joe-ness, your voice like a soft, sleepy pillow for my head, your phone number tucked in my pocket like a candy heart.

I dutifully fetched the coats for the knitters as they were leaving. Everyone was clucking and smiling, and being that I'd just entered the gates of love, I thought this happiness had everything to do with me. After the last of them had trickled out the door, I helped clean up the plates, cups, and leftovers. I was so happy I might have been humming.

"Thank you for helping, sweetie," Mom said to me. She stopped as if a fuse tripped inside her brain and swung her head around to face me, her eyes accusatory. "Shame on you. You acted like a boy-crazy teenager." The sound of her voice grated my brain.

"What are you talking about?" I pretended not to understand.

"That phone call. I've never seen you run through the house like that. You should have told him you were too busy to talk." She turned the faucet on hot, squirted soap into the sink, and let it fill. "That's what you should have done. You embarrassed me, tromping up and down the stairs."

I had no idea how she knew it was you who'd called, and it spooked me. She was so good at deflating my balloon. I swore I'd never do that to my own daughter. Of course, I did just that when my Michelle proclaimed, at age fourteen, that she'd found the love of her life. "Like anyone cares. They were busy gossiping. Ruby said Mr. Pasik is going senile, and Dottie said Mr. Schakowsky had an affair with his secretary. That's so disgusting." I hoped to shock her into thinking about something other than you.

"I don't like that Vadas boy calling here." She tugged her yellow rubber gloves on with a snap.

"His name is Joe. He asked if he could come over to see me. I told him no because I was helping you. Now that everyone is gone, I'll call him back and tell him it's okay. Okay?"

She froze with the dishrag in her hand and then plunged her gloved hands back into the sudsy water. "No. You certainly cannot call him. That would be chasing him. For crying out loud, slow down. Next thing you know—"

"Half my life will be gone before you let me live it." I shut my eyes and prayed for patience. "I'm not chasing him."

Grandma waddled into the kitchen. "Chasing boys? What's

next? Lifting your skirt?" she said as she opened a prescription bottle on the counter and shook out a heart pill. "Give me a glass of water, Marta."

Mom grabbed a glass from the cupboard, filled it with cold water, and shoved it at Grandma. She swallowed her pill like a chicken guzzling a golf ball.

Mom waited till Grandma left. Her voice was a hiss. "Listen to me. You're too young to get all wrapped up in some boy. You'll end up like that other girl—I'm sure a baby wasn't what she wanted when she went on a date with a Vadas boy."

I was sure I knew more about sex than she did.

Just then Dad came breezing in with a big "Hallo." He reeked of booze and cigars after whooping it up, watching football with my uncles. He punched my arm. Mom stiffened in case he might sock her too, but when he saw her face, he wisely checked himself. "What are my beautiful girls bickering about now?" He picked up a leftover sandwich triangle with his finger and thumb. Ham salad oozed out before he popped the whole thing in his mouth.

"Nothing." Mom gave me a pointed look, then went back to vigorously scrubbing cups and saucers that didn't need scrubbing.

"Mom's bent out of shape because Joe called. She thinks he's going to knock me up." I'd lowered my voice but wanted her to hear. There was a splash in the sink as she whipped her head around to look at me—if eyes could slap faces, hers would have.

I bit my lip, afraid I'd gone too far, but Dad said, "Oh, for Pete's sake, Marta. What are you all up about? You sound like your mother. Let the kids be already."

Her hands froze, and she breathed deep and slow, trying to contain herself. The tendons in her neck pulsed, making me think she was trying to keep from chucking dishes at him. She didn't like it when he drank with her brothers because she said their so-called brutish behavior rubbed off on him, and he would come home feeling full of himself.

The day after you'd called, Mom appeared behind me in the bathroom when I was washing my face and said, "And another thing, don't even think about going steady." Then she startled me when I turned the corner in the living room. "Did you know he's practically failing his classes? The principal called him in for truancy last year? Don't be stupid for this boy." I wondered who she was shaking down for information.

Dad would stroll into a room and find Mom and me chopping at each other, and he'd slink back out, not wanting to be caught in the crossfire.

Was she jealous of me? What was making her so angry and discontented, what vague disappointment snaked through her restless mind? Did she think she'd made a mistake marrying Dad? Maybe she once envisioned a rewarding career or a different kind of life. Maybe she dreamed about having an affair at the Cardinal Motel with Mr. Schakowsky, and during the day she scrubbed the passion away with Bon Ami or sucked it up with the Eureka. Maybe I was a reminder of what she could have been.

There was something disturbing sliding around under the surface of my family, but the truth was more than I'd bargained for, and Mom was practiced at lying about it before I was even born.

You and I slid into a world of wet kisses and illicit touch—our mouths and hearts opening wide, sealing us from the outside world. You could undo me with a kiss, and make me feel as if I was swimming underwater, naked, with my eyes shut. I loved the odd lines of poetry you fed me, how you said my eyes were "big love-crumbs," my kiss made your heart wise, the "voice of my eyes" was deeper than the roses, and not even the rain had hands as small as mine. I had no idea where or how you came up with these things until, years later, I read Cummings myself.

Mornings before school were a blast, riding around in your car, singing along with the radio or debating whose theory about black holes made more sense, Hawking's or Einstein's—not that we fully grasped either, but wasn't it cool to think about what would happen if we were sucked into a hole in the sky? Most fun was making up dirty knock-knock jokes: "Knock, knock. *Who's there?* Camelot. *Camelot who?* Came-a-lot is what I did in bed last night." You recited dozens of comedy skits from Firesign Theatre—"The Whispering Yeast Hour," "Beat the Reaper," and "Porgie Tirebiter"—imitating characters with speech impediments and bizarre accents. Your memory amazed me, but I wouldn't have known if you'd made it all up.

Gavin could imitate voices, too, but he never made me laugh as hard as you could.

To avoid a bloodbath at home, I never talked about you to my parents. That's why I wanted to plan our dates at school, why I asked you not to call me, and I called you only when I knew Mom was out or too busy to listen in on the extension. That's why I had you meet me at Paige's or another girlfriend's when we went out. As far as Mom knew, she could count the number of dates we'd had on one hand, and that's the way I wanted to keep it.

We both know how that plan worked out.

You opened my sheltered eyes, took me to places in the city, and in myself, that I never imagined existed. The first time we went to Mickey's Saloon in the Flats stands out in my mind because of what happened after we left.

I had been on Route 21 over the steel and iron mills only a few times before then. Cuyahoga Iron Works, Republic Steel, and Cleveland Steel & Tubes pumped the blackest, most foul-smelling smoke into the sky, but the open-hearth furnaces fascinated me. Flaming tongues rose from orange mouths that could have swallowed men's lives whole. I imagined the steelworkers' eyebrows and lashes were singed, their every pore packed with dirt. What would it be like to be married to a man who coughed smoke into his wife's and children's faces at night, who left soot on his pillow in the morning? When he left for work, a dark smudge where he had slept would remind me that he defied death every day. I told myself if that man were you, I would love you even more.

I stepped out of your car to find myself encircled by cavernous, boarded-up buildings, places where a man with murder on his mind might drag a woman into. Dad told me that the Flats, the half-mile-wide valley where the Cuyahoga River snakes under the Superior Viaduct, once teemed with wildlife, until the refineries, chemical factories, and warehouses turned the sparkling Cuyahoga into a sloshing mess of oil and chemicals that once caught fire. Did you know *Cuyahoga* means "crooked river" in Iroquois? It was ruined. Dozens of factories closed, and the docks were abandoned. The ground was coated with black ice, men with yellow eyes huddled around trash barrels that spit ashes. I held your hand tightly. Mom would have locked me in a tower like Rapunzel if she'd known where I had been.

The hand-lettered sign taped on the door of a painted brick building read: 18 AND OVER ONLY. My stomach sank. I was just seventeen, but you assured me, "It's cool." Just inside the doorway was a bouncer with a square face and flared nostrils. He stood with one leg on a stool and the other planted firmly on the floor. I was sure I'd never get past him, but his eyes brightened when he saw you.

"Hey, it's the weasel," he said, then nodded toward me. "This the girl?"

"Fuck off," you said, then turned to me. "This is my asshole brother Fabian."

Fabian grinned, his slash of a mouth exposing big teeth and pink gums as I stammered a hello. He took my hand in his fat paw and rubber-stamped it with a red star, told us to have a good time, and then whispered something to you that made your ears flame. I was dying to know what it was.

In the back, near the bar, we found a small, sticky table that wobbled disagreeably until you shoved a matchbook under the base. You hung your jacket on your chair, told me you'd be right back, and wedged your way to the bar to get us something to drink. Bass guitar from the jukebox shook the floor. The bar swarmed with wiry men with gaunt faces, hulks in leather with chain wallets, and women with hair teased up like tumbleweed. The room smelled like rotting apples and tobacco smoke. A pock-faced man in a bomber jacket and rolled jeans watched me closely as I took off my jacket and arranged it on the back of my chair. I slouched, wishing I hadn't worn such a body-hugging sweater, relieved when you finally returned with two mugs of 3.2 beer and a pack of Lucky Strikes.

"You and your brother don't look anything alike," I said.

"Thank God." You made the sign of the cross. "Don't pay him any mind if he winks or leers at you. He's a pig."

Someone bumped the back of my chair. I scooted closer to you, excited to be at a downtown bar drinking a beer as if I did this every weekend.

You offered me a cigarette, but I passed. I didn't pick up the habit till later. You said, "I'll tell you a story about Fabian," but your story told me more about your father than your brother. "When we lived in the old neighborhood, off West Twenty-Fifth, my brother Laz bought a Schwinn bicycle for his paper route and a Saturday job at the butcher. Well, Fabian kind of borrowed the bike one Saturday without asking, so Laz had to hoof it to work. Fabian was still gone when Laz came home. His bitching and moaning got my mother all upset, which got the old man wound up, and soon the whole house was up in arms. When Fabian finally waltzed in, my father's face was purple. He flattened Laz's bike by backing his car over it a few times." Cigarette smoke streamed from your nose. "To this day, Fabian is still on Laz's bad side."

I nearly choked on my beer. "Why did he do that? It wasn't Laz's fault."

"Well, yeah, but the way my old man saw it, the bike caused false pride in Laz and jealousy in the rest of us. Getting rid of it solved everything."

I didn't say it, but your father's logic was deeply troubling.

People began to whistle and clap. The stage was a two-foot riser along one wall with strands of twinkle lights hanging above it. I couldn't see the performer, and we could hardly hear in the back. A girl, oblivious to everyone, danced with herself, her head down and her long hair waving in her face. Near the bathrooms, another girl, with tears running in black streaks down her cheeks, sobbed into the pay phone. A scream rose from nowhere. It was bizarre, like being in a Hieronymus Bosch painting I'd seen in an art book. So, of course, I didn't object when you pulled me onto your lap and started kissing me as if we were all alone. The guy at the next table backed his chair into us when he dumped his beer, and I was glad when you handed me my jacket and said, "Let's split."

Our breath streamed from our mouths in the cold, sulfurous air outside as we ran to the car. You started the engine, then turned to kiss me. When it was hot as a toaster and the windows were steamed, you killed the ignition and climbed into the backseat, pushing your books and cassette tapes to the floor. "Well, come on. I didn't come back here to get away from you. The doors are locked," you said.

My stomach flipped as I slipped over the seat to join you. Before I could orient myself, I was on my back. You tasted like malt, your hair tickled my face, and the only sound was our heavy breathing and the suck-smack of our lips. I went soft, boneless when you slipped your hand up the front of my sweater. It was warm on my bare stomach, so amazingly warm that I didn't stop you when you worked your hand higher, or when your fingertips ran back and forth along the top edges of my bra, making me writhe, and not even when you pulled the cup down to lay that hand on my bare breast.

"You're such sweetness," you whispered into my neck, and little noises of pleasure, like mewling, rose unexpectedly from the back of my throat. You locked your lips around a nipple and sucked as if you were a grown baby. Beyond sensibility, I thought I'd wet myself.

Meeting your family was an evening of abrupt turns. It left me concerned and upset, yet feeling intensely alive. Mom called the south end of town where you lived "the sticks," but it wasn't country, and it definitely wasn't farmland. I stepped from your car onto a gravel driveway, and a crackle ran up my spine to think this was where the beautiful boy I loved with all my heart came from. A huge pine tree obliterated the brick half of the front of the rambling ranch. The concrete front step was broken. A rusted dog chain lay near a birdbath filled with dirty ice.

My apprehension must have showed because you looked at me and said, "Welcome to paradise." I took your hand and smiled. Why should I care where you lived? You had brought me here because, of all things, your mother wanted to meet me. Earlier that day, I'd spent a half hour in the drugstore trying to find a card for a woman I didn't know but appreciated simply for being your mother.

All houses have their own particular scent, and when I entered your house, I thought of boiled beef bones and dogs. What did you smell when you stepped into my house? Was the Lowsleys' signature scent furniture polish? Bleach? Pine-Sol? Two dogs came bounding at me as I walked through a hall: "Moon Pie and Potato Chip," you said. Low to the ground like a straw boot mat, Potato Chip poked my ankles with wet whiskers. When I bent over to let her sniff my hand, she looked up at me, one eye as bright and black as a bead, the other bulging and cloudy, as if dunked in bleach. I drew back my hand.

The dogs trotted alongside us into a cozy kitchen that spilled into an open family room. It was heartwarming to watch you hug your mother and kiss her on the cheek. I hadn't expected her to be glamorous, but I was taken aback by the white roots of her thinning, reddish-brown hair, the age spots covering her ruddy face, and how her breasts swayed beneath a blue dress with fat cabbage roses. A gap between her front teeth took my attention away from her smile. Yet she cupped her rough, dry hands around mine and spoke to me in a way that captivated me, and I decided she was beautiful.

"Angelica, how good to meet you. I hear nice things." Her thick, singsong accent made you wince as you shifted your weight from one foot to the other. She swept her hand over a table laden with pie, cookies, strudel, and cake. "Make yourself at home. Eat. Have something to drink. Jozsef, make sure to introduce her to your sister and brothers and all the kids."

You took two cans of Schlitz beer from the fridge and handed one to me. I didn't know anyone who drank in front of their parents. I sheepishly glanced around, but no one seemed to care, so I figured, Why not? I smiled politely at your mother while you steered me into the cluttered living room to meet the rest of the family. Your excitement felt like a current when you held my hand.

You introduced me to your sister, Mariska, her husband and two children, then waved your hand toward the man sitting next to him. "That jive turkey with the ponytail is Adam. His little girl, Rachel, is hiding behind the chair—I see you! Watch out for her. That's his wife, Bobbi, over there, with the basketball under her shirt." You lowered your voice. "We call her Fertile Myrtle."

Was it fair to label her Fertile Myrtle? After all, she didn't get pregnant on her own. Pink faced with a sugary pout, she looked comfortable in a wingback chair with a pillow behind her back. She smiled, but her sharp eyes assessed my minidress and shoes, whittling me down to my bones, making me feel as if I'd stepped into your house from another country. Of all your brothers, Adam resembled you the most, with his full jaw, slender nose, high cheekbones, and muttonchops. I imagined you and Adam as shiny muscle cars with jazzed-up, high-velocity sperm, able to reach top speed in seconds. I thought about what it would be like to risk everything for a boy, especially when you casually draped your arm around my shoulder and I felt weak in the knees. Your display of affection in front of your family made me uncomfortable, because touching and hugging were not the norm in my house.

A jittery-looking man in a fitted shirt with rolled sleeves and Ban-Lon trousers walked into the kitchen with a woman holding a baby. You said, "That guy there with his head up his ass is Laz. Thinks he's the big shit because he races stock cars at Northfield." Laz heard you and laughed loudly. "And this is Laz's wife, Doreen, and their monster baby, Mick." I have to say, he was a rather large baby. Doreen gave you a look of exasperation, and you whispered to me, "Kid came out weighing nine pounds, fourteen ounces. Tell me that's not a monster."

You surely wouldn't call him a monster now. Neither of us could have guessed the role Mick would one day play in our lives.

In the midst of the good-natured warmth your family showed, I was struck by my feelings of longing and envy. Adam and Bobbi's little girl, whose untimely birth had been the topic of hot gossip in town, came out of hiding to rush at your legs, making you stagger back. Bobbi was pregnant with her second baby now, but with a spot of acne across her chin, she didn't look much older than I was. Had she wanted a baby? Did she ever resent her toddler? What about Adam? Was he happy? Always romanticizing, I saw his brooding expression as poetic and passionate, like yours.

You asked me if I'd mind if you talked to Laz for a minute. I don't know what made you think I'd feel alone or bored. Your sister said, "Like I give a flying fuck," as clear as day, but no one except me seemed startled by her language.

Your mother studied my platform shoes as if they amused her. Her eyes rose to my face, brightening. "Jozsef told me you are a pretty girl. *Csinos lány*. Is true."

"Thank you. You have such a big family." It was silly of me to state the obvious. I tried to picture myself cooking a huge pot of stew with six young children underfoot, and you as their daddy. The fantasy didn't mesh with my college/working girl plans, but I was taken with the idea nonetheless. Mom couldn't have been more wrong about you and your family. They were perfect, everything I didn't have and pined for.

"Yes. Good children…mostly," your mother said, and shook her head as if amused. "Please, have something to eat. Try the *dobos torta*. Drummer's cake. It's my special." She leaned over the table and cut a wedge from a cake decorated to look like a drum. The flesh of her upper arm quivered. "You like my Jozsef?"

Both she and Doreen looked at me, waiting. Heat spread across my face as I set down the beer and took the plate from your mother's hand. What did she want to hear? Was she as wary of her Jozsef getting too serious as my mother was about me? You were standing with Laz near the bar. You each raised a shot glass and downed it at the same time, then your eyes telepathically found mine. You cocked your head and smiled at me. I told your mother, "Yes, I like him. A lot."

She looked pleased. "He not so good in school, but plenty smart." She tapped her finger on her temple. "Maybe too smart."

I nodded in agreement as a piece of sweet, tender cake that tasted of rum melted in my mouth. Bobbi walked slowly into the kitchen, one hand supporting her belly, the other on her back. "Ugh, I can't stand another day of this. Did you and Joe meet at Huggs?" she asked as her eyes roamed over the table of food. When I said yes, she peered sideways at me as if testing to see what I knew about her. "I went to Huggs. Class of '72. I missed graduation."

Avoiding looking at her middle, I said, "Really?" She stared at me for an awkward moment as if unconvinced, so I looked her in the eye, hoping to convey that, even if I did know, it didn't matter. A quick sip of beer tasted medicinal after the sweet torte.

A loud slam made us both jump, and the man I assumed was the head of the household emerged from the shadowy hallway. He looked shopworn, with a slack tie around his neck, half of his wrinkled shirt flapping outside his pants, and a disorderly hank of hair across his forehead.

"Great. The party's just beginning. I have to pee for the thirtieth time today. The bathroom is as good a place as any to hang around until he passes out or something," Bobbi said, and lumbered down the far hall. Doreen announced she had to change the baby and headed in the other direction, toward one of the bedrooms. The atmosphere in the living room shifted, as if the adults held a collective breath, hunkering down for a storm. Mariska pulled her little ones, Avery and Ryan, over to a corner and spilled a barrel of Lincoln Logs onto the floor for them. Avery didn't stay put for more than three seconds. Adam seemed to be scrutinizing his father while trying to make it look as if he wasn't. You ignored him, walking over to the table to stand near me and slurp your beer while staring absently at the food.

Fabian addressed your father first. "How's it going, *Apa*?"

"Colder than a witch's left tit," he answered as he hitched up the front of his pants and adjusted his belt. "Hard day, hard day, and I'm still under the frog's ass." I almost laughed out loud. I'd never heard such a thing.

He clumsily fell back into a recliner that groaned under

his weight. Your mother poured a drink and Mariska took it to him. He raised the glass to his wife as if in thanks. Rachel sat on the floor and mined her nose until Bobbi returned from the bathroom and promptly smacked her plump hand away.

Your father's watery eyes, circled with dark rings, swiveled around the room and then settled on me, the one piece that didn't fit, the wiggling fly in the soup, but he didn't make any effort to greet me. He lay there like a sack of mulch with the middle button of his shirt open, his flabby cheeks dragging his mouth into a frown. I turned to you, puzzled. Good manners told me I should greet your father, maybe introduce myself if you didn't intend to.

Looking from you to me, your father evidently made the connection. His brows clamped together, and he spoke in what I presumed was Hungarian. Fabian turned to him and said, "What the hell you talking about?" I swallowed hard, fearing he'd said something about me.

Your father grunted and said, "You deaf?" He leaned toward Adam, jabbing a finger at him with the hand that held his drink, making it slosh. "Hey, girly boy, when you gon' cut that ponytail off? Eh?" He hooted.

"When you cut your nose off your face," Adam said.

It was no surprise that any niceties slid fast. Your father pushed the recliner upright, making the footrest snap, to sputter at Adam, "*Nyald ki a seggem!* You of anyone should know, you with the mental capacity of a sock. And while you're at it, tell your piss ant brother over there to keep his *fasz* in his pants, or he'll end up in the same pickle barrel." He then pointed his finger at you. My stomach shrank into a tight, hard mass.

"Okay, *Apa*. Okay. We'll watch him," Fabian said.

You seemed to retreat to the far corner of the kitchen. Ryan, who was contentedly building a log house, parroted his grandfather, "*Nyald ki a seggem.*" Rachel ran out from behind the chair, kicked him, and ran back. The log roof tumbled in, and he screeched, "She kicked me! For no reason!" Rachel barked like a dog from her hiding spot. Ryan wailed louder.

"Stop that! Crybaby! For fuck's sake, I didn't come home to listen to this racket," your father said. Whimpering, Ryan twisted his fists into his eyes. Your mother rescued him by bringing him into the kitchen to give him a crescent cookie.

Mariska walked over to stand closer to your father than I would have dared and told him to sit down. He glowered back at her. "Take your 'sit down' and put it...," he said, but his voice went too low to hear. She firmly said, "Enough of that. You're talking *dilis* now." He waved her away while he glared at me. His nostrils flared like a bull's. Fear tingled like tiny claws on my back. I wondered how loud things would get. Would fists and dishes fly like curses in front of the children? Strangely enough, my nervousness was for you, though, not me.

After taking another beer from the fridge, you said something to your mother, who was standing at the sink with her eyes closed and her back to everyone. You pulled me into the hall, tossed my coat at me, and ushered me out the door by my elbow before I could say happy birthday, thank you, or even good-bye. You didn't bother with your jacket.

A sloppy winter rain was making pockmarks in the snow. My shoe slapped into a puddle of slush. Water soaked my foot; the cold shot up my leg. I remember asking you what was wrong as I pulled on my coat and hopped into the car. You said, "Nothing," and jerked it into gear. You'd never barked at me like that before, and I don't mind saying I didn't like it. The tires chewed gravel as we flew backward out the driveway, then you shifted into drive, and we were off. I started to pat my dampened hair but had to grab for the door handle to keep from flying across the seat as you took a hard turn, feeding the Bel Air gas. The car must have reached sixty in five seconds. The can of Schlitz rolled back and forth on the seat. The defroster was blowing cold air.

Your hands were tight on the wheel, knuckles like white

clubs. The Chevy screamed down Pleasant Dale and bounced up from a dip in the road. The tires spun out when we crossed the bridge, making the back end swing. I was terrified we'd hit a patch of ice, skid through the wooden guardrail off the bridge, and plow headfirst into the cold, black Cuyahoga canal.

My panicked shriek must have startled you. You gawked at me as if I'd dropped from the sky into your private universe. A rocking trailer zoomed past, sending stones flying, making us both recoil. Finally, you eased your foot off the gas. I only allowed myself to breathe when you parked the car, at last, at the Meadowlands picnic area in the Park. I unclenched my hand from the door handle and shook it.

You retreated again into a brooding world that didn't include me, your shoulders tight, chin tucked down. The muscles in your jaw flexed. I couldn't stand another tick of silence. "Okay, what just happened?" I asked.

You popped the beer and drank deeply, looking mean. "You don't want to know."

"Don't tell me what I don't want," I said. Did you expect me to beg you to talk, or did you plan to keep your anger all to yourself? I thought you owed me an explanation after dragging me out of your house like you did. "If you're going to stare out the window without talking, take me home. I don't want to sit here and watch you boil your brains. You can do that by yourself."

You sighed, offered me your beer, then reached for the pack of Lucky Strikes on the dash, shook out a cigarette, and lit it. "I'm sorry. If you understood half the crap my old man said, you wouldn't want to be around him either."

"I can judge for myself." I took a drink, then handed the beer back. I was glad you apologized and softened my tone. "What did he say?"

You chugged the rest, your Adam's apple jerking, and then crumpled the can on the dashboard with one hand as if you hated it and shoved it under the seat. My blood rose when you told me some of the things your father had said. What kind of man calls his son "the ass valve of a pig" or tells him he has "piss in his head instead of brains"? What did your father mean when he said I was going to give you nothing but grief? Insulted, I motioned for your cigarette, and you passed it to me. After two quick drags, I passed it back. We were like a married couple who understood each other's habits and gestures so well that we didn't always need to speak.

You stared up as if you could see through the roof of the car to the black needles of rain. It dawned on me that you weren't sulking over what your father had said about *me*; it was what he'd said about you. I scooted across the seat to sit close to you, ashamed to have been concerned only with myself.

This may sound strange, but I was glad when you said your father called Adam a stupid sucker and told Mariska to sit on death's penis. At least he didn't direct all his verbal abuse at you. You explained that Hungarians curse better than anyone else. "No one bothers sending anyone to hell. That's too gentle. They say, 'May God's horse put his dick up your ass.' They start out with stinky and whoring and end up with disgusting body parts. You'd slap me if I repeated it to you."

I was shocked to learn that "*Nyald ki a seggem*" meant "lick my ass." I hoped your nephew didn't understand what he'd repeated.

A clump of ashes fell onto your thigh. You watched as I brushed it off, as if surprised to see me tidying up after you. You said, "Gypsies have a way of making poetry out of cursing. My old man's got a little Gypsy in him, but he's got no sense of poetics. He just sings his sad songs when he's got a drunk on."

I'd never heard that before, "a drunk on." I've never heard anyone, since you, pepper his speech with such creative profanity either. A couple of times I threw a few choice curses at Gavin just to shock him. I never told him where I learned them.

You cranked open the window to toss out the cigarette butt.

"My old man managed a big textile company in Hungary. My family came here in the fifties during the revolution. I was the only one born here. Now he sells steel-toed work shoes to factories. He drives a whole fucking shoe store in a truck." I laughed, and you grinned as if you couldn't help yourself. You got serious again and said, "Shit. I don't know what to do now. All I wanted was to graduate and get as far away from my old man as I can. But that would mean leaving you."

I took a quick breath, pleased that you might be envisioning a future with me. You casually pushed your shirt sleeve up to show me something on the inside of your forearm. There, just below the crease, was a crude tattoo in blue letters: *ANGEL*. I couldn't believe it. "Is that what I think it is? You did this?" I asked. The top of my head buzzed.

You looked down at your arm as if proud. "Yeah. Needle and ink. Couldn't sleep last night. I didn't do your whole name. It was too long." You sounded so apologetic.

You were made of layers, and as they were peeled back, I never knew whether I'd find something marvelous or terrible. Filled with awe and dread, I ran my fingers across the puffy red skin, disturbed to know you'd been compelled to alter your body for me. My name on your arm—it was so reckless. My mother would have had a cow if she knew. I bet your father would have killed you.

I admit I wondered if that was why you'd done it—if the tattoo was an act of anger or defiance, done for the same reason that I felt compelled to do things just to separate myself from Mom. This possibility that the tattoo represented something other than your love for me made it seem somehow impure. I felt as if you were standing a great distance from me, and we would never understand or know all there was to know about each other. It was the first time I understood that love is not all encompassing. A person can never really enter the one they love, not the way I'd once thought was possible.

The wind smacked a branch of shriveled leaves onto the

windshield, making me jump. It occurred to me that your father might beat you. I'd never considered how good I had it, despite all my complaining. Mom might have been a phobic mess, but at least Dad didn't booze it up and ruin parties, or call me horrible names. In comparison, our family seemed as plain as boiled potatoes.

Our relationship intensified that night, desire making us more restless and unsettled than the storm. We climbed into the backseat. You gathered me in your arms and kissed me, and the thought of how quickly things could change made me never want to let go. I remember an urgency in the way you clutched me, too, and the force of your mouth on mine. Do you remember how the sleet drummed the windows and roof of the car? You unbuttoned my jacket and slipped your hands under my dress. Your fingers toyed with the waistband of my drugstore panty hose that could stretch to accommodate another person inside and then pulled. I squirmed away. No boy had touched me there, under my clothes.

"Don't be afraid. Kiss me," you said, and so I offered my mouth. I wanted to trust you, tried to concentrate on the kiss, your tongue, and the hard white teeth behind your lips as your fingers tunneled like untamed beasts. Soon I was clawing for something to keep me from skidding off the seat: your hair, shirt, arm, anything. The feeling of being so utterly out of control, as if splashed across the seat like a glass of milk, took me unaware. Once it started, it lasted until I couldn't take any more. I tore my mouth from yours and gasped for air.

The insides of the windows dripped with condensation. Beyond that, it was all darkness and shadow, shuddering sheets of rain, the black pines yielding to the wind. Your breath was a rasp across my body. You held yourself up with one hand and unbuckled your belt with the other, telling me I was "everything good and sweet in the world." Jackrabbit fear leaped in my gut. You wanted more of me, and if it felt anything close to what had just happened, oh, I wanted it, too. I wanted it so bad that all the warnings and lectures about sex fell away. But I didn't want it in the feverish backseat of a car, nowhere to put our elbows and knees, our clothes twisted, our bare skin against the creaking vinyl. That wasn't the memory I wanted to carry with me for the rest of my life. What had I wanted? A heart-shaped bed with a mirror on the ceiling? Jim Morrison crooning "Strangers in the Night"? I don't know. I wasn't fussy. I just prayed you would understand when I told you no.

Your eyes begged as if down on their knees, your body pushed against mine with insistence. "I love you. Please, just let me—"

"Not here. I want to, I want to, I do, but not like this."

"God, Angelica. I, oh, shit—" you said, then buried your face in my hair. For a moment I thought you were crying, making strange noises as you rocked your hips against my thigh, your heavy buckle mashing my hip. A low groan escaped your lips, and then you stilled. I could guess what happened but wasn't sure what to do. Should I have told you it was okay? Offered you a couple of tissues? The last thing I wanted was to embarrass you. I breathed in the iron smell of the car, the oil and perspiration in your hair, and caught an unfamiliar, oddly sweet odor.

"I better take you home," you said. You smoothed my dress for me, apologizing, then stepped out of the car for a moment before getting behind the wheel.

My thoughts were messy as I crawled into the front seat. That you couldn't hold yourself back alarmed and thrilled me. Did you have any sense of what you'd done to me? Did you know how I'd want more? You drove slowly with your arm around me and kissed me at every red light, making our desire feel right again. The sleet had stopped, but the roads were slick. The people of Nopiming were snug and sleepy inside their furnaced homes, feet propped up, ready to watch the weather report on the eleven o'clock news, their children tucked safely in bed. The two of us were driving toward something we couldn't see. The snow in the yards shone as if coated with glass,the bare branches of the trees were thick fingers of ice. It was the beginning of everything. The end would come too soon.

I wanted to take your hand and put it back between my legs, where it was still burning.

‹▲›

‹›‹

CHAPTER SIX

At the time I believed Dad had given me his unspoken
complicity to date you. After all, I was sure he'd seen you
and me mashing lips in your turquoise boat of a car, idling on
a side street near our house. I'm sure you remember. It was ten
minutes past my curfew, and each time you kissed me I told
you, "This is the last one." Finally, you rolled the car into gear
and headed down the street. There was Dad, less than half a
block away, watching us while Cookie sniffed in the bushes.
Well, he never said a word.

After that night I would catch him staring at me or, rather,
through me as if reminiscing about the days when he had been
the most important man in my life. Maybe he remembered
something from when he was a teenager, a longing of his that
had never been satisfied. I worried that my loss of innocence
was somehow apparent, but if he suspected I saw you as much
as I was, or doing things I shouldn't, he didn't let on. Maybe
he thought it was better to stay safe in the dark than to risk
hearing me lie to him. Maybe he kept his thoughts to himself
because he didn't want to deal with Mom's histrionics.

You wouldn't believe how good he was at keeping secrets.
I had no idea he was in the middle of another conspiracy
of silence right under my nose. But there are some truths
one could never imagine, even if brightly colored threads
connected the dots. I can't say that I would have cared, then, if
had I known the truth. I was busy falling in love.

Gavin once asked me to tell him how I'd lost my virginity,

saying it would turn him on. Telling him turned me on, too. I didn't tell him the exhilaration I felt or the deep bond I was sure you and I had made, but it certainly wasn't because I forgot. For some girls their first time is painful and humiliating—all push and grunt and gouging fingers, the man snapping their body open like a cheap doll's. For me it was a shock, like a dive into a cold lake, but when I surfaced for a gulp of air, it felt as if summer had just begun. I owe that to you.

You wanted to hear how the new lyrics you'd written sounded with the band, something along the order of "You're moving in slow motion / to the tune of desperation / The monkey pulls the trigger / and it's assassination." I thought you wrote the strangest things. Then again, I hardly ever listened to the Doors, not until you were gone, anyway. We sat on a tattered couch in Skip's basement, where blankets had been hung along the cement walls to deaden the crash-bang of guitars and drums. Skip, who was practically parentless, let his friends do whatever they wanted in his house as long as they didn't break anything or pee in the potted plants.

I didn't see much in Skip, then. His girlish voice held a tune, but his wide-legged stance and the way he thrust his guitar out with his hips was too theatrical for me. The bass guitarist played with the kind of concentration that girls hoped he'd give to them, bobbing his head in a trance, his blond hair hanging in his eyes. Ammo was a wiry drummer who spun the drumsticks like batons with his long fingers. All three of them dressed as if they'd been spit out of a tree shredder.

We passed around a bottle of sangria that tasted syrupy sweet. The band started playing, then stopped to discuss when the bass should come in, started again, then stopped to argue about the tempo. Skip kept shaking his head while messing with a "piece of shit" amplifier. Having lost interest in the music, I studied your profile, handsome and focused, as you took a drag from a cigarette held deep in the V between your fingers. I felt wise around you as if you were unlocking mysteries, stripping my essence down to all that mattered. Was it lust or love? You don't know how hard it was getting to keep my grades up.

I never knew love and sex were so entwined, how a person's entire body yearned for intimate connection. Where had the idea that sex was bad and boys were the devil come from? My mother was like a skipping record. Well, if you were the devil, I was going to be your equal. I crawled into your lap, straddled you, and gave you a wine-soaked kiss, grinding my hips until I felt your cock grow hard.

Did you ever meet Mrs. Kincora? It was odd that we never once saw Skip's mother. Her bedroom smelled like stale potpourri and cloves. A yellowed slip, a bra with cone-shaped cups, and panty hose lay on the shag carpet as if she'd floated from her body and left her skin behind. Magazines, brassy jewelry, tissues, lipstick-rimmed coffee cups, and an ashtray with crushed cigarettes cluttered her dresser and nightstand. The dresser mirror was cloudy as if inhabited by the dusty ghost of a husband. There was a king-size bed. However, the door had a lock, and I was wet from wanting.

After stripping off our clothes, we slapped our bodies together as if suddenly shy and embarrassed to be seen in our entirety. Then we discovered that the intimacy of being skin to skin was euphoric. We couldn't stop rubbing our bodies together, as if polishing each other smooth, the satiny orange bedspread bunching beneath us.

I had this flowery notion that we would create a bond that would keep us together forever, and it all came down to this single act, what we were about to do, you and I, for the first time. As much as I'd wanted to have sex, I found myself swamped with ridiculous fears: you were too big to fit, you'd swell to some gargantuan size inside my little body, or you would poke in the wrong direction and rupture something, batter my spleen or liver. Anything could happen, I thought, even as I watched how skillfully you rolled on a Trojan, as if you'd done it a hundred times, having begun at age twelve when one of your brothers threw a couple of packs at you and told you to practice.

Guitars screeched, and cymbals crashed like a catfight in the basement. It was a stall tactic when I asked, "Have you ever gone this far before?" It was also a no-win question. Yes would have felt like a slap in the face, and No would have been hard to believe. I stared very hard at your right ear and thought about other girls in school you might go for: Cindy in her clingy dresses, Marilyn with her teacup-size breasts. There had been rumors. Jealous, and still hedging, I wanted to know who.

You said the right thing. "Just once, and you don't know her. And it wasn't like this. I never felt like this before."

"How?"

You kissed my neck. "Can't you tell? It's all for you, my wintertime love." That was what I needed to know, but it didn't quell my other fears. My teeth were rattling inside my skull. My heart thudded against my ribs. I know you felt me shaking, because you asked if I was okay.

I told you I was, but your rubber-coated cock, which hadn't diminished in hardness, felt ominous against my thigh. This is it, I thought, the beginning and the end. You crawled on top of me, watching my face with a round-eyed kind of wonderment. Every muscle in your body felt tightly bunched, ready to launch, like a sprinter coiled at the starting line. I innocently nodded when you said you had to push. What happened next wasn't expected. I couldn't help it—I screamed when I felt my body give way, imagining my insides tearing to let you in.

You froze. "Oh, shit! Did I hurt you?"

I whispered no, closed my eyes, took a few sharp breaths, and let my fear go in tiny shudders. It wasn't painful. Not really. It felt strange and unfamiliar, as if a new body part had been lodged inside me, not at all what I'd imagined.

You asked if I was ready, but I wasn't sure what I was

supposed to be ready for. I said yes, anyway, and you pumped as if a starting gun had fired. I squeezed my eyes shut, clapped my hands onto your backside, and hung on. I didn't yet know how to match your moves, but you whaled away hard enough for the both of us, making grunts and gasps that startled and thrilled me. I opened my eyes for a second and saw your face hovering above mine, contorted as if in pain, eyes half shut, tongue suspended in your open mouth.

You convulsed with a groan and then collapsed, panting. I lowered my legs, thinking, That's it? This is what I'll do at least a thousand more times in my life? How long had it lasted? The time it takes to brush your teeth? To put on your socks and tie your shoes? You felt as heavy as a horse on top of me. My thighs trembled. War whoops and drumming punctuated a screeching guitar solo. You stirred, mumbled something, and shuffled to the bathroom. I was afraid to move or get up—as if my insides might spill out. I wondered if I bled on Mrs. Kincora's bedspread. I wondered if she'd notice.

When you returned, we lay together, nose to nose, and smiled like simpletons at each other. Your cheeks and lips were cherry-red, as if you'd been playing in the snow. I put my hands on your chest, felt the rise and fall of your lungs, and the beat of your heart in its bony cage.

You asked, "Was it good?"

"I don't know...yes. Did you think so?"

"Hell, yeah. I'm so happy."

"Me, too."

Most of the snow had melted, leaving blackened curbs and matted grass while unveiling surprises, such as a lost key, an orange Wham-O ball, a soggy glove. The plants in Mom's flower beds were pale and stalky, nothing visibly ready to bloom, although deep in the hard Ohio soil, life was germinating, and farther below, the earth's red-hot core was roiling.

Things were bound to erupt.

I no longer cared where you and I did it as long as we did it a lot. In the backseat of your Chevy, parked behind the church rectory. In my parents' detached garage when it was only forty-six degrees; we dropped our pants and fucked standing up while I held on to the seat of the Lawn-Boy. You were so excited you came in less than a minute. I remember when we dragged a couple of scratchy wool blankets into the field on a sunny afternoon when the ground was still frozen, hoping we'd keep each other warm. We didn't, but I was delirious to get naked with you, despite my chattering teeth. The clinking noise when you unbuckled your belt was like Pavlov's bell to me. It was hard to understand why anyone would *not* want to do it all the time.

At school it became a game to tease each other to madness. You slipped your hand up my sweater to the bare skin at the small of my back or petted my thigh under my skirt in the cafeteria. I remember sitting close together in the back of the library, pretending to study, as you stroked your finger along the side of my breast through my clothes. You whispered that you wanted to touch the place where dreams were made. "A silken altar. A crazy girl and a mad boy in a holy temple, feasting on love." Whatever that meant, your warm breath in my ear was all it took to push me to the edge of orgasm. I was afraid I left a wet spot on the chair. How did anyone not know what we were up to?

I believe it was a Tuesday, that horrible day in March 1975, when everything went haywire. You and I were in the hallway behind the gym, where we often met during the second-to-last period on the days when you went straight to work after school. I had study hall. I can't remember what class you had. You told me I looked like a million dollars. The clean smellof Doublemint gum floated on your breath. "I want to feel your trembling—"

"You can feel it later."

"Why wait? Let's cut class," you said, and guided me down the empty hall through a set of doors that led through the athletic director's office to an equipment storage room. Ever cautious, I questioned you as if I could ever be rational while anticipation was drumming inside me. You said Coach Kaspersky was timing the sophomores on the quarter-mile run as you pulled me into a room with shelves of rolled mats and wire baskets filled with sports equipment. It smelled like sweaty boys and rubber balls. The door sealed with a heavy clank behind us, turning the closet as dark as night.

Teenage boys consider themselves invincible. They take chances with stunts that defy logic. It's true, they think about sex an awful lot, but girls think about sex too. More than Mom or even I ever imagined, and they make equally poor choices. There were times you and I acted very adult. Other times, well, we were plainly idiots. That day nothing could have stopped us.

I clutched the muscles of your back under your shirt as you lifted me up so I was sitting on the mats. When you touched me between my legs, it felt as if a flock of doves flew under my skirt and stayed there, beating their wings. We tried to be quiet, I know that much, whether or not we actually were. There wasn't much to talk about: part A goes into part B. It was one of those times when we prudently tried to keep as much of our clothes on as possible, just in case. The threat of getting caught is part of the thrill, but who expects it actually to happen?

"Come on, hurry," I might have said.

"Lift your knees," you might have said.

"Right here. Yeah."

A bright light momentarily blinded us. A shaft of lightning? A camera flash? An explosion? Exposed. Kaspersky stood in the doorway. He shut the door, as if he'd seen something so wrong he couldn't believe it, and then opened it again. "What the...? Holy crap. What's going on here?"

You and I stared at each other with wild horses' eyes. You hoisted your jeans, and I lowered my legs and smoothed my clothing. Despite the obvious, I prayed Kaspersky wouldn't know what we'd been doing. The athletic director was ugly and barrel-chested, with Popeye arms and no neck—a typical, hot-headed coach with a silver whistle around his neck that he loved to blow. When I think back, I'm surprised he didn't use it then. His nose flared with anger.

When he asked for my name, my mouth was so dry that my lips stuck to my teeth. Clearly he knew who you were, however. He told us in clipped words to follow him to the office. You tried to convince him to let us go with a warning, but he said you were out of warnings. I always wondered why.

"Let her go, then. She's a good student. She's never been in trouble before," you said as you kept pace with him, pitching like a salesman. "It was my idea. It was my fault. I talked her into it."

"Too bad she listened to you."

We sat on the hard wooden bench outside the principal's office while Kaspersky talked to Greers. I tried to imagine what he was telling the principal, what he might have described, and if he used vulgar terms. I couldn't hold still, needing to pee in the worst way. Your arms were crossed tightly in front of your chest, and both your legs were bouncing. A pock-faced boy stared with curiosity at us as he waited at the counter for a late pass. Phones rang. The secretary smiled benignly at us. I didn't even want to consider how we might be disciplined— my biggest concern was how to keep this from my parents. I began to worry, though, when I asked if you knew what might happen, and all you did was shrug.

Greers gave us a hard look when we went into his office and took seats opposite his desk. He'd been teaching for thirty or more years, and worked as the middle school administrator before he became the high school principal. He liked to say that guiding us was his life's work. Today he told us that in all his years, nothing like this had ever happened. "Never." He cleared his throat, adjusted his checkered blue tie, and said, "There isn't even anything in the handbook that addresses such behavior."

You campaigned on my behalf again, but at this point I just wanted you to shut up because it was prolonging the inevitable. Greers let out a burdened sigh as he leaned back in his swivel chair as if trying to determine how innocent I was. He told you to beat it, much to my surprise. "I'll be calling your parents. You got a full suspension, starting today. Get out of here."

You mouthed, "Tell him: my fault," as you walked past me. The door shut, and I was alone with Greers. He studied me quietly. My pulse beat hard in my neck. I squeezed my legs together and tugged down my skirt. My bare knees looked obscene, and I nearly wet my pants.

Ours was a strange exchange:

"You don't have to be afraid to tell me what really happened. Did that boy pressure you?"

"No."

"You can tell me the truth."

I didn't say anything, confused because I was telling the truth.

"Mr. Vadas did not in any way force you?"

"No." I wanted to tell him I loved Mr. Vadas.

He smacked his lips, eyebrows raised, as if I'd not only done the wrong thing, but said the wrong thing. A sudden wave of nausea hit me. This was going to be bad. "All right. I have no choice but to suspend you and call your parents." He might as well have committed me to an asylum.

The principal's grim face and stiff behavior tipped off my folks that he hadn't called them in to tell them I'd won a scholastic achievement award. Mom sat perched at the edge of her chair as she twisted the straps of her patent leather purse in her lap.

Dad adjusted his suit jacket, his eyes darting around the office.

Greers explained that students aren't allowed to demon-strate affection on the school grounds. "Our policy is clear. No kissing. No hand holding. No touching." He paused to wipe his brow as if growing anxious under my parents' intense stares. "Coach Kaspersky found your daughter and Joe Vadas in an equipment storage room in his office. I understand your daughter is a good student, but we can't let inappropriate behavior slide. We have to set an example. I gave Joe a ten-day suspension, and I'm giving Angelica five."

There was a stunned silence, then an involuntary burst of air escaped Dad's lips, like gas venting. Mom went as pale as a candle. I stared at my blatant knees. Suspension was bad enough, but it was the nature of the crime, what Greers called "inappropriate behavior," that apparently stumped them. "Exactly what kind of behavior are we talking about?" Dad asked.

I wanted to shake him while I struggled to contain my tears of shame. From the corner of my eye, I saw Mom pinching and pulling at her neck. Greers's intercom buzzed, making us all jump.

He ignored it, clicking the top of his pen with his thumb a few times. At last he said, "It was an act adults do in private. Something teens shouldn't be doing, in school, or anywhere. That's all I need to say. If you want details, ask your daughter."

◄▲►

CHAPTER SEVEN

"They get it from television," Grandma said, slapping another spoonful of chicken-and-rice casserole on her plate. Three sharp cracks of her spoon rapping on her plate rang in my ears. My plan was to starve myself until I disappeared. Mom was so upset she could hardly sit at the table. Her hand trembled as she poked her fork at the lump on her plate. Dad would eat no matter what happened. A foot of raw sewage could fill the basement, and he'd still expect dinner.

"I warned you about this, didn't I, Marta? She's turning out to be a *hure*." That's *whore*, in German, in case you didn't guess. "And you know the reason why. The root cause of her—"

Mom set down her fork and held her hand to her forehead. "Please, Mother. Just stop." Grandma straightened her back, her thin lips in a straight line.

"How could you do something like this, Angie? I thought you knew right from wrong," Dad said. Unable to meet his surgical-steel glare, I stared at his sagging chest and the wiry white hair that peeped out from behind the collar of his shirt.

"Nothing happened. Kaspersky didn't see anything. He just thinks he did. We were horsing around. That's all."

Mom said, "I don't believe you. Why would the coach and principal lie? These boys—"

"Joe isn't one of 'these boys.' Whatever you think happened, it wasn't anything wrong."

Mom gaped at me, aghast. Dad's face fell as if I'd discoed it flat with my platform shoes. They'd rather have blamed you for leading me astray than hear me say I didn't think fornication was wrong. Dad said, "Goddammit. I knew I should have said something. How long have you two been carrying on like this?"

His accusatory tone upset me. I spoke without thinking. "You knew I was seeing him. You knew! And you were okay with it."

"I didn't know you were seeing him like *this*. I trusted you. I thought you were smarter," he said, his blood pressure visibly pushed into the red zone.

Mom let out a little squeak. "You *knew*? For God's sake, Ed."

Grandma smacked her lips, chewing and talking at the same time. "Lot of good you do. Can't even put the milk back in the refrigerator," she said to Dad. "Neither of you has the backbone to raise a child. If she were my—"

"You kept this from me?" Mom asked Dad. "What's been going on?"

"You don't want to know." He pointed his finger at me. "That's it. No more. The two of you are history. Concentrate on your schoolwork. Your reputation is shot to hell, and I hope I don't have to spell out what the bigger issue here is. I won't have your life wrecked by some sex-crazed boy who doesn't know a brick from shit."

Cookie, lying near the doorway, lifted her head. Dad seldom raised his voice or swore.

"You can't keep us apart. I love him, and he loves me."

"You don't know the first thing about love," Mom said.

"What do you know? You and Dad don't even touch each other."

"Angelica!" Mom said, her fingers fluttering at the base of her throat. Grandma clucked her tongue. Cookie hopped to her feet and let out two warning barks as if to make us settle down.

Nearly purple in the face, Dad steamed like a cartoon version of himself. He spit bits of food across the table. "Someday you'll understand why parents make the rules. It ends here. You're grounded for a month. Seeing him is not an option. You're not to go out with him. You're not to speak to him on the phone. It's over. Kaput. We have plans for you, and I don't want some boy derailing them. Go to your room."

I was already running from the table.

My alarm clock glowed: 2:23 AM. Two days of our suspensions had passed. I thought I heard a rap on my bedroom window but wasn't sure. I lay still and quiet in bed until I heard another rap, then leaped up and peered out to see you standing in the backyard, looking up at me. I will never forget how your face brightened when you saw me. I threw on my chenille robe and scuffs and raced downstairs. I couldn't get to you fast enough.

The moment I opened the back door, you took my hand, and we ran together through the backyards to your car, parked a few houses down, on Sunset Drive. I shivered. It was cold out, but you were warm as you wrapped your body around mine and kissed me. Whenever I was with you, the world was right.

I told you what my parents had said, that I wasn't allowed to see you anymore, and asked what your folks had said. I was surprised to hear they didn't know. How did you manage that?

You parked back by the dumpster behind the movie theater, partially hidden behind the trees, and we climbed into the backseat. We kissed with our mouths open wide as if to crawl inside each other and hide. You tasted like beer and smelled like cigarettes. Your face felt rough against mine. You were an animal. I was in heat. We didn't bother with foreplay. I don't know about you, but I wanted to connect as if the only way to straighten the mess we were in was to do it again and again. I remember making a lot of noise that night.

You put your hands in my hair and inhaled deeply. "If this is madness, I love it. I can't stand being away from you."

"What are we going to do, Joe?" We could go anywhere or do anything, I reasoned. You knew how to navigate in the world. You owned a car. You'd been working for years, and to me that meant everything. You could handle money. For whatever reason, I assumed you had a bank account. I envisioned us driving out West where it never snowed, and we wouldn't have to worry about where we slept. Who thinks about gas money, the next meal, or where to shower at a time like this?

You said you'd figure something out, and that was good enough. I trusted you. Slipping out at night to see you didn't seem that hard. We'd have a secret life that began at midnight. So be it. I would show my parents they couldn't control me.

I had left the back door of the house unlocked so I could steal back inside. My slippers were wet from dew, so I slipped them off and left them by the door. Cookie was sleeping in the breezeway. I never thought she'd bark at me, but she did. Then she wagged her tail, making a low noise in her throat as if in apology. "Shh," I scolded before I crept through the house to the stairs. Wouldn't you know it, she followed, panting, nails clicking on the pine floor. I tried to shoo her. "Go back, stupid dog." She lay down, head on her paws.

The upstairs hall light flicked on. I cursed under my breath as I scuttled back to the kitchen. I tried to fill a saucepan with milk, but my hands were shaking. I probably smelled like you. I patted my face with cool hands, hoping my cheeks and lips didn't look sandpapered from your face.

Dad came into the kitchen and turned on the light.

I looked away. "Ow. My eyes. Turn off the light."

He did. Before he could ask what I was up to, I told him I couldn't sleep so I was warming a glass of milk. All he said was "Oh." He stood there as if calculating things, looking at me. I feared he was going to supervise, but he left to check the back door, supposedly to make sure it was locked, as he always did. He came back holding one of my damp slippers.

"You went somewhere, didn't you?" he asked. I couldn't speak, afraid he'd know I was crying. "Angelica, answer me. You went to see Joe, didn't you?" I shook my head no. He asked why I was lying to him. Between sobs, I managed to say, "I love him. You can't make me stop seeing him."

He told me he could.

Every night after that I lay awake, waiting to hear the clink of a stone at my window. After my five-day suspension was up, I thought you'd pick me up as I walked to school in the morning, or you'd wait for me in the afternoon. But you weren't anywhere to be seen. When your ten-day suspension ended, you didn't return to school. I was baffled.

Meanwhile, everyone at Huggs was agog over our suspensions. Paige was the only one I dared tell what had happened. Anyone else who asked was given the sanitized version that we'd been caught making out. Wildly exaggerated stories blew like a March wind through the halls anyway: we were found groping each other behind the stage, I was giving you a blow job in the boys' showers. The rumors ballooned when you didn't return to school. Bella Doyle, homecoming queen runner-up, and bitter about it, too, said we'd been caught doing it doggy-style on Kaspersky's desk. Girls gave me dirty looks. Boys watched me through sly eyes. There wasn't much I could say or do. Stopping a slut rumor by defending yourself is like trying to put out a fire with a blowtorch.

Nopiming looked stark and brown, like a faded Polaroid, the roadsides bleached from salt, no leaves yet on the trees, the grass matted flat like a child's hair in the morning. The weather was enough to depress anyone, and the atmosphere at home was intolerable. I refused to talk to my parents. I hated the sounds Dad made when he chewed his meat, the gulp Mom made when she swallowed her coffee, the way Grandma's left brow shot up when I walked past her. Mom's gray eyes followed me around the house as if she knew intimate things that mothers should not know about their daughters. She cleaned with an angry vengeance, slamming drawers and cupboards, rattling pots and pans, fire ants crawling up her back. It was as if she smelled sex on my body: an oily muskrat, a filthy cat howling in heat. And Grandma was right behind her, sniffing me out, too.

Mom finally plugged the phones back in, and I called your house whenever I could. The phone rang and rang. Your mother answered once. She said, "No, no, I can't say where Joe go. Sorry." Her voice sounded sad and distant, as if she held the phone at arm's length. I wasn't sure if she meant she couldn't tell me, or she didn't know where you were. Which was worse? Paige drove me past your house when she could. Your car was never there. I asked at the police station about filing a missing person report, but the officer told me that family members had to file such a report. Besides, eighteen-year-old boys who took flight, especially the kind who get suspended from school, didn't interest the cops. Skip and the rest of the band were content to shrug off your disappearance. "He probably got sick of all the bullshit and took off." It crushed me to think that you'd go anywhere without me.

You were different from any other boy I'd known, smart about particular things, not necessarily what was taught in school. When I shut my eyes, my hands remembered the arc of your body, from the dimpled curve of your backside up to your flat shoulder blades. I could splay my hands and feel the flat expanse of your chest, imagine running my fingertips through the sparse hair down to your navel, then lower still, to the most infinitely interesting part of your anatomy. Day and night, I wore the heart locket you had given me on Valentine's Day. Every time I thought of you, I kissed it and then circled my thumb around it ten times for luck. You told me not to open it, because the kiss you placed inside would escape. The thought of carrying your kiss in a locket nestled between my breasts was far more romantic than a photograph would have been.

I still have that tarnished charm.

There were mornings when I had to force myself to roll out

of bed to grind through another day, not knowing where you were. The possibility that you didn't care about me anymore brought me to tears. I wanted to throw myself on the ground until something solid gave way, or the earth cracked open to reveal you. My parents' calm, expressionless faces over your absence read as smug and cursory. They didn't have to say what they were thinking—your lack of communication was evidence that you hadn't really loved me. I began to think you were a coward for not standing up to my parents. You could have come to the house and made things right by apologizing and begging their forgiveness. You could have told them you intended to marry me. You could have said we were already engaged.

If you'd gone to California to sleep on rooftops and write music like your dead hero, Jim Morrison, it was obvious I wasn't to be your Pamela Courson. You didn't need or want me.

The bond I once had with most of my friends vanished. Becca admitted her parents told her to stay away from me. Imagine how that felt. Thank goodness Paige was sympathetic. It had been a long time since we'd hung out, flipping through magazines and dipping Cheese Doodles in peanut butter, so I felt a little strange calling her, as if the only reason was I'd been dumped by my boyfriend. It was understood.

I envied her freedom. She even had the use of a car, an orange AMC Gremlin, while her sister Alisa was away at college. I wanted to start classes for my driver's license, but Mom steadfastly refused to let me get behind the wheel of her Buick Century, as if she thought I'd drive straight into the armpit of Cleveland, get hooked on heroin, and prostitute myself. The two times Dad let me take his new Lincoln for a spin around the block, I thought the vein that ran up the side of his forehead would burst.

When I last inquired at Huggs about lessons through the school-sponsored drivers' ed course, they told me there wouldn't be an opening for six months. Dad, who could be incredibly cheap, refused to shell out money for a private driving school. He said, "You already proved you can't act responsibly. Just concentrate on your schoolwork."

"If I could just get my license, I'd show you—"

He shushed me at an apparent crucial moment in the dumbest TV show, about the detective with a cockatoo named Fred. Mom and I would cringe whenever Baretta kissed his bird on the beak. She'd pick up her knitting and leave the room, disgusted, and then Dad would spend the rest of the evening trying to justify to me why he liked the show.

"What makes you think we'd trust you with a car?" Mom asked.

"Shh! I'm going to miss this." Dad hopped up to raise the volume.

I retreated. My parents were going to punish me for my transgressions with you for the rest of my life, a handy "Go to Jail" card to deny me whatever I asked for.

But the brilliant future my parents planned for me, the one without you, was derailed on a Saturday afternoon. It was a day with the kind of gusty wind that knocks squirrels out of buckeye trees and whisks hats from people's heads. It was early spring in northern Ohio, where it can snow even after the dogwoods start to bloom. So much of my life seemed outside of my control that I decided to take whatever small steps I could toward independence on my own. I'd stashed away more than enough cash from babysitting for classes at ABC Driving School in Cuyahoga Heights, and Paige volunteered to take me. As long as my parents didn't bar the doors and windows, I could do this. All I needed to enroll was proof of age—my birth certificate—and that was what proved to be my undoing.

◄▲►

CHAPTER EIGHT

The most likely place for my birth certificate would be the fireproof safe in the basement where Dad kept his will, insurance policies, and other family records. Mom was knitting at Dottie's, Dad was doing his monthly charity stint at the free clinic, and Grandma was engrossed in *The Afternoon Movie* on television.

As I walked through the family room to go downstairs, she asked me to bring her a glass of water. Her feet were propped up on the ottoman, stout ankles covered with an orange, green, and pink afghan, one of Mom's more ghastly color combinations. She licked her chapped lips before she took a sip, and I swore I heard her tongue rake across the cracks. Neither age nor thirst had diminished that tongue's ability to lash, though. "Thank you. At least you're good for something when you're not flat on your back." Her feet wiggled gleefully under the blanket.

"And what are you good for?" I asked. In an odd way, I missed her zingers after she was gone; the two of us had sparred in a manner that I couldn't with Mom. Grandma invited my comebacks, and I knew better than to take her seriously.

"I finished my life's work, and it wasn't done with my legs up in the air. You have no idea what real work is. You think life is a party," she said.

"I do not. I have chores. Notice there's not a speck of dust in here? Anyway, my main job is to finish school. News flash to

Grandma—I'm going to be more than a *hausfrau*. I'm going to college." Ill-fated words.

"Ha! Not if some boy puts a baby in you." She waved me away.

That last one smarted, but I let the nanny goat have the last word and padded down the stairs into the cool hush of the basement, where it smelled like damp wood and rusty cans, despite a rumbling dehumidifier. Squatting on the cement floor, I unlocked and pulled out the long drawer of the cabinet to leaf through the hanging folders. You wouldn't believe the stuff Dad had saved. I flipped through folders of yellowing insurance records, mortgage papers, tax statements, warranties, instructions from the Amana Frost Free and the Whirlpool washer, even the receipt for the aluminum siding the house was wrapped in years ago, but did not find my birth certificate.

I found my parents' records, though, and was stunned to discover Dad was a whopping thirteen years older than Mom. She'd told me the difference was just a few years. Both of them claimed they stopped counting their birthdays because they didn't want to remember how old they were. According to these papers, Dad would have been thirty when Mom was seventeen. No wonder she hadn't wanted me to know. I was shocked to think Grandma would have allowed her young daughter to date such an older man, doctor of feet or not. What would they have said if I'd brought some old fart home, instead of you, my Gypsy Joe?

Then I came across what proved to be the most baffling find: a decorative, hand-lettered document "Celebrating the Union of Edgar Mortimer Lowsley and Marta Margaret Bauer." It was marbled parchment with a floral border, the kind of thing most people framed and hung on the wall. It seemed a shame to hide it, but Mom didn't like pictures cluttering up the walls or fussy knickknacks crowding shelves and tables.

After paging fruitlessly through the safe for the second time,

I had no idea where to look next. I glanced at the marriage document before I tucked it away and caught the date of their wedding: 1961. I would have been three years old.

Stumped, I stared at the numbers. Odd, don't you think?

It had to be a mistake. On the other hand, anyone who'd take the time to hand letter a marriage document surely would have checked the date. I sat back on the floor. Maybe there had been a clerical error when my parents were first married, so they had another ceremony to make the marriage legally binding. Maybe they'd eloped. Maybe they were married by a justice of the peace to save money and had a church wedding three years later.

What else could it be? The aluminum Christmas tree in the corner of the basement glinted in the stark light from the bulb that hung from the rafters. On the shelves were boxes and boxes of knitted blankets and sweaters, outgrown clothes, and seasonal decorations—a ceramic Easter rabbit, baskets full of plastic eggs, a Nativity scene with a chipped baby Jesus and missing a wise man—things that were familiar to me as far back as I could remember. The cold floor seeped through my thin jeans and made me shiver.

I couldn't sit in the cellar all afternoon when I needed answers. I placed the paper back into its envelope and took it with me as I ran up the stairs. My sock caught on the metal strip on the top step, and I sprawled into the kitchen, whacking my chin. My teeth bit into my tongue, the taste of iron filled my mouth. Tail wagging, Cookie trotted over to poke me with her nose as if I'd thrown myself onto the floor to play with her.

"Angie?" Grandma said from the other room, irritation in her voice. "What are you up to, making all that racket? I hear you all the way over here."

So much for being stealthy. Shaken, I told her I everything was fine, then limped upstairs to my parents' room to get my baby book and Mom's old photo album from the cedar chest at the foot of their bed. My birth certificate could be there, and maybe the picture album would provide some clues.

My *Baby's Early Years* memory book opens to my first photograph, a round-faced newborn in a wicker bassinet. Even then you can see the girlish pout in my bottom lip and the perfect baby chin, looking almost like an afterthought, no more than a little bump to keep the lips in place. On the next page, where the birth certificate is supposed to be, a hand-written card with the date and time of my entrance into this world is scotch-taped in place—*midwife Rose Rumble delivered Angelica Marie on June 30th, 1958, at 6:13 AM, healthy and whole, weighing 6 lbs., 5 oz., measuring 18½ inches.* A plastic bag with a locket of hair from my first haircut is taped in the book, too, but not my birth certificate.

Disappointed, I paged through the photo album, filled mostly with pictures of me. Me trying to squirm out of Mom's arms. Me with Grandma and Grandpa. Me sitting on Grandma's lap. What do you know, she's actually smiling at me. Pages of photos, none of them with Dad. Then he appears as if literally dropped into the picture. In the only one of him with Mom, he's squinting at the camera, and she's wearing a light-colored suit with a corsage pinned to the lapel. She looks as stiff as crinoline, with her hands clasped in front. Dad has a full head of hair, dressed in a dark suit and tie, and stands more than a head taller than Mom, holding her elbow. The two of them don't look particularly close, much less in love. They look like cutouts from two different photographs glued together.

I studied a picture where I'm sitting on Dad's lap at a table in front of a cake with candles. Mom is standing behind him, smiling, pleased. Determination shows on my face as I take a deep breath, ready to blow out three tiny flames. My scalp prickled. I'd never noticed his absence in the earlier photos, but it sure looked as if Edgar wasn't around until I was nearly three. I paged through them one more time, thinking I'd simply missed him, as if the photographs might reveal something different.

Maybe I was their "Love Child," as Diana Ross sang, "Never meant to be..."

I laughed at the idea. My parents were beacons of good morals. Dad wasn't in the photos because he was the one who'd taken all the pictures. I clapped the album shut and shoved it under my bed. Lying back on the carpet, I stared at a strand of dust hanging from the ceiling, still puzzling about the dates on that other document and agitated because I couldn't find my birth certificate.

No teenager thinks about their parents having a dark past if they have any past at all.

Each passing minute tied my stomach into another knot as I waited for them to come home that afternoon. My head ticked like a nickel-plated watch. I tried to study biology, but the words—*lipid bilayer and nonpolar tails of phospholipids*—swam like fish all over the textbook pages. I heard Mom's car pull into the driveway and raced downstairs to be waiting for her the moment she stepped into the house.

She hung her raincoat in the breezeway. Frizzy strands of flaxen hair had blown loose from her chignon to make a halo around her head. "It sure is windy. The weather's going to change," she said, bringing a crisp, earthy scent with her into the kitchen.

I casually studied my fingernails. "Yeah. Sure is. Hey, Mom, I was wondering, where's my birth certificate?"

She froze for a second, the flinch imperceptible before she slowly set her purse on the table. "Oh, why, it's..." She hurried to the sink to wash her hands. "I'm not sure. Let me think about it while I get dinner started. Dad will be home any minute, and he'll be starving, as always. What do you want it for?"

"You can't remember where it is?"

She snorted. "I can't possibly remember everything. Wait

until you're my age." Pink dish soap bubbled in her hands. She looked sideways at me, as if testing my seriousness, then her eyes skittered away. "I'll find it, but I don't understand why you need it."

She took a butcher-wrapped package from the refrigerator and set it in the sink, searched through the cupboards until she found the Pyrex cooking dish she wanted and then poked around in the box that held the packaged seasonings. It was a good show of pretending everything was okay, but her jaw was working like a grinder. Cookie circled her, tap-dancing on the linoleum, begging for a biscuit. Mom stole another glance at me. "What happened to your chin?" She raised her own so I'd do the same, giving her a better look.

"Nothing. I tripped. Just tell me where you think it is, and I'll get it."

Her hips and upper arms shook as she briskly rinsed pimpled chicken parts in cold water and picked at buttery globs of fat. "Don't use that tone with me. You always expect everything right away. Why are you in such a hurry? You'll have nothing to look forward to when you're an adult."

Impatient over her deflecting, I pressed ahead with my questions before I lost my nerve. "When did you and Dad get married?"

"What? For goodness sake, Angie. What is with you today?"

I set the paper on the counter. "This says you and Dad got married in 1961."

Confusion registered on her face. Her brows pressed together as she wiped the hair from her forehead with the back of her dripping hand. "Oh, that…it was a mistake." Her neck turned red as she patted the chicken parts with a paper towel, then she plopped them into the casserole dish and washed her hands again. "What were you doing, snooping around in the safe, anyway? You could misplace something.

Those are important papers."

"Were you and Dad married when I was born?"

She slapped the faucet off, snatched a checkered towel from the rack, and wiped her hands more vigorously than she needed. "You get some strange ideas sometimes, missy. Of course we were married," she said as if unjustly accused.

I started to argue, but then Dad walked in through the back doorway. The wind twirled the long flap of hair he combed over his bald spot. "Hello. How're my girls?" He paused before he came into the kitchen, detecting something disagreeable in the air.

"Everything's fine," Mom said.

"No, it's not."

"Oh?" He fussed with his hair as if checking how much damage the wind had caused.

She turned to me, putting on a big show of exasperation as if hoping he would rescue her from me. "Can't it wait until after dinner? I will get it for you then. All right?"

I rolled my eyes and sighed, having little choice but to wait.

"What's going on?" he asked.

"Angelica's been nosing around, and now she has some fancy notions going around in her head," she said.

Fancy notions, as if I were making things up. Apparently, it was her intention to discount anything I said to Dad. I spoke through gritted teeth. "I need my birth certificate because I'm going to take driver's ed. I can pay for it myself. If you won't take me, Paige will."

"That's what the fuss is about? If you're paying, you can take lessons on the moon for all I care, but don't think you'll be driving my car anywhere soon," Dad said, smiling at his cleverness. "If Mom says she'll get it for you after dinner, then that's what she'll do. So, what's cooking?"

Mom stared at the raw chicken parts as if thinking about whether to fry them or fling them at the wall. I went to my room and stayed there, frustrated. All I cared about was getting my hands on my birth certificate. When my parents had actually married didn't matter to me anymore.

It was an official birth certificate, issued by the Ohio Department of Health, Division of Vital Statistics. Nothing seemed out of order: mother's maiden name, age at delivery, father's name, age, occupation, my full name, date of birth: 1958—everything looked as I'd expected. Mom stayed in my room for some reason, sitting on my bed, watching me read it. I could always tell when something was under her skin, not just because her forehead would be creased and her pupils shrunken to pinheads, but because her anxiety seemed to leap in an arc from her nervous system to mine. This time the sparks were palpable.

"Angie, honey, there's something I need to tell you. See the date of notarization?"

That hadn't occurred to me. The notary date was 1961, the same year as the marriage certificate. "What does that mean?"

She kneaded her small fists into her thighs. Her eyes began to move as if she were reading from a teleprompter. "First of all, I want you to know I didn't keep this from you on purpose. That was never my intention. It's just that some things are hard to talk about. Some people avoid talking about them altogether, or they put them off until they're ready, and that can be a long, long time. Sometimes they're never ready. What I want to tell you is…is…I was married once before, before I met Daddy. I was no older than you, actually."

I looked at her, stunned, mouth open as if to catch a fly, trying to imagine her being married twice. When she took a breath, shakiness seemed to dampen her determination to plow ahead, as if she thought I wouldn't understand. What could possibly be so bad? Did she have an affair with Dad, get pregnant with me, and divorce her first husband to marry him? There was a part of me that couldn't wait to hear more, not yet aware of the depth of the story.

Her voice sounded far away. "I was living with Aunt Harriet, in Wisconsin, for a spell, helping her with the farm after she had surgery, and I met someone at her church. He was in the service, and he was going to leave for Camp Casey, in South Korea, in a month. We got married before he went. We were foolish. We thought we were in love. And, well, he never made it home. He was killed in North Korea."

I was having a hard time following her but nodded to let her know I was on her side.

"That man was your father. I met Daddy a few years later when I came home to live with Grandpa and Grandma. He legally adopted you when we got married, and your birth certificate was amended and notarized."

I was struck dumb in the face of this bizarre fact: my father wasn't my father? I stared at my birth certificate. The letters of his name seemed to float out of place, like the words in my textbook. My knees went weak, my face felt hot as I tried to digest this, thankful Mom kept quiet and allowed me to think. It made sense, considering I didn't resemble the man I'd grown up believing was my flesh-and-blood father, not physically, or in mannerisms. Even you surely noticed that. I used to think it was dumb luck that my father and I bore no resemblance. With his off-kilter jaw and nose, he looked as if a mule had kicked him in the left side of his face and rendered it permanently askew.

I suddenly felt different in a way I can't describe. "Why didn't you tell me earlier?" I asked, remembering two class-mates who had always known they were adopted. It was no big deal to them, just a fact of life. I supposed it could have been worse.

"It's hard for me to talk about. Believe me when I say I never meant to deceive you." Her arms circled protectively around herself as she studied me, gauging my reaction. "Besides, Dad is the only father you've ever had."

Just the same, she had deceived me. Not telling me that Dad wasn't my birth father and letting me grow up thinking he was equaled deception, don't you think? A rising unease that I'd been cheated out of something, a chance to have a different history, bothered me. "Do you have a picture of him? My real father?"

Eyes heavy with sadness, she said, "No. I don't. It happened so long ago that I hardly remember it. And then I didn't want to remember. Don't you see? This is the marriage I was meant to have. This is the father you were meant to have. What else matters?"

There was a lot that mattered. My real father sounded like someone to be proud of, a war hero, a decorated veteran, not a gawky doctor who scraped calloused feet. We might have a Purple Heart, a folded flag in the closet, a letter commending his bravery from the president. "This is about me, not you. It's *my* father. My *real* father."

"Your real father is here in this house." She pursed her lips.

My voice rose. "Just because you want to forget something that happened doesn't make it right for me. You can't drop this in my lap and not expect me to want to know more…what he looked like, what he did. He's a war hero. It's not fair to keep this from me. I have a right to know!"

She looked as if shot in the stomach, her blue eyes wide, her face pale, her jaw hanging. She searched my face, shocked that I'd demand such things. I sensed her pulling away as if some unthinkable terror inside her head was reeling her in. She seemed so fragile whenever she got rattled like this. What could be upsetting her? Why wouldn't she want to talk about him?

I could think of only one reason, the same reason I wished I could forget you. "You still love him," I said, crumbling inside, projecting my pain onto her. I wanted to cry for her.

She squeezed her eyes shut. "Oh, Angelica. Oh Lord." The

groove in her forehead deepened. Apparently she did love him, which explained her discontent—Dad wasn't the man she'd wanted, even though she'd said, seconds ago, that their marriage was meant to be. It was as shocking as it was sad to think she'd once been so deeply in love and suffered such grief. My desire to know about my birth father was even stronger now, wondering what kind of man had captured my mother's heart. She wasn't a cold fish, after all.

I bit my lip, trying so hard to be patient. "Can't you tell me something, anything, about him? Please? What was his name?"

Her lips were a wavy line of anguish. She put her hands on either side of her face, and her body seemed to fold inward. "Oh...oh...I don't know how to...I don't think I can."

She hurried out of my room, leaving me alone, feeling stupid and useless in the wake of her sorrow. After a few minutes had passed without her return, I went to her room, my nerves tense enough to snap. The opportunity to learn more would slip away if I didn't grab it with both hands and hold tight.

She was looking out her bedroom window at the gray, lifeless sky.

"Please, Mom? It's important to me."

"Angie, sweetheart, I'm sorry. I...I don't want to lie to you about this. I can't. You have a right to know the real story." She took a huge breath. "I was young and naive, and, well, I should have known better." She sat on her bed and folded a thin white hankie with purple flowers into a tiny square on her lap, opened it, and then refolded it. Her face was splotchy, and the skin of her throat was red from being pinched and pulled. "I met a boy at the roller rink. He said he was the cousin of a girl from school. Susan, I think." She slumped and took a deep breath that made her chest and shoulders slowly rise and fall.

"Someone you had met before you married my real father?"

I was completely in the dark about why this mattered.

"No, no, no. That's just a story," she said, shaking her head, irritated over being misunderstood. I wanted her to tell me something that made sense. Roused by her voice, Cookie trotted in and sat at her feet, ears folded back, panting nervously. "There was no first marriage. Your grandmother made that up. She said the family would be disgraced if anyone knew the truth. She said it was shameful. She said, 'No one can do that to you unless you let them.' I was seventeen, for God's sake. I had no idea this kind of thing could happen...." She paused as if to choose the right words. "He took advantage of me. I tried to stop him, but he was like a mad bull. Inhuman. He forced it on me. The next thing I knew, I was pregnant."

I struggled to connect the disjointed scraps of information she'd given me. There was no first husband. No marriage when she was young. That was a ruse, thanks to Grandma. The words *mad bull*, *forced*, and *pregnant* rang like alarm bells. "What are you saying?"

"I'm sorry. I'm so sorry. I didn't ever want to have to tell you."

"You mean you were forced, like, raped?" I prayed she would say no, prayed it wasn't true. She squeezed her eyes shut and gave me a quick nod, one so slight that I would have missed it if I had blinked. My skin seemed to shrink. "By *who*?"

"He said his name was Phil something or other."

"And he got you pregnant?"

"Yes."

I forced a swallow. "With me?" She nodded again. My mouth went dry. Panic and disbelief made my body prickle. Her fears, obsessions, and warnings took on a new significance. Mom had been raped. This was why she hovered over me, why she scorned all things carnal and talked as if she despised men. It had to be true. Of course it was true. Why else? I felt my blood drain as I slid onto the floor by the bed.

Cookie poked my arm with her wet nose, then licked my ears and neck. I batted fur with my hands, then pushed her head away. She yipped at Mom to get her attention.

"Shh. It's all right, girl. Sit," she said, and Cookie sat, panting dog breath in my face.

"Don't you know his full name? Didn't you ever see him again?" I asked. On some level I thought I could talk her out of this version or show her that it was a fabrication, as in *Let's go back to the beginning and start over. What really happened? See, it wasn't rape after all.*

Her face twitched as if she'd gone through this a dozen times before. "Do you think a man like that would give me his real name?"

"Couldn't the police find him?"

She groaned dismissively. Cookie let out a howl that echoed Mom's, a strange noise that, under different circumstances, would have made us laugh. Maybe that was our collie's intention.

"What about Grandpa and Grandma? Didn't they do anything, like hunt the guy down?"

Her face hardened, and the muscles around her mouth pulled tight. "Your grandmother called it a sob story. Your grandfather didn't want to hear about it. They didn't even know I went out on a date with someone. At least, I thought it was a date." She blew her nose. It sounded like a trumpet blast.

"But there are laws." Typical teenager, I wanted to argue everything.

"Oh, laws. Yes. Laws. Lot of good they do. It always comes down to the woman's word against the man's. They'll ask you what you were doing, what you were wearing, if you flirted, if you said no when you really meant yes, why you didn't fight harder, why don't you have bruises. You had to get shot or stabbed for anyone to believe you. Maybe it would've been better if he had strangled me like he said he would. All this talk about shame and disgrace, like it was my fault, like I asked for it. I didn't ask for it! And I didn't want a baby either!"

I gasped, sucking a dog hair into my mouth.

Her upper lip rose in revulsion. "'That's what happens

to girls who sneak around,' they said. And they shipped me off to Aunt Harriet's like I was trash. I was supposed to give you up for adoption. They said 'Don't you bring that bastard baby home, that child with blood from God knows where.' I wouldn't do it. Keeping you made them mad. I was glad it made them mad. And then I had to live with your grandmother's cockamamy war bride story." Her voice was shrill, scraped raw from living with anger and shame.

The dog hair fluttered in the back of my throat, making me gag. Was she mad at me? I didn't do anything, did I? Yes. I was the baby she didn't ask for, the baby she kept to spite her parents. Mom hadn't wanted me. My birth father was a rapist—the truth seared as if I had been branded with a hot iron. I wanted Mom to stop talking, but she kept ranting, much of it making no sense. What was she thinking? That the truth was a good thing? That it would set her free? Sure, I'd wanted to know about my birth father, but you can see this was more than I could handle.

"What did I do that was wrong? He was the villain. My only sin was being naive. That's all! How dare they say I slept with a man? It wasn't sleeping!" She spat. Mom actually spat. "They could take everything else from me: my pride, my self-respect."

Something big and hot was trying to claw its way out of my chest. Unable to listen anymore, I stumbled downstairs, snatched Dad's car keys from the table, and ran outside to his precious Lincoln. I needed someone to blame. I shouted every obscenity I could think of, every dirty curse you had taught me. I shouted at the house and its bland facade, its smug shutters and winking window shades, and the idiots who lived inside. I started the car, zigzagged in reverse out the driveway, and took off toward Brecksville Road.

What had been written on my *original* birth certificate for my father's name? *Unknown Assailant*? Was he some dirty tomcat who lurked in alleys, a yellow-toothed wolf crouching behind a tree? He sounded like a snake charmer with greased hair and a pencil thin mustache.

No love was involved in my creation—only violence. What did that make me?

Why did he pick my mother? Why did she have to get pregnant? Why did it have to be *me*? A car honked at me. My heartbeat ratcheted. I had two tons of steel to keep under control. I veered to the right to avoid being sideswiped. *Concentrate.* I headed for the Metropark, hyperalert, focused on the task at hand: watching the other cars, traffic signals, lights, and signs, and staying in the proper lane, at the proper speed. I was thankful you'd let me drive your car around the school lot a few times, but it was harder than I'd thought to handle the mechanics of driving *and* watch the world around you as you're moving through it, especially in shock.

I kept checking the rearview mirror, afraid Dad would come chasing after me in Mom's Buick. I pressed easy on the accelerator, bringing the car up to thirty-five mph, and loosened my grip on the wheel. *Stay mellow. It's fine. You're fine. Steady on the gas.* The light ahead was green. I gassed it too hard when I took a turn and swerved across the centerline before I straightened out. Another horn blasted, making my heart race, and a man in a station wagon shook his fist at me. Who did he think he was? Some flabby-faced slob who thought everyone in the world owed him respect just because? I gave him the finger. I'd earned the right.

After that declaration I began to feel at ease. Soon I found it exhilarating to be in command for a change, maneuvering through the world by myself. I executed a near-perfect, right-hand turn onto Chippewa Creek Drive, tires crunching along the gravel shoulder. I could get to like this. I was doing great. I was willing to bet I could have aced a driving test. You would have been cheering.

Winter-flattened leaves still clotted the ground at the park, but the buds on the towering hemlocks were heavy and full, on the verge of bursting into leaf. Fiddlehead ferns would soon unfold, dogwoods would blossom along the parkway, and wildflowers would be strewn like confetti across the fields. The air would be sweet, and I could go wherever I wanted. I could be whoever I wanted. I imagined myself behind the wheel of an orange Rally Sport with racing stripes on the hood instead of driving this old-fogy car. Looking classy, I'd cruise with the radio up and the windows down, my hair blowing all around. In anticipation of spring, I cranked open the window as I turned onto Valley Parkway and headed to the picnic area where you and I used to park.

A gust of cold air from the window blew across my face like a sharp slap. I was the daughter of a rapist. At that moment, I understood what it was like to have an out-of-body experience as if I'd crash-landed on another planet. I was no longer the same person. I could not escape this. Dad's car wouldn't get me where I wanted to be, which was sitting next to you in a Bel Air with a clanking heater, headed toward a glittering future. "Joe, where are you?" I cried out, circling the empty lot. We could have run away together. We could have left our rotten families and started our own. I wanted to go back, back to when we were together, before I knew this sickening truth. I spun the wheel and stepped on the gas, trying to get back to my other life, the one with you in it.

The realization that it was gone forever hit me, and the pain that awareness brought hurt so bad it blinded me. There was a jarring crash, and everything stopped.

◄▲►

CHAPTER NINE

I sat beside a desk as big as the state of Montana. The desk belonged to a big cop who was talking on the phone. Officer Fielding of the Nopiming police department. He must have told me his name, but I couldn't tell you when. His short-sleeved shirt was stretched tight across his back and bear-like shoulders. The hair on his forearms was bushy enough to collect pencil shavings, eraser shreds, and small insects. A framed photo on his desk needed a shot of Windex to clear up the picture of a woman with bouffant hair and a pink dress. The busy room was filled with several other desks, all of them burdened with stacks of paper, gooseneck lamps, and multiline black telephones with blinking lights. The policeman behind us had bristling eyebrows weighing heavily over his eyes. The cop on the far side of the room looked permanently pissed off, tired from tangling with deadbeats who robbed convenience stores or listening to uptight citizens bitch about yapping dogs. Beyond a gate was a hallway where people hustled back and forth with businesslike efficiency. I sat still, taking it all in, but had no sense of self. Numb, I was a girl who'd detached herself, pulled the tooth of herself out by the root.

Fielding put the phone back in the cradle and caught me staring at him. He switched the toothpick to the other side of his mouth and said, "Your daddy-o is on the way. You can wait here. That okay with you?" I nodded. My nose and throat felt clogged with dust. I wanted to go home and sleep this off like a bad case of the flu. "Good. No sense taking you to a holding cell. You don't belong there," he said, winking at me as if I were a young plaything he'd found in a sticky downtown bar, an innocent he wanted to take somewhere and slowly undress while kissing her bare neck, not caring what her name or age was. He would wrap his stubby fingers around me; and, after he was finished, he'd sing an Elvis tune in a voice as deep as a sinkhole on Route 21, *Are you lonesome tonight,* proud of himself as he buttoned his shirt while I lay like a transparency in a motel bed. He'd write my phone number in his little book. Maybe he'd call, maybe not. I wouldn't have cared.

Instead, he asked me if I wanted a Tootsie Pop.

I imagined him wrestling a rapist down onto his stomach and sitting on his back while cuffing him. Later, he'd call his wife and lie about having to work all night again so he could sleep with me. That skewed sense of righteousness seemed attractive.

He stared back at me, the toothpick teetering between his teeth. "Sure you don't want a Tootsie Pop?" I wondered if *Tootsie Pop* was code for something.

"Sure, if you want one," I said. He frowned as if he recognized the need in my eyes. It was a look I would later try to hide, although Gavin was one of those men who was able to hone in on the vulnerability in a woman.

"Hey! Where's that file on Stokes?" asked a man with a Fu Manchu mustache and long sideburns. "Am I the only one who gives a shit? Christ Almighty, do I got to beg for it?" He kept talking as he walked out. "Everyone treats me like a goddamn workhorse. That's all I am. A goddamn workhorse." Another officer slapped him on the back and laughed.

Despite a coarse blanket draped around my shoulders, I had the chills. I wondered who else this blanket might have comforted, if it had ever been spread out over the grass for a family picnic or been dragged into the woods to make love on, as you and I did with the blanket in your car. The fluorescent bulb above me flickered and buzzed, casting a strange light over gravy-colored walls. When I shut my eyes, I saw the front end of the Lincoln up against a pine tree, jade-green boughs flopped across the hood. I hit a tree. I wrecked the car. Dad was going to kill me.

As if conjured by my thoughts, he appeared at the far end of the room, standing behind the gate, his pale eyes searching for me. I slumped low in the chair and pulled the blanket closer. The man who could fix anything, from a tiny earring post to a washing machine, looked as if he'd lost his needle-nose pliers. He was wearing a sweatshirt, something he never wore out of the house unless dashing to the hardware store for a new faucet head. His sparse hair was plastered to his forehead, and his face shone like parboiled meat.

I wondered what my real father looked like, if I resembled him or had any of his traits, good or bad. Bile rose in my throat.

Dad wasted no time getting over to me. For a moment I feared he might hug me. "Angelica. Dear God. What did you think you were doing?" He brushed the hair from my forehead with a cold hand. His finger ran across a tender spot where I assumed I'd hit the steering wheel and knocked myself out. Not wanting his pity, I moved my head away. He set aside the blanket and draped my pea coat over my shoulders, then sat across from the officer and proceeded to wring his hands. My stomach growled.

Fielding asked him my full name, date of birth, and half a dozen other questions, verifying what information I'd grudgingly given him earlier. He finished his report by typing with two fingers on an electric typewriter on a roll-away next to his desk. When he asked if I was always this quiet, Dad raised an eyebrow at me. My stomach rumbled again.

"Lucky she wasn't speeding. Some kids get all liquored up and wrap themselves around telephone poles," Fielding said as he leaned back in his chair. He suggested I be taken to a doctor to be sure everything checked out, but other than being disoriented and having a "goose egg," I seemed all right. He gave me a ticket for driving without a license. That was it.

I hated to leave the insulated anonymity of the police station. Dad drove me home in Mom's car. I didn't ask about the damage I'd done to the Lincoln. He kept stealing glances at me, clearing his throat, adjusting himself in the seat as if about to say something. He never did. Presumably he was afraid he'd say the wrong thing, so he said nothing at all. It was as if a dead animal lay on the car seat between us, a dog with congealed blood on its coat, long mouth open, yellow teeth bared, something that would leave a bad odor between us for years.

I rested my forehead on the cool glass and remembered the neighborhood tour you once gave me: That's Sheffield Paints. Lenny's Auto Tune-up. An office building. Houses. Houses. More houses, obviously a residential zone…How I wished I had you to talk to. Even if you hadn't known the right thing to say, you would have done something to show me you cared. Then I wondered if you ever cared for me.

I hung up my coat in the breezeway and kicked off my shoes. Dad took my arm to pull me close and gave me an awkward, rigid hug, patting my back as if I were a baby. I stood with my arms at my side, resisting, much in the same way I initially resisted Gavin. I didn't deserve comfort or love.

"I don't blame you for running off like you did, but, please, don't do this again. All right? We'll get past this. You'll see," he said.

He was an optimist to the point of absurdity. To even suggest that we could get past this was insane. I pulled away from his scarecrow stiffness. "So you know what Mom told me?"

"Yes. I'm sorry you had to find out this way. She wanted to tell you on your own terms, when she was ready, and I felt I didn't have the right to say otherwise. It's difficult for her to talk about. But I love you like you were my own little girl.

Even more so. You understand that, don't you?"

"How can you, when you know who my father is?"

"Well, I don't know him, of course, but from what Mom says, he was a good man." He smiled down at me as if to show me he was okay with it. I gasped at his calm acceptance of something so heinous that it made me want to vomit.

"He's a rapist, Dad! I'm the daughter of a rapist. That doesn't bother you?"

He shrank back, staring at me as if I spoke in Martian. "What?"

It hit me then. He didn't know the truth. Mom must have told him the cockamamy war bride story, and he'd bought it. Embarrassed and ashamed, I ran from him. I passed Grandma, who was watching like the Amazon queen she thought she was, her hands moving like small rodents in the pockets of her cotton housedress. She knew everything. That's why she gave me those evil looks—I was her bastard grandchild, the daughter of a *hure* who became a *hure*. I wanted to poke her in the eye for the awful things she'd said and done to Mom, and for trying to pawn me off on strangers to raise.

I told her, "I hate you. I hate you more than I've ever hated anyone in my life."

Her wrinkled eyes widened.

I slammed my bedroom door and pushed my chair in front of it. I hated Dad for gaping like a carp at me, for not telling me he wasn't my real father when I was younger, for not being man enough to have figured out the truth about Mom. Unable to understand the little ways we deceive ourselves on a daily basis, I thought he had to be the stupidest person on the planet for not knowing her irrational behavior was more than typical motherly worrying.

I lay, stomach down, on my bed with my head hanging off the edge. I was an analytical person, a conscientious honor roll student, a quick learner. I'd studied literature and ancient history, read Shakespeare and Salinger, yet none of it, nothing, had given me the skills or words to make sense of this.

The following morning I wouldn't have been surprised if I had opened my curtains to an ash-filled sky, charred houses, trees burned to stubs, the ground still smoking. Instead, the sun had risen like a relentless machine, and the sky wafted like a freshly washed blue sheet above us. My house was the same house, with the same eggshell-white ceilings, dark-wood floors, and braided rugs. The only difference: I understood reality was a dark beast, capable of shifting under my feet.

I fingered the silk edge of my blanket, trying to reframe my past in light of what I now understood to be the truth. Everything I'd thought about myself had been a falsehood. In many ways, our family operated like any other family. Dad paid the bills, fertilized the lawn, and kept us free from foot pain. Mom knitted and purled, chased after flesh-eating germs, and smothered me until the sound of my own name made me cringe. We played Uncle Wiggly and Chutes and Ladders. I went trick-or-treating on Halloween. I had a sandbox. I pushed my plastic baby doll in her flimsy buggy back and forth along the sidewalk while squirrels scolded me from the trees. We had two cars, one-and-a-half baths, and a color television. Hot and cold water. Electricity. We ate pot roast on Sunday, spaghetti on Wednesday, and tuna casserole every Friday and we weren't even Catholic.

My friend Becca was terrified to stay in the house alone with her addled grandfather because he would forget who she was and try to kick her out. Lizzy was ashamed to be seen with her mother, who was so obese she couldn't walk to their mailbox without wheezing. Jessica's father owned a motel where a man was found shot in the head in room thirty-six. Paige suspected her parents were swingers who went to sex parties. Skip seemed to have been deserted by his folks. I had a hunch there was more to your relationship with your father than you'd let on. Yet I was certain no one's family had a secret as hideous as mine.

I walked downstairs to the kitchen. Grandma's door was shut when I thought she'd be up and about, poking at our sores, swinging her machete into the thick of things. Dad was sitting at the table. *The Plain Dealer*, still folded, was in front of him. There was no plate of fluffy yellow eggs, no stack of pancakes, no waffles steaming in the iron. Like Grandma, Mom must have slept in, too, which was so unlike her that I wondered if she'd swallowed a bottle of sleeping pills.

Dad cleared his throat and said simply, "Morning." How could he possibly love me, now that he knew who my father was?

I must have been four when he sat me in an examination room chair as deep and wide as a mountain valley to a little girl, then raised it high and tilted it back so my feet were in the air. He tickled them until I begged him to stop. He let me play with a plastic skeleton of a foot and ankle that came apart like a puzzle. Once I stood in front of the X-ray machine in his office, my small pink feet placed exactly so on the painted feet on the floor, and Dr. Dad pretended to X-ray me. He said, "This is very serious, Miss Angelica Marie. I can't see your bones, just the dirt between your toes. The good news is, I've solved your stinky problem." Then he let me pretend I was the doctor, even though I couldn't even pronounce *podiatrist*. "Turn this way, turn that way, stand on one foot, now jump in place," I had said, making my sternest face. "We have to remove the bunnies on your toes." He cried, "Oh no, anything but bunions." His desk was big and shiny, and I'd spin around in his wooden chair until I was dizzy. His receptionist, Miss Quinn, had a phone, an intercom, and an electric typewriter. I'd play secretary and peck out a letter to Mom: *Hi eMomm i am dsittgjn aj dfads offce.*

He and I had sat together at the kitchen table while I colored a family tree for school. I colored every little leaf with a waxy green Crayola, creating a beautiful, shiny world. He talked about Grandpa and Grandma Lowsley as if they had been my blood grandparents, helped me spell *Henry* and *Astrid* in the branches, and said his family's English roots could be traced back to Virginia in the 1700s. How carefully I had printed his name on the branch for *Father*, having no reason to question him. How could he have let me done that?

Maybe if a person told a lie enough times, he could convince himself it was true. When I looked at him, I no longer saw the father who dazzled me with the sweep of his hand over a deck of cards or helped me nurse a fallen baby wren by feeding it raw hamburger and bread soaked in milk every hour. When we let the fledging go, we cheered as it managed to flap clumsily up to a low branch on a tree. The next day a smatter of downy feathers trembled in the grass beneath the tree, and one of Mrs. Wozniak's mewling cats was slinking away under the fence.

What would my truth be? Was I supposed to lie about who I really was, just as Mom had to lie about me? It wasn't as if I'd been a paragon of truth to begin with, but I'd always expected, at some point in my life, I could be honest with others and myself. That idea vanished like the baby wren. This was something I could never tell anyone.

That morning I didn't need to ask Dad if Mom had filled him in on the details; it had settled like a bad dream on his crooked face and drooping eyelids. The truth about me and the fact that his wife had lied to him was likely more than he'd bargained for in marriage. I'd have felt badly for him, too, if it wasn't for the fact that he had willingly deceived me.

After pouring myself a glass of orange juice, I searched the bottom cupboard for strawberry Pop-Tarts, pushing aside corn-flakes, puffed rice cereal, and the Quaker Oats barrel with the picture of the wholesome, white-haired Puritan. Later, I crossed Oat's eyes out to keep him from staring at me. We always had strawberry Pop-Tarts, we bought stock in them, we hoarded them in case of a tornado or atomic bomb. Why today, of all days, would we be out?

It was a conspiracy. A deliberate plot to make me crazy. My teenage brain was outraged and confounded, wondering how Mom had managed to get herself raped anyway. If she hadn't wanted a baby, why did she have me? She could have aborted me. I would never have known. Try twisting your mind around that idea. Or she could have left me on the doorstep of a church so a normal couple, who had no idea who my real father was, would have adopted me. I could have led a life unaware of the abhorrent circumstances of my conception. "It's not fair!" I stood up, swung around, and knocked the glass of juice. It spilled across the counter and onto the floor.

Dad was on his feet. "What do you want? Tell me. I'll go to the store. I'll get it. Whatever you want." He was so appeasing it made my stomach turn.

When I realized my actions had upset him, a sense of power rippled through me. Under these new circumstances, how much bad behavior could I get away with? Would my parents let outright belligerence slide? What about swearing, drinking, smoking, staying out late? Were a few psychotic episodes to be expected and, therefore, excused? How long before this silver lining grew dingy with use?

A high-pitched, inhuman scream, like a cat being stabbed, reverberated from the upstairs. Dad ran to investigate. Cookie followed me as I chased after, only to collide with him in the second-floor hall as he rushed from Grandma's room, saying, "Ambulance. I have to get an ambulance."

I peeked in from the doorway. Grandma, dressed in a housecoat, was flat on her back on the floor, her head tilted back, jaw slack, lips pulled in. Her pinned curls were a garden row of gray whorls under a spiderweb hairnet. Mom's face was as white as crushed chalk as she gently patted Grandma's shoulder. Next to Mom, Cookie lay with her head on Grandma's hip. I flattened myself against the wall in the hallway, trying to stay steady. Yesterday, I'd wished her dead. I'd wished my entire family dead.

Three medics burst into the house and up the stairs, only to have Cookie rush at them from the bedroom to growl them back down. Glad to have something useful to do, I shut her in my room, where she barked and pawed at the door. One of the medics interrogated Mom, and she answered in worried bursts as the man jotted notes on a clipboard. The other two men shifted Grandma's limp body onto a stretcher and carried her gently down the stairs to the ambulance. My parents followed, Mom's hands fluttering nervously at each other. From the front door, I watched the medics hoist Grandma into the ambulance. Mrs. Plutchnek, standing post on her porch across the street, waved at me. I didn't acknowledge her.

Dad asked if I wanted to come with them to the hospital.

I shook my head. "Definitely not."

"It might be a stroke or heart attack. I'll call when I know more. Sure you'll be okay?"

I said what I knew he wanted to hear.

Gertrude Grund's failing heart overshadowed my crisis. Rehashing the fact that I'd been deceived, or demanding restitution from my parents for raising me under a falsehood, would have been denying Grandma the attention she expected and deserved. What did I have to complain about? She was dying. I was alive. The upside was that wrecking Dad's car, as well as my trespasses with you, seemed to have been forgotten.

Mom couldn't focus on anything for more than two minutes; her anguished thoughts rippled and circled like an oil slick on the Cuyahoga. When she wasn't at the hospital, she had angry explosions of hot tears that made me want to cry with her. One afternoon I found her sleeping on Grandma's bed. For a moment I wanted to curl up next to her, but when I remembered her saying she hadn't wanted me, I might as well have been kicked down the steps. Overly cautious, Dad looked around me instead of at me as if I were a glass ballerina that might break if handled the wrong way. I avoided both of them, peering out of my room before I walked down the hall or the stairs, listening for footsteps, pausing, watching for the shadows of who they used to be, so I could slip past unseen. If not for my existence, perhaps a different kind of family, one with different issues but none nearly as horrible as ours, would be moving around within the walls of this house.

Every morning I felt as if I had awakened from a nightmare in which I was trying to fly away but some dark, indefinable shape had me by the ankles. I had trouble reconciling the whole idea of rape with my mother, unable to fathom such a horrific assault. Her anxiety became something I could feel for myself now—how it seizes your heart and shoots holes in your lungs. In bed at night I'd pitch and flip until I thought my arms and legs would run off without me if I didn't get up and walk it off.

That was how I discovered Dad was sleeping on the couch. I saw a bulky shape there in the dark and nearly jumped out of my skin. He simply snorted and turned over. I stood, frozen, my heart hopping erratically. His face had fusty wrinkles from being pressed into the pillow. His snore smelled like sour juice.

Desperate for sleep, I poured myself a shot of whiskey from the cupboard. The fumes were strong enough to make me gag; I wasn't yet accustomed to hard liquor. I searched through the upstairs bathroom for cough syrup or sleeping pills, anything that might bring me relief. I found a nearly full container of Valium that Dr. Borage had prescribed for Mom more than a year ago and pocketed it.

You would think I'd have been elated when I opened a letter of acceptance from the University of Virginia, Charlottesville, since it was my first choice, but now I wasn't sure I wanted to go. The world was too scary. Maybe to you or anyone else I looked the same, but I felt damaged inside. I wanted to burrow in like a sand crab. I considered waitressing north of here, where no one knew me—Howard Johnson's, or Bob Evan's on Rockside Road—serving overweight truckers and slack-jawed salesmen while trying to decide which one might be my father so I could poison his chicken soup or stab him with a steak knife.

I decided I had to be strong. I had to mold myself into a tough girl who wouldn't flinch or feel pain. I had to pound nails like weapons around each of my fingers.

In the weeks it took Grandma's stringy heart to give up the fight, daffodils and tulips bullied their way out of the sun-warmed earth. On the one occasion that I visited her in the hospital, I envisioned her bolting upright, tubes flying, her eyes flashing at me as if I were the last person she wanted to see before she left this world. But nothing moved, not an eyelash or a ridged fingernail, and it hit me that she wasn't going to get better.

When she died, flowers came from people who worked with my uncles, Dad's office staff, Mom's knitting club, and neighbors, filling the viewing room in Troychek and Son's Funeral Home with lilies, mums, and carnations—feathery petals, cool, soft, and quiet. Grandma's willow-whip body made barely a wrinkle under the white-satin blanket in the casket. The thick blue veins under the skin of her hands had eerily disappeared, but the age spots remained. The skin on her face was stretched like plastic wrap over her stony cheekbones and pointed nose. Overall, though, I'd have to say she looked well rested, as if pleased she'd never need to correct her *dummschwallen* son-in-law, never need jab a crooked finger at Mom or give me a lip-curling, disapproving look again. Her silence told us we were all on our own now, and may God help us.

Mom turned Grandma's silver wedding ring so the diamond setting was on top, but it spun back around to the bottom of her boney finger. Mom's shoulders started to shake, and she stifled a sob with her hand over her mouth. Her eyes, small and wet, were lost in her puffy face. "Oh God, this killed her. This just killed her," she said in a barely audible quiver.

What had killed her? The shame of having a rapist's child in the family? Who else knew? I looked around the room for my uncles, aunts, and cousins, wondering what they knew about me. I was an outsider. Tears ran quietly down my cheeks—not for Grandma's passing or the pain Mom felt—but for you. I cried because I needed you, and you weren't there.

Paige and her parents came to the evening visitation. I never thought Mrs. Schmidt and Mom would have anything to say to each other beyond a polite hello, but their conversation was animated and expressive, with commiserating pats on the arms, as if they were the oldest of friends. I took Paige by the elbow and steered her outside. It was a cool April evening. Spotlights in the bushes shone upward on the white brick of the funeral home, making it appear to glow. We walked away from the canopied entrance to the back. Paige shook out two Eve cigarettes—as long and slender as we imagined ourselves to be when we smoked them—from the pack in her purse. We nervously exhaled while we talked about what a pill my grandmother had been.

"I remember she told us we'd get hepatitis and die after my sister pierced our ears with a needle and cork. What was it she said about my sister?" Paige asked.

"That Alisa wore her jeans so tight she could save money by not wearing any, and she could put a sign on her back advertising her tail while she was at it, too."

"Your grandma was a trip," she said with a smoky laugh. "Hey, Doug Schreyer asked me out."

"No kidding? That's cool." I was glad for her.

She asked if I'd heard any news about you. I shook my head. She scuffed the ashes at her feet and apologized for asking. "It's okay. Thanks a lot for coming. Really," I told her as I inhaled deeply and looked up to see a cloud passing over the full moon.

I missed you as much as I missed the person I once was. Losing you and learning I'd been conceived during a rape rolled into one massive, throbbing ball of pain.

What do you suppose my birth father was doing at that moment? Getting a free meal from the Salvation Army? Lying on a grimy cot in a subsidy-rent apartment on Fifty-Fourth , staring at a bare lightbulb hanging from the ceiling? What did he keep in his refrigerator? Salami? Eggs? A soft tomato with a cancerous black spot? He might have his own family, a basketful of smiling children with chocolate-coated grins and a wife in a ruffled apron who served him barbecued ribs and mashed potatoes, knowing nothing of his illegitimate daughter.

I saw him with a swim cap of dark, wavy hair like mine, a fat, stubby nose, and eyes with the intensity of a quick-moving summer storm. He focused on some distant spot, an invisible panorama, a sordid scene from his past, as he tore the meat from the ribs with his incisors, and his greasy lips moved in a silent monologue as he chewed. Suspicions, cold Midwest winters, bad city water, and clinging women made his teeth grind, no matter how many bones he sucked clean of flesh.

◂▴▸

Chapter Ten

Principal Greers didn't call your name at graduation. Saigon had been renamed Ho Chi Minh City by the Communists. Dulled by stolen Valium, I stumbled through the commencement ceremony. I had to stand in the front row with the other vertically challenged students, such as Ricky Papp, who stank like the pet store his father managed, and Melinda See with her dented nose. My cap kept falling forward on my head, and my legs ached, as if I had shin splints from running all night. A few crude hoots echoed in the auditorium when my name was called. "Wanna meet in the supply closet?" some guy said. I imagined you gallantly punching him square in the nose.

Oddly enough, once I had my driver's license, there wasn't anywhere I wanted to go. I decided I wasn't going to college but kept it to myself. My friends urged me to find someone new. I'd taken a summer nanny job for Mrs. Rossini, who had paid me well in the past to watch her two children. She said I could take the kids to the city pool or down to the lake in her Impala. I reasoned I could easily check out the lifeguards and fishermen, scour the shipyards, or look under rocks for suitors. I could lay in the sun, glossy with baby oil, and let them come to me, like vultures to roadkill. No.

Dad wasn't around much, and Mom looked the other way as I pushed my curfew back later and later. She seemed afraid to set limits, and I took full advantage of her hesitancy. She didn't need to worry, anyway. I wasn't doing anything outwardly dangerous, other than self-destruct.

There's no tactful way to say this: I let your friend feel me up for dope. Skip Kincora's penchant for altered states of mind had grown into a healthy appetite for any and all drug consumption, and Blue Bus became a band of pot-smoking, post-hippie anarchists disillusioned by their lack of commercial success. The band's absence of musical talent would have stunned you. The screech of glam rock permeated Skip's house, like the Spiders from Mars. Thick clouds of patchouli incense masked the smell of cheap marijuana that popped loudly from seeds and stems.

Skip kept a stash of pills in a plastic divider case from Andy's Hardware but couldn't be counted on to remember which were uppers and which were downers, if you were supposed to take half a tab or whole and swallow it or let it dissolve under the tongue. I stayed away from the hallucinogenics and stuck with weed, alcohol, and Quaaludes. They turned my jagged world into something white and muffled, and helped me sleep despite nightmares of poisoned DNA spiraling through my veins.

Other aspiring musicians, stoners, potheads, and fans floated in and out of Skip's. The girls who occasionally dropped by watched me from the corners of their eyes while I moved around the house as if I lived there, cleaning ashtrays, collecting empty bottles, spraying the smoke stench with air freshener, like a good wife or mother. They knew who I was—the girl who was caught in the act with her boyfriend at school—and there were times their eyes widened with misguided admiration.

I felt numb in a peculiar, throbbing kind of way, like a stubbed toe soaked in ice water. Skip could have done anything he wanted with me, but he was passive and uninspiring. His lips were often so chapped, I feared I'd swallow a loose flake when he kissed me. I wanted someone to rattle me, inundate me, or swallow me whole like Jonah. I wanted to forget you, and everything else that had gone wrong.

Unfortunately, Gavin was the only man who could do that.

Anyway, the best thing about Skip was that I didn't have to put on pretenses. He was as benign as a stoned pup and ignored me if I was rude or mean, which was often. I think it's because he didn't care enough about me to get hurt. I don't mean to say your old friend was hard-nosed or cruel. He found one of your notebooks under the cushion of a couch he was getting rid of and gave the book to me, saying, "I can't throw it out, man. It's his life's work. You take it."

My mind retreated from Skip as I ran my fingers over an inked cartoon, a single eyeball with legs. The sunken grooves your pen had made in the cardboard cover of the spiral-bound steno pad seemed to warm under my fingertips. I had seen this book in your room. My stomach quivered. I remembered how you doodled or wrote with your head hanging down and your hair in your eyes.

The pale-green pages were filled with more eyeballs, intricate geometric patterns, winged dragons, lists ("Reasons Why School Is Fucked Up," and "Twelve Ways of Looking at Barry Manilow") and poetry:

> Angel:
> winter blows mean and cold
> the fire (inside) is bright
> my blood runs hot
> my heart spills
> secrets; yes—
> these dark nights tell all
> your copper eyes
> apricot lips
> fields of hair
> I want to get lost in
> and yes

all of that, too, but
hush now—
to touch you is (to know) desire.

My heart ached anew when I read the poems you'd penned for me. There were no dates, nothing to mark time, and the last ten pages were blank. Unfinished work. Your life cut short. I clutched the book to my chest, wondering if you were even alive.

Only once did I question Mom about the time she'd said she didn't want a baby.

My nanny stint with the Rossini kids had just ended. Most days I slept till noon and, later, took part in dope fests at Skip's. One particular morning Mom was knocking at my door. When I didn't answer, she opened it and popped her head in to tell me she'd been sorting through Grandma's things. "I put a pile of clothes on her bed. Could you fold them into a bag, mark it, and put it in the garage for Goodwill? I just can't bear to do it."

"Angie?" she asked again. "Angie, honey? Do you hear me?"

"Yeah," I muttered from under the sheet. I had been dreaming she tried to leave me in the care of a hooker on the corner of Prospect and Ninth in downtown Cleveland.

Her voice grew near. "Are you feeling all right?"

"I'm tired. I'll take care of it later." My brain felt swollen. The bed shifted when she sat on the edge. When I felt her soft hand rubbing my shoulder, I scrambled to the far side of the bed, pulling the sheet with me. The last thing I wanted was for her to touch me. "You said you didn't want a baby. So why did you have me?"

She exhaled, seeming resigned, more tired than I'd ever seen her. "It's not that I didn't want you. It's that I had no say in it. To get pregnant like I did. I mean, who would want such a thing to happen?" She looked at her hands as she wrung them together. "But when I held you in my arms, I thought differently. I believed I was being shown a way to heal. I had something else to focus on instead of my pain. I wanted give you the love I never got."

I felt myself turn red. As far as I could see, the love she gave me had been suffocating, and I did not want the god-awful responsibility of being her reason for living. Unable to get past my own hurt, I'd thought she was self-centered for bringing me into this shitty world just to help herself heal.

"I named you Angelica because you were my angel. You still are. Don't you know that?"

"How can that be?" The possibility that I reminded her of the monster who assaulted her lurked in the back of my mind.

"I know it's hard for you to understand. Maybe when you have children of your own—"

"I don't want children. Ever."

Mouth open, she froze for a brief, staggered moment, looking as if I'd dumped a basket of raw eggs into her lap. "Oh, please, don't say that," she said.

I stubbornly shook my head. The thought of passing my dirty genes on to another generation disgusted me. I didn't want to bring children into a world full of evil.

When she saw I was serious, her glassy eyes went distant in her slack face. "I hope someday you'll change your mind. Life doesn't always give you what you want. If you think it will, you're in for a rough ride." As she left my room, she said, "Don't forget about Grandma's clothes."

After she left, the house was still and quiet. Just as Mom had told me, Grandma's clothes were piled on the bed. Dust floated in the sunlight from the window. I snapped one of her five-and-dime house dresses up the front and laid it flat and smooth on the floor. The soft fabric was covered with a tiny rosebud print. One of her silver bobby pins, tacky from hair gel, was in the pocket. For nearly an hour I sat there, snapping and unsnapping those silver utilitarian snaps and pinching the pads of my fingers with the bobby pin. My very existence had pitted my mother against her mother. No wonder there had been so much animosity.

I gathered a fistful of hair and spread the ends across my forehead to see how I'd look with bangs. No one else in our family had my eyes: fawn brown with gold flecks, like flashes of amber lightning. Everyone else had blue eyes and fair hair. My cheekbones and round nose were definitely Mom's, although her face was fuller. Maybe I inherited my high forehead, thick upper lip, and pointed chin from my birth father. I stripped off my clothes and stood on my toes to see as much of my naked body as I could in the bathroom mirror. Would he want to rape me, too? I caught my breath. My father was all that was evil in the world, a demon that sucked women into its center, then spit them out in broken chunks. And I was part of that awful machinery.

You understand I had no choice but to transform myself to fit this new, altered sense of self.

Combing out sections of my long hair, I cut until the bathroom wastebasket was full. Coloring my hair was a drippy ammonia-laced affair that took over an hour. The fumes stank and made my eyes burn, even with the fan on. The brassy yellow hair I was left with felt as if coated with laundry starch. I dried it straight out from my head using gel and a flat hairbrush.

Mom came home from the supermarket and bakery. "What are you up to in the bathroom? What is that smell?" She padded lightly up the stairs.

"I'm coloring my hair." She was going to hate this look, a thought that sent a current of short-lived pleasure through my veins.

"Oh." There was a pause as she digested this strange information. She tested the doorknob; I'd locked it. "By yourself?"

"I brought a Boy Scout troop in to help."

"Oh no, Angie. What did you do? Your hair is so pretty." Her voice drifted, carried by a northerly wind over the Great

Lakes. I leaned against the door as if I could feel her leaning against me from the other side, the weight of her body matching mine. *Mother.* I wanted to crawl into her lap and pull everything back with me—every plum pie Christmas, every birthday party balloon, sweet bedtime story, hug and nursery rhyme—take it all back to the beginning. I wanted to start over, with Dad as my birth father.

"Don't have a cow. I'm fine. I just have to clean up," I said. When I heard her retreat, I hurried into my room so I could entertain other ideas about how I might mold myself into someone a man would take one look at and decide to leave alone. It wasn't so long ago that I'd wanted the world to know who I was, confident and full of myself, much of it because I was madly in love with you. That wonderfulness had turned to dust, something that stuck inside my throat like a thick wad caught in a vacuum hose. I wanted you to hear the high-pitched whine before the motor blew. I wanted you to hate the new me. The girl you'd left behind no longer existed.

Dad came thumping up to speak to me through my bedroom door. "I'm concerned because Mom is concerned," he said. I reasoned that might be good since it meant they were both on the same page for once, but that togetherness wouldn't last long. "I just want to talk to you. Please open your door, Angie."

I've thought a lot about the word *talk* since then. Even as we talk, we deceive ourselves. Like dense fog, a barrage of words can hide the issues we don't want to reveal. You did it by telling funny stories to hide the truth about your father's drunken abusiveness. Gavin told jokes to hide his self-loathing. Mom told another story altogether.

When I told Dad my door was open, he entered, wearing the concern of a doctor who hoped to diagnose and fix what was wrong. That quickly changed when he saw me. Poor Edgar. He gasped and stammered while trying to process this strange new look. Mom was behind him, craning to see. I laughed, which, judging from their ashen faces, further alarmed them.

Mom said, "Oh dear. Don't worry. It'll be all right. I can get you into the salon tomorrow, and they can fix it."

"I'm not worried. Are you worried? I think my hair looks good. In fact, I love it," I said. Her face fell like a cat shooed with a broom. Dad stared, goggle-eyed, as if I were a stranger.

Since trying to be a tall, lithe princess in a ball gown was like a tunneling mole aspiring to be a mink, I went for the crusty decadence of torn and patched recycled clothing, with an element of glam to further cheapen the look. I was able to create a stunning wardrobe from a thrift shop on Euclid Avenue for less than thirty dollars. Dark makeup made my brassy blond hair look all the more extreme. My attire and attitude complemented Skip, who slunk around in deliberately torn jeans and black t-shirts with hand-painted obscenities, studded leather belts, and wristbands.

My parents were ill equipped to handle the change, apparently worried that setting limits might make things worse, that I'd shave half my head next, so they said next to nothing. We had become so emotionally frozen that being zapped with cattle prods would have been preferable to talking. Mom fell into a sad, quiet funk. Dad took up residence in Grandma's room. He would slip quietly out of the house in the morning, then blow back again late in the evening, and, after a few short-circuited exchanges at dinner, he would retreat to his study to watch television on the small, black-and-white set that he'd brought in from the garage.

Late one night when I came home, I noticed the kitchen light was on, so I snuck in through the front door, wanting to avoid whoever was still up. Once inside, I heard Mom holler, "You're drunk!"

This spooked me—how could she possibly know my condition from the other end of the house? I was even more agog when I heard Dad's loud, slurry voice.

"But it's true, isn't it! Your mother told you I was the best you could get, that I would make things right. I'd be a father to your daughter. I'm nothing more than your caretaker."

I wavered in the foyer, holding my breath, one hand on the wall for balance. His tone changed to a pitiful whine. "I did everything for you. I went along with everything. You promised me you'd tell her, and then I find out it was all a lie. And now look at her. She's gone off the deep end."

Mom cried that it wasn't her fault. She cried that she did the best she could. Cookie barked at the back door from outside, wanting to get in. Dad insisted that she'd never loved him, and it was her fault I was "going to hell in a hand basket."

Did you ever think you were to blame when your parents argued? I was nothing more than a messy consequence in their lives, a lug wrench jamming up the gears. If it hadn't been for me, they might have been happy together. Let's go even further back—if it hadn't been for me, they might have never married.

When I peeked around the corner, Mom was at the counter, sobbing. Dad stared at her as if holding himself back from hugging her or punching her—I couldn't tell which. At one time I was really good at reading my parents. I knew when to protest and when to shut up, but this was over my head. When he saw me standing in the doorway he stared as if his eyes were sending him the wrong information. Can a drunken mess detect another drunken mess?

He feebly lifted his hands and then dropped them at his sides. "I can't live like this anymore," he said. He let Cookie in, then tromped upstairs, presumably to pack. Mom slumped down onto her knees, and Cookie circled her, licking her hands and nudging her arm. I pushed the dog away and bent down to ask her if she was all right. Her head turned at the sound of my voice. I flinched in case she came up swinging.

She brushed her hair from her forehead with a trembling

hand and said, "God damn him." At least she hadn't damned me.

It's not hard to understand why Dad thought he had to go. I'm not defending him, but you can imagine the circumstances. He felt used. How could he live with her, sleep with her, even sit across the dinner table from her, if he believed she'd never loved him, not to mention she didn't trust him enough to tell him the truth? It was the end of any semblance of family as I knew it. When he came back a few days later for the rest of his clothes, the second TV, and whatever else apparently belonged to him, Mom locked herself in the bathroom. Like a coward, I ran to Skip's and got stupidified.

For a few days Mom bravely tried to act as if nothing had happened. Then she told me she was glad Dad was gone, and burst into tears. I didn't know what to say or do. Once a week he slipped a check in a sealed envelope under the door in the breezeway. He and I had a few heated arguments when he realized I had no intention of attending the university, but after I explained that I needed to stay home to make sure Mom didn't hurt herself, he didn't ask me about college again for months.

I took care of the grocery shopping, raked leaves, cleaned out the flower beds, and took Cookie for her nightly walks; she was the one thing in our lives that stayed constant. Mom sat on the couch, watching game shows as she absently knitted long scarves for nobody, as if she thought she could stitch our lives back together. For the first time I noticed gray strands in her long hair which she wore slapped up against the back of her head like a horse's tail, stabbed full of bobby pins.

On our first Christmas as a splintered family, she went to Uncle Tim's for dinner, but I stayed home, hoping Dad might stop by. He never did. I'd dusted off the old aluminum tree and set it up in the front window. The rotating color wheel clicked as it turned, casting the room in alternating blue, green, red, and yellow light. The first time Mom put it up in our front window, Dad swore it was a sacrilege. She told him it was all the rage, but he wasn't convinced. "Boy, they sure saw you coming," he'd said, and after that Christmas it was banished to the basement and kept there as a reminder to Mom not to waste money on fads.

She didn't seem capable of pulling herself together. As for me, my life was about to take another turn, but I can't say it was for the better.

A lime-green, two-door coupe magically appeared in the driveway one morning. The hair on my neck prickled when I saw it. Who was here? I cautiously checked the house for visitors or intruders, but there was no one around except Mom, who was still sleeping. I slipped a pair of boots on my bare feet and a jacket over my pajamas, and went outside to take a look around. The car was a Ford Maverick. An envelope with my name on it was propped on the steering wheel. The door was unlocked, so I hopped in and tore the envelope open to find a Thinking of You card. The message scrawled inside read: "Got a deal from a patient too good to pass. Only 23,000 miles. Auto trans. Thought you could use it to take classes at the local college, if you don't want to go to Virginia next semester. Dad."

Disregarding the reference to college, I whooped out loud, ecstatic, until I realized there were no keys. I searched the entire car: under the sun visor, beneath the worn mats and seats. It took me a moment to realize the silly car didn't even have a glove box, but I wasn't going to quibble over minor details. I hurried back inside and roused Mom, but she didn't know anything about it and refused to speculate on anything concerning Dad. I kept grilling her until she told me to please leave her alone.

Dad's receptionist, Miss Quinn, didn't recognize me in my garish getup until she heard my voice, and she had been my father's receptionist ever since I could remember. Under her front desk she kept a fishbowl full of stickers, hard candies, and kazoos. When I was a girl, she'd let me pick a toy *and* a piece of candy, saying it was all right, even though Mom had told me no sweets. Mom said Miss Quinn was a spinster who had her own ideas about how Dad should run his practice. Sometimes I wondered if there was ill will or jealousy between the two women.

Miss Quinn stared, slack-jawed, at me as I walked down the hall to Dad's office. His door suddenly opened and he charged out, his nose in a patient's file. "Say, Marilyn, where's Mrs. Bell's chart? I just thought of something. Oh, Angie." He stopped just before he barreled over me. "What a surprise."

Somehow I doubted that. He asked me to wait in his office while he took care of something. I settled into one of the cushy chairs, mulling over the fact that he'd called Miss Quinn by her first name. I wondered if this was a recent development, or if he'd always called her Marilyn. He seemed heavier in the middle, and I soon saw where the extra weight had come from. On his desk was a Styrofoam box with a half-eaten double cheeseburger with special sauce, tomato, and lettuce ruffling out from under the meat patties, and next to that was a milk shake and a bag of glistening fries.

He came back into his office, looking like someone who had a few good tricks up his sleeve. "Fries?" he asked nonchalantly, holding the bag in my direction as he sat down at his desk.

"No, thanks. Hey, the Maverick is really cool. Thanks for putting it in the driveway for me because I just love, love, love looking at it." I smiled as sweet as sugar pills. He did the same, but when he didn't say anything, I asked him if I had to roll over and beg for the keys.

"You get the keys when you get your butt into college. You were accepted at two excellent universities, and you're not attending either of them. You're sitting around at home instead. It's been over six months. What's the problem?"

I stared at the plastic, cutaway model of a foot on the corner of his desk, remembering how I used to enjoy playing with it. I told him, "I lost my enthusiasm." His pursed lips told me he wasn't giving me any sympathy, so I said, "I'm not just sitting around. I filled out job applications at all kinds of places. Apple Tree Vets, the Family Health Clinic, Mirror-Me Salon, Stickney's Rentals. I'm waiting to hear back from them." I won't tell you how long I'd been waiting.

"Looking like that?" he asked, peering over his lunch at me as if I were as dumb as a quart jar of sand. "Angelica. You know better."

"Hey, I can't make things look pretty when they're not. My life sucks. Did you know I have these awful dreams and—"

He held up his hand to stop me from going further. "Enough. I don't need to hear about it." The way he cut me off always infuriated me. He pivoted his chair to look out the streaked window at the overgrown shrub and the parking lot. His comb-over had gotten sparser. "What's your mother think about you not attending college?"

"We don't talk about it." I found it interesting that he asked about her. I cleared my throat and added, just in case it still mattered to him, "She misses you."

He rocked back, tapping his fingers on the arms of the chair. "No. Not me. She misses having a husband."

"Just the same, she's not doing so hot."

"I'm sorry to hear that, but I was her caretaker for too long. I think it hurt her more than helped her. It's time she learns to take care of herself."

"She needs help, Dad. I'm not doing a very good job."

"Then don't make it your job."

I blinked in surprise. Was it that easy? He reached into his top drawer and threw me the car keys, ringed to a rubber footprint that read Dr. Edgar M. Lowsley for Family Foot Care.

"Here. You need to think about your future. Nothing else. If you're not going to school, you better find a job, because the only way I'll pay for car insurance is if you're in school. Otherwise, that bill will fall on your shoulders."

◀▲▶

CHAPTER ELEVEN

The first time I stood at the cash register at Rego Rini's, staring at the rows of buttons, I felt like a grade school dropout. The floor supervisor plowed through the instructions while her sourball breath wafted in my face. After the first week my legs throbbed, and I couldn't have faked a smile if a gun had been shoved in my back. The upside was the store manager didn't give a whit what color my hair was, how much makeup I slathered on my face, or if my t-shirt was raunchy or see-through, as long as the blue smock covered it. Dad's work ethic had apparently rubbed off on me because, by the time I'd earned my name pin, I could void receipts, verify sale items, ring up food stamps, and get the bag packers to stick around at my checkout instead of wandering off; and I knew where to find anything from denture powder to baby zwieback. You would have been amazed, considering you're a former grocery store employee.

You may find this common, but I was taken aback to learn my coworkers were squabblers and foot draggers who regularly committed petty theft against their employer. Then again, the district manager alienated everyone with his strange, weekly staff meetings. "Moment of Truth," he said to us once. Stumped, we stared back into his one good eye. "Ask yourself that every time you walk out onto that floor. Who are you? Who are your customers? Perform your job like it matters." He posted a sign that read M.O.T. above the break room door in case our duty slipped our minds.

Thia, a clerk with zebra-striped hair and a silver ring on

every finger, spoke loudly to me from the other register. "If you stick around, you know, you'll get a raise. You can actually advance here. If a douche-bag like Rita Vogrin can work her way up to floor supervisor, who knows what the future holds for us winners?" She threw back her head and laughed. Alarmed, I looked at my customer, a woman in pink foam rollers, to see if she'd overheard; but she was trying to balance her checkbook, so I carried on, ringing up her frozen pie crust and canned cherries.

"What's the raise? Five cents after six months?" I asked.

"Something like that. By the way, sugar water works better to spike your hair than that dippity-do glop I bet you use. Hey, you want to go trolling at the Pantheon with me on Friday?"

I did.

I came home from work one day to the smell of coffee and the murmur of familiar voices and laughter from the living room. The knitting club was over. They hadn't been to our house in ages. I poured myself a cup of coffee, overhearing Ruth say there were times she wished *her* husband would pack up and leave. "Then I could have some time to myself for once instead of always waiting on him. I can't ask him to wash a dish without it causing a commotion." When Mom asked her what she'd do with her time, Ruth said, "Redecorate the goddamn house. Pete's sake, the old goat won't let me touch anything. Our living room set is going on forty years already."

I believe it was Ida who said she wanted a job so she could spend her own money on herself and not feel guilty. "I'd love to get a twenty-dollar makeover at the beauty counter."

When Mom mentioned she liked the idea of a makeover, Dottie said, "Marta, forget the makeup. You need a new wardrobe. You're shrinking right out of your clothes. We don't see or hear from you for forever, and then, *bam!* You look like a different person. How'd you lose so much so fast?"

After a few moments Mom said, "I call it the down-in-the-dumps diet." Even though she sounded more sheepish than wry, it was good to hear her crack a joke. "I hate shopping for clothes. I have no idea how to pull an outfit together."

"Why don't you get your daughter to take you? I bet she knows what's in style."

Mom clucked dismissively. "I don't think so. Angie's got her own ideas of fashion these days. You know, she tore a perfectly good pair of dungarees all the way up the sides and then pinned them back together with the pins showing. I don't know what kind of style she calls that. We used to call it poor. I can't imagine what she'd dress me in. Fishnet stockings and chain link?" The women's tittering made a slow burn creep across my face.

I made my presence known. Mom paused midbite into a gingersnap cookie, and her face reddened when she saw me. As I walked through the room to get to the stairs, the fur collar on my vinyl vest rose as if it were my own fur, and the floor creaked under my trashy boots. Ida was the first to say hello, then greetings from the others quickly followed, even as they averted their wide eyes. My hello and smile were hasty.

Mom came up to my room after the women left, presumably to apologize for what she'd said about me. "I just don't get it."

"Get what?"

"Why you dress like this. Why you color your hair. What are you trying to prove? I watch you walk out of the house every day looking weirder than the day before. Don't you care what kind of impression you make on other people?"

"Don't you?"

"Me? What about me?"

"Mom, you're swimming in your clothes, and no one tucks a shirt into an elastic waistband. You look ridiculous. Of course, you never really do anything or go anywhere, so who cares what you look like? Dress like a slouch if you want to." I wanted to be honest, but my words sounded regrettably mean.

"A slouch?" She brushed the front of her blouse and slacks,

looking hurt, and then lifted her chin and took a deep breath. "Well, I don't think I'd look good wearing a dog collar or tutu either. You dress like you belong in a circus."

"I am in a circus." I sat down on my bed to unlace my boots and pull them off. "Don't lose sleep over what I wear. Do something for yourself. There are people at department stores who can help you if you don't know what to buy. That's their job."

A few weeks later she went to a stylist in the mall instead of the blue hair salon on the corner and had her long hair trimmed into a chin-length bob, which took a few years off the gaunt face she'd been left with after she lost weight. She also bought her first pair of "dungarees," even though jeans with pleats and creases weren't what I would have dressed her in. The point is, she began to evolve.

After all, she no longer had to prepare dinner at five o'clock every evening, no longer had to wash and press Dad's shirts or fold his Clorox-white briefs and undershirts, and no longer had to duck from Grandma's sniping shots. She volunteered two mornings a week at the library's adult resource center. Then she and Dottie started watercolor classes at the Arbor Township Art Center. Before long she'd transformed Grandma's former bedroom into a studio with a secondhand easel and a wheeled cart for her paints and brushes. Instead of anxiously knitting from sunup to sundown, she painted flowers, wobbly fruit, and snowcapped mountains with impossibly blue lakes on stiff, machine-pressed watercolor paper. It didn't matter how ugly or simple her paintings were—she was breaking out of her gloom.

That was my opportunity to break free.

Thia and I rented a two-bedroom flat with a crumbling cement balcony on Fulton Avenue. The building stank like varnish with an undercurrent of urine on humid days, and the windows except for the one in the closet-size bathroom were swollen shut.

You wouldn't think my independence would leave me feeling insecure, but it did. All I knew was this was not where I wanted to be. How long would it take before I figured it out? I still had nightmares. In one recurring dream I walk along a highway in the dark, picking up dead women lying on the side the road and bagging them, the way you'd bag soda pop cans. A car zooms past. Dust and trash blow in my face. The taillights fade, and then it's quiet again. As I continue walking, the grass turns dark and slick, and the stench of rot worsens. I stumble over something: a woman with thin skin, like film on scalded milk, and arms and legs as spindly as crib rails. I reach down to take her arm, and when her body turns, I see it's my mother. Something wet and black slithers from her eye socket and leaps at me. I drop my bag and take off running along the broken yellow line of the highway. When I think there's enough distance between us, I feel compelled to go back for her. She can't be left alone. It's my job to bag her.

Then Thia would be shaking me and yelling in my face, making my heart race. "Wake the fuck up! You're screaming again!"

I believed it was best to jump headfirst into what you are most afraid of. For me, that had become a certain type of man: dangerous, huge, and hairy, a skewed vision of my birth father. I went after the spitters and snarlers. I attracted them the way rancid meat draws flies, then dropped them before they could leave me, just to prove I couldn't be hurt. This was how I intended to make myself impervious as metal and Teflon slick. The high point of my work week was Friday night when Thia and I would clock out of the store at nine, paint our faces, and go bar crawling. You wouldn't have recognized me.

She knew some of the best places to go outside of the college bars, such as the Pantheon or the Down Under. Sometimes we went to see Blue Bus play at the Local 453, even though I no longer hung out with the band. Near the end of the night, when everyone was wasted, Skip would let both Thia and I onstage for their last number, the Ramones' "Blitzkrieg Bop."

On the few occasions when we went to Mickey's, I hoped I might run into your brother Fabian, but I never did. Not there, anyway. It was at The Utopia. To tell you the truth, I would have been better off not having seen him.

Thia noticed the group of bulked-up men standing at the bar first, the biggest one wearing a short-sleeved shirt to show off his flexing bicep when he lifted his drink. "How'd you like to have that brute tear your clothes? Ooh, pump it," she said as she toyed with the velvet choker around her neck.

"Wait. I think I know that guy," I said, staring at him as if trying to read the small print. When he turned, I pinched her arm, making her yelp. "I do know him! Come on." I recognized his boxer nose, the dark hair, his fat paws. Your brother Fabian could have doubled for Lou Ferrigno as the Incredible Hungarian Hulk.

I gave him a hip bump. "Hey, hey, Fabian. What do you say?"

He swiveled around. "Hey, baby, what's shaking?" he asked, greedily eyeballing the cleavage brimming from my laced, vinyl bustier. His expression changed when he saw the rest of the package, evidently not keen on short women with flaming red hair, my color du jour.

"You don't recognize me?" I asked. For a second he seemed alarmed, as if I were some twisted chick he'd bedded who had come back to haunt him. "I was your brother Joe's girlfriend, Angelica."

The dawn came slowly. He took a step back. "Whoa. I never would have recognized you. Not in a million years."

"I take that as a compliment. You look buff as ever. How are you?"

"All right," he said. He didn't ask how I was, still staring outright. One of his cohorts in crime gave me a sidelong look, then Thia caught his eye.

"That's great. How's Joe?" I had to swallow after I said your name, suddenly nervous. "What's he up to these days?"

"Uh, he's fine." Composed now, he straightened like a puffed rooster and cracked his knuckles.

"What's he doing?"

"I really don't know." He reached for his beer and took a long drink with his head turned, eyes drifting away, clearly uninterested. I was full of questions about you: Did you finish high school? What kind of work are you doing? Do you have a girlfriend? Are you happy?

"Come on, Fabian. You have to tell me something. I mean, really, what's he up to?" I deliberately stepped into his line of vision, my head cocked.

"I don't have to tell you squat," he said sharply, as if I were a mutt with mange, humping his leg. I wondered if he faulted me for your suspension. For the first time I questioned how you might have explained what happened in school to your family, if you'd pinned the blame on me. Why else would Fabian shun me?

"Fine. Whatever. I don't care. Tell him—" I stopped. My first impulse was: Tell him I said hello, then I thought Fuck you both might be more appropriate, considering his hostility and the fact that you were doing fine. How could you be fine? How *dare* you be fine? You had no idea what I'd gone through, the emotional hurricane I'd weathered since you'd taken flight. For all you knew or cared, I could have slashed my wrists over you.

"Never mind. Don't tell him shit," I told Fabian, and retreated, feeling like a nobody, sitting alone at the table. Thia was writhing on the dance floor with one of Fabian's mugger pals while the house band mangled "Boogie Oogie Oogie."

What would I have said if Fabian asked me how I was doing? As I poured myself another beer from the pitcher on our table, I thought about all the losers I'd been with, the one-night stands, the grabbers and the players. It was pathetic and desperate. I felt conspicuously jilted and embarrassed, my tough-girl cover shot full of bullet holes like a state road sign. I was tired of playing the angry, wounded soul. The realization that I was responsible for myself hit me in a way that filled me with alarm. I didn't want to be clerking at a rat-ridden dump for the rest of my life.

That fall I started taking classes at the community college, aiming for a degree in education or business while I kept my job at Rego Rini's. After that, I figured I could transfer to Cleveland State. I quit smoking dope after I tumbled like a dropped marionette down the apartment stairs at three in the morning. That's what I was told, anyway. I don't actually remember what happened, which made the incident truly frightening. I had awakened on the couch of the Indian guy in the apartment below ours, smelling like cilantro chutney, a small chip in my front tooth.

I still found it hard to sleep without having bad dreams. Thia was the only person I considered telling about the circumstances of my conception. I didn't think it was possible to shock her. After all, her bombshells were deeply disturbing, especially in the offhand way she dropped them. Once when we were talking about uncircumcised penises, she'd said, "The tip of my granddad's was like a little peeping eye." I didn't ask how she knew. So one day we were sitting at the table behind the supermarket, the wind whipping our cigarette-smoke breath from our lungs before they could be blackened. "My mother was raped when she was seventeen," I said, testing her reaction.

The hood of her parka didn't move, so I saw only half of her face when she turned to look at me. "Holy fuck. How?" When I said I didn't know, she said, "Well, I guess that's good. Who'd want to know? Not me."

I dropped my cigarette to the ground and crushed it with

my boot, the courage to tell her the rest of the story just as flat. As we walked back to the store, I said, "There are times my life doesn't seem real to me."

"Me, too. I feel like I'm flapping around like a kite without a tail, and the only thing holding me to the earth is a string. I'm waiting for someone to reel me in," she said. I wasn't sure what I was waiting for: someone to reel me in or cut me loose.

By now I'm sure I don't have to tell you Gavin was that someone. He may not have realized it, but he was searching for a needy woman when he found me at the Round House. He reeled me right in.

◀▲▶

CHAPTER TWELVE

On the night I met Gavin Schirrick, Salvador Dalí had already put me in a dark mood. It was fall 1978. *Un Chien Andalou,* was playing at Cleveland State's art theater, and since I'd heard it was inspired by dream logic, I hoped to get some insight into my own crazy dreams. You would have loved the absurdity of the film, but, if there was any meaning to Dalí's dream world, I didn't get it.

After the show I went to the Round House, a quiet neighborhood bar with televisions and pool tables. It was a good place for me to ruminate until I drank enough to forget what it was I was ruminating about. I sat with my back to the door and laid my jacket on the seat next to me. The jacket was black leather and suede, with padded shoulders and metal studs, garish and cheap looking, something I'd picked up for ten bucks at Goodwill. A wad of dried gum made a thick lump in the left pocket, and a grease stain marred the lining. Thia thought the stain looked like Jesus's face, but to me it resembled a bearded Jim Morrison. "Leave it to you to see the Antichrist," she said, but the image of Mr. Mojo Risin' reminded me of your fondness for the Doors, so there you have it.

The bartender, Rufus, poured me a Chivas and soda without needing to ask. Seated across from me was a couple—a middle-aged woman with pink hair like spun cotton candy and a man who looked as if he'd lost more than a few fistfights. The woman touched his arm, and he leaned toward her, as if on the edge of something sweet. Through the haze of cigarette smoke, I could see the players in the billiard room; and from the corner of my eye, I was aware of someone taking a stool near mine at the bar. Rufus greeted the newcomer, holding up his palm. "Gavin, my man, how's it hanging?"

"Smokin'," said the man named Gavin, drawing out the word like a hissing snake as he slapped Rufus's hand. He looked conspicuously out of place in a suit and tie. "What's shaking?"

"Not much. Spent my day off watching my car rust," Rufus said.

"Wish I'd been there to see it happen." Gavin kept talking while Rufus poured him a shot of top-shelf tequila. "I buzzed two execs out to Columbus the day afore last. Didn't catch more 'n two winks of sleep. Then, coming back, I drove smack into a major crack-up on I-90."

Loud cheers followed the sound of clacking balls from the poolroom. I slipped off my seat and walked to the bathroom. I suspected that Gavin was watching me because he'd paused midsentence. I was wearing tight pants and stacked boots that screamed overcompensation for lack of height, still dressing in what can only be described as an aggressive antifashion fashion. I'd show you photos if I hadn't burned them all. You'll have to imagine.

When I returned, Gavin's tie was in his jacket pocket, and he was talking like a bullet train to Rufus. "Honest to Pete. Rent the video, man. The bloopers are better than the fucking story," he said, then looked at me as if he'd just noticed I was there. "Oh, hey, apologies for the potty mouth, sweetheart. Where's my manners?" He patted himself as if checking his pockets for them. He had a broad forehead and thin nose, poker-straight hair the color of coffee ice cream, long sideburns, and a blond mustache. A puckered scar nicked his chin. So different from you. He said, "I never seen you here before."

I winced at his grammar. "You must not come here often. What's with the fancy threads? Hoping to make a big impression on someone tonight? You look like you fell off a hearse." I laughed. My forwardness was a front, nothing more than alcohol bravado. His comeback was to say I looked like a groupie who fell off the tour bus. Touché. Tapping my pack of cigarettes on the bar, I offered him one. He shook his head. A nonsmoker. Not to be trusted. I asked Rufus if he had matches, and he tossed a pack my way.

Gavin deftly snatched them out of the air and then struck a match for me. I noticed a slight tremor in his hand. "So, you seen *Smokey and the Bandit?*"

"You'd have to pay me to see a movie like that," I said. "Wait. I take that back. A car chase with a wisecracking hillbilly and a fat cop would have been better than the flick I just saw. *Un Chien Andalou*, by Salvador Dalí. You know, the artist?"

He shot me a scathing look as he ran his finger across his mustache, and I chided myself for assuming he wouldn't know Dalí. "What'd you go see it for? You an artist?"

"No. It sounded interesting. It's supposed to imitate a dream state, a kind of Freudian free association. It starts with a man slicing a woman's eyeball in half with a razor and ends with the hair from her armpit attaching itself to his face. At least I don't feel so crazy anymore. My dreams aren't half as strange as Dalí's."

He squinted his mouth in a frown. "What kind of strange dreams you have?"

I rolled the ashes from my cigarette. "I don't like to frighten strangers."

With a snort he said, "Bet it ain't half as scary as the chick I was with last week. Come on. Tell me. It worth a drink? Hey, Rufus, one for this hot young thing sitting next to me. Hit me, too, while you're at it." He knocked his drink back, then held up the empty glass. I noticed the top joint of the middle finger on his left hand was missing. "Okay. Come on, let's hear it. Pretend I'm Dr. Freud. Lay down on my couch and tell me your dreams, baby doll."

Shaking my head, I deferred, but he seemed okay with that.

Maybe my dreams were too surreal for him. We had a conversation that jumped from dreams to fears to roller coasters before we slipped into a back pocket of silence that felt easy. He agreed with me that the wooden Clipper at Cedar Point was still the best. His goal was to travel the world and ride every single coaster. I was on my third drink, willing to believe that anyone who was a friend of roller coasters was a friend of mine. I thought that the longer two people could go without speaking and still feel comfortable with each other was a good indication of compatibility.

He finished his drink and ran his tongue back and forth over his bottom lip, his chin up, eyes taut. "What are you most scared of?" His voice curved around me like seduction.

I stared at the different bottles of liquor on the shelves behind the bar, rows of transparent colors reflected in the mirror behind them—green, peach, dark amber—a toxic river I could drown myself in. "I'm not afraid of anything."

"Liar. How about this? I tell you something and then you go." He eyed me like a con man, someone with enough bad dreams and hastily packed suitcases of his own to be asking someone else about theirs. I focused on his face, trying to decide what it was in the thin wire of his sly smile that intrigued me. "Here it is: I'm scared of going crazy."

That was unexpected. I sat back, doubting. "Really?"

"Yeah. Nuthouse, certified c-r-a-z-y."

"Why?"

"It runs in the family." That shoulder tic again. "Your turn."

My attentiveness rose a notch. "Well, you could say evil runs in my family. I find that scary."

"You're lying."

"All right, I am, but the truth could be worse."

"Yeah? Well, that goes both ways. You might think I'm an easy-going guy, just another Good-Time Charlie, but watch out. I'm the one's evil." He laughed in loud, embarrassing snorts. I did not for one second think he was a Good-Time

Charlie, especially when his knee pressed against my thigh like a bad proposition. Maybe he thought we could be evil together, or two evils equaled something virtuous. "Hey, what kind of ring is that?" he asked as he reached for my hand.

I froze at his unexpected touch. A rush of blood made my jaw slacken and my mouth water with desire. "A nail. I hammered it to fit my finger."

"That's different." His grasp was firm as he examined the top of the ring where the pointed end and the head overlapped, but you and I know he wasn't really interested in the ring. He rubbed his thumb in the center of my palm, studying my eyes. A buzz ran up my arm to my scalp as if he'd pressed a button or a trigger. "What's a nail wrapped around your finger mean?"

"That I'm tougher than I look." It sounded silly, spoken out loud, and I regretted telling him.

"Man, you're one weird chick...the way you dress, the things you say." He didn't let go when I tried to take my hand back. Instead, he brought it to his mouth and kissed the inside of my wrist. The devil's breath on my pulse. "Do you know how to love, or is being tough all you know?"

I gave him a cold, quiet stare, but he didn't back off the way another man might have. He held me fast with black eyes that slid down my throat to settle between my breasts. My resolve melted like a chocolate drop in his hand. I'll be honest: I imagined him picking me up from the stool and throwing me onto my back on one of the tables behind us, legs apart, right here in the bar, and me liking it. This push-pull game with a stranger in a business suit troubled and intrigued me. Pool balls clicked like cap guns. Child's play. Double dare yous. I reminded myself I was done with one-nighters as I wriggled my hand away from his. I swallowed the last shot and set the glass down. "Thanks for the drinks and the barstool analysis, doc. Session's over."

He hopped up to help me with my jacket, a gentlemanly gesture that made me self-conscious, as if I were undeserving.

"It's late. Let me see you home," he said, as smooth as a key turning a lock. I knew his routine. Next he'd be pushing his way into my place, and then his way into me. He slapped a couple of bills on the bar for Rufus and said to me, "Wait a sec, gotta drain the monster first." His audacity made me laugh.

The minute the cocky bastard turned his back, though, I was out the door. And I almost got away, too. My heeled boots jarred against the concrete sidewalk as I passed the familiar darkened storefronts: Flip's Art Supply, My Goodness Bakery, Renaldo's Barber Shop. My open jacket flapped in the wind, but I was too drunk to feel the autumn cold.

"Hey, wait up. What's your hurry?" I heard him call after me.

The word *prey* rose from my stomach and lodged in my throat. My mother's face flashed in front of me as I turned to look at him. Everything inside urged me to keep walking. He could easily outrun me and pull me down from behind, like a yellow-eyed cat on a gazelle. I read in a magazine that meeting your attacker's eyes is the key to survival, so I pulled my jacket around myself and stayed focused, ready to push all my energy into hitting back or knocking him off balance, even though I could hardly stand straight. Headlights illuminated the street, throwing shadows; three teenage boys inside a car looked menacingly at me as it passed, exhaust spewing a noxious smell.

"I say something wrong?" Gavin asked. I clenched my teeth and held steady, giving him nothing. He tipped his head to the side. "Hey, I'm not the bad guy. The bad guy's the one hiding between the buildings, circling you in a low-rider. You shouldn't be alone on the streets this late."

I straightened up, trying to look taller as he closed the space between us. My nipples pulled tight. "You can't hurt me."

"Hurt you? Why would I do that?" He put his hand under my chin and asked me my name. I wondered if he could tell I was shaking when I told him. He said, "Pleased to meet you, Angelica. I'm Gavin Schirrick, protector of lost women and stray cats. Or is it lost cats and stray woman? You make me forget. You make me forget everything." I saw the flash of his teeth as his lips caught mine before I could turn my head. Maybe I didn't want to turn away. He was 80 proof: smooth, clean, and potent with a peppery bite. His hand went to the back of my neck as he teased his tongue inside my mouth. I didn't think to ask what he wanted to forget.

I dropped my keys and purse onto the table and kicked off my boots. The apartment was dark and still smelled like the burned cheese sandwich Thia made for lunch. I assumed she wouldn't be home until the wee hours, but just in case, I'd flipped the mat outside our door to tell her I had a guest in my room. Gavin took off his suit jacket and laid it over a chair, then unbuttoned his white shirt. It seemed to glow as he draped it over the jacket. I turned away as he shed the rest of his clothing. Not one to waste time, he pounced. His hands pawed and kneaded me. His kiss was solid and deliberate; his teeth hit mine with a clack. I knew there was more to this twitchy jokester than his smile.

As he yanked off my clothes, he whispered what he evidently thought was flattery: "Man, are you stacked," and "Wow. What tits." You described my body with poetry: my nipples were flower buds, I had a wild sea between my legs, I tasted like the sun in your mouth. I still remember what you said after our first kiss in the winter of '74. "Kisses are a far better fate than wisdom." I was sure those weren't your own words, but it didn't matter—I will never forget them. You breathed flutes and songbirds into my ears. If I couldn't have romance like that again, what else was there?

I stood motionless with my hands at my sides, wanting Gavin to show me. He gave me a tight squeeze, as if to bring me back to the present. "What's the matter? You got second thoughts?" My heart was sinking fast. I wanted nothing. I wanted too much. I wanted things I wasn't sure I was worthy of.

I told him to slap me. He blinked at me as if he hadn't heard right. "Slap me," I said again.

What I will tell you is, light exploded behind my eyes when Gavin Schirrick complied. Whatever he lacked in poetics, he made up for with a physical presence, confident and solid, moving his body over mine as he punched his way through a wall to get at my core. He was energy that crackled through my circuitry and left me with rug burns. He was thrashing sex that bit the soft flesh of my backside, forcing me to respond, to tear back into him. There was something about his missing fingertip that excited me. I grabbed his hand, sucked it, and tasted myself. That's all I'll say.

We lay next to each other on my bed and stared at the ceiling. A low chuckle rose from his chest. "That was so fine I bet your neighbors are smoking a cigarette. Jesus, Mary, and Joseph."

"Don't forget the Holy Ghost." I sat up to look for my clothes. The party was over as far as I was concerned.

He grabbed my arm and pulled me back, saying, "You should paint stars on your ceiling. Then you'll always dream good dreams." He rubbed my arm as if consoling me when he said, "I can't stay, baby doll," as if he thought I'd be upset or hurt.

"No shit." I pushed his arms off, wondering if he really thought I'd want him to stay. He was good, but not stay-the-night good. Well, maybe he was; I tried to convince myself he wasn't. He hopped up and kissed me hard as if he meant business. When I dodged his eyes, trying to hide my hollow bone vulnerability, he held my face so I was forced to look at him. He told me I was "the hottest babe ever," but he had a red-eye run to Toledo in the morning, a long drive from my place.

"I'm a driver. Bankers, politicians, lawyers, hacks, rats and their whores. I shuttle them to airports, hotels, trysts, the moon—you name it. Hence the fancy threads. But I need some shut-eye before I go. Hey, why don't you come home with me?"

"Where's that? And how you gonna drive anywhere after all that tequila?" Oafish from hard liquor, I picked up my shirt and slipped it on without my bra, then stumbled around in search of pastel underpants.

"Vermilion. My chariot could drive itself there and back," he said, and I felt a tiny ping inside, remembering how you called your Bel Air a chariot. Gavin hugged me as if I were a small package that he needed a better grip on. His tightly muscled body was naked except for black socks. "You're such a fox. Come on. You can stay at my place and get some sleep. Job won't take more 'n a couple hours at the most, and I'll be back by nine. We got all Saturday to mess around."

"Mess around? As if I don't have any plans of my own?" I threw back my head to bare my neck, wanting to believe he knew what I needed.

"Not anymore. You're coming with me," he said, and I believed.

I would later learn that Gavin had cut his teeth on the white lines of the highway—his father was in the service and his family moved every two years when Gavin and his brothers were growing up. I remember long road trips with my parents to Florida, Myrtle Beach, and New York when it seemed as if we drove forever. Half of it was just to get out of flat, boring Ohio. Whenever I would sit up from sleeping on the backseat, thickheaded from motion sickness, cramped, and thirsty, the view was the same: barns, corn, and cows through smeared bugs on the front windshield. Mom would be in the front seat, grappling with a crumpled map while Dad hummed. I didn't get carsick when Gavin drove forty-five miles from Cuyahoga County to Erie on I-90, following the contour of the lake in his black Cadillac Seville. His driving was as sleek as his seduction. He obviously held his liquor well, not necessarily a good sign.

It was after midnight when he parked his car in front of a cluster of rattrap apartments. "'Rock the boat,'" he sang as he walked me to the front door with his hands on my back, guiding me forward. "'Rock the boat, baby.'" I leaned against him as he unlocked the door, and we both fell inside. His place was sparse—a cheap couch, a card table covered with paperwork, folding chairs, a standing lamp, half-melted candles along the window ledge. A small TV on a two-shelf bookstand. Pull-down shades. No curtains. No pictures on the wall. I didn't think his lack of decor meant anything more than he was a man of simple needs. His king-size bed was unmade, and there was no dresser, but he had more stuff than I'd ever seen before in a man's bathroom.

We didn't get to sleep until 3:00 AM, and when I awakened, Gavin Schirrick was stepping out of his trousers, already back from his job. He crawled over me, pressed his mouth onto mine, and reintoxicated me before we lapsed into heavy sleep. I was content. I felt safe. I was not.

Gavin took the telephone call lying down. I tottered into the bathroom to wash my face with cold water, trying to get my eyes to stay open. It was past noon. I brushed my teeth and fuzzy tongue with my finger and his gritty toothpaste. My hair was flat on one side and going sideways on the other, so I dampened my palms and slicked it all back.

"No, not really. What'd you expect?" he spoke into the phone when I returned to his bed. In the daylight, his flat chest and stomach, narrow shoulders, and defined muscles shone. The hair in his armpit was straight and light brown. I pulled back the sheet and crawled in.

"Look, Terry, I can't—" He inhaled sharply when I took his sleepy cock into my mouth. "Ah, oh—" he gasped, and looked at the phone in his hand, horror-struck. He pushed my head away and swung his legs off the bed. "What? Nothing. I dropped the phone."

I got it: Terry was a woman.

He looked sideways at me, expressionless. My face grew hot. I climbed from his bed, hurriedly gathered my clothes, and went into the bathroom, thinking about how eager he'd been to bring me home and toss me onto his bed a few hours ago. I hooked my bra in front, twisted it around, and hiked it up into place. I made several attempts to step into my leggings before I finally sat down on the toilet. I felt like a magazine in a doctor's office: the edges of the pages curled and covered with greasy fingerprints, the best recipes ripped out. I hated men, and I'm sorry to say, that included you.

I hurried into the living room to find my boots. Finished with the call, Gavin walked in, wearing nothing but unbut-toned jeans. He watched me with lidded eyes. "Don't run off."

"When do you want me to leave? Ten minutes before Terry gets here?"

His jaw muscles flexed. "It's not what you think."

"What I think doesn't matter." I stepped into my boot; something sharp bit my toe. I drew back and then remem-bered I'd dropped my earrings in them when I took them off so I wouldn't lose them. I shook them out and threaded the posts through my earlobes. I should be horsewhipped. I needed a lobotomy. Why did I continue to cheapen myself? *Hure*, Grandma had called me.

Hobbling around, trying to pull on my other boot, I fell back against the wall. He helped me up and then put his hands on my shoulders to pin me to the wall, his groin pressed against me. "Terry's just a chick. You're something else. Even with your clothes on."

"You got your kicks, I got mine. Just call me a cab. No, never mind. I'll call my friend."

He snaked his hand up my shirt. I looked at the half-melted candles on his windowsill—six of them in different heights and colors—and pictured them burning and dripping wax onto the brown carpet. What kind of man has candles? Most likely a woman had bought them, trying to soften the room. I wouldn't fill it with anything but ugliness, and he was a lying dog who smiled like a thief. Both of us were as deep and treacherous as a coal mine.

It made sense we ended up together.

"Stay. I can slap you around some more if you want. Whatever you want, little rocker." He pinched my breast hard enough to make me jump. "You have a bad dream last night?"

Plastered against the wall, I went weak in the knees, despairing and exhilarated at the same time.

"I don't remember dreaming."

"See? I'm good for you."

It was true. I had experienced a rare, nightmare-free night when I'd slept with Gavin. He was good for me in that way—my bad dreams receded as we started seeing more of each other. It's too bad I didn't understand the trade-off was that he'd become the bad dream. Anyway, when I had the occasional night spooks, he wanted to hear all about them. He got a kick out of putting his own spin on it in some ridiculous way, consulting a pseudopsych book, *Symbolism and Totems*, that he picked up at the Goodwill. He said that my dream of being chased by an elephant-size toad suggested that I was trying to hide my true self. He was so incredibly earnest, not to mention he was partly right, that I smiled despite myself.

The fact that I occasionally asked him to slap me was a source of fascination to him, and he obliged as if he'd been doing it to women all along. I asked him once what was in it for him, if he liked slapping me. He said he did it only because I asked him to. "I don't analyze shit like that. I'm not that deep. I'm shallow," he said, which I know he didn't actually mean. Besides, if he was shallow, I was subterranean.

We didn't date, not in a conventional way. We just had sex.

He stopped by my apartment whenever he came through the area, which was often, or he would call. "I'm lonely," he'd say, and ask me to drive out to spend the night with him. One time when I told him I'd made plans to meet Thia at The Cellar Door, he joined us. He boogied on the dance floor like a juiced-up jazzman, entertaining if not amusing, his feet moving a half beat too fast on the blinking squares. He flirted outrageously with Thia. "Just clowning around," he said, but I felt a curious stir of jealousy.

Painfully aware that everything I thought was real could be jerked out from under my feet tomorrow, I tried to keep emotion out of our relationship. I did not want to fall in love. He was the one who started to act as if he cared. He gave me gas money. He asked me to stay the weekend. I was working less at the store to be with him. He gave me space to study, since I was still in school. Soon I was keeping a toothbrush and clothes at his place and then I was cooking for him: stuffed green peppers, stir-fry pork, chicken cacciatore. Easy to please, he would smack his lips at anything I made, scorched or soggy. I remember the time he pulled a hair from my spaghetti sauce and said with a grin, "Aha. I discovered the secret ingredient."

He'd been living in Vermilion for a year. Before that Toledo, Indianapolis, St. Paul, Chicago, and too many other cities to recall. He was born in Jacksonville, Florida, had two brothers, didn't like to talk about his family, and didn't ask about mine, which I appreciated. I pictured his parents as either rail thin or morbidly obese, uneducated and unable to afford braces to fix his wayward bottom teeth. He had taken enough business courses at various community colleges that they should have added up to some kind of degree, but there were times I thought his intellect was rivaled only by a Cadillac that could drive itself. The idea of making a living off the wealthy appealed to him, and he jokingly called himself a parasite.

After I passed my final exams for my associate's degree, he told me to pick up a cake at the store before I came home from work. Astonished, I thought he was kidding. He was making me buy my own cake? Then he said, "And quit that stinking job. Right now. Tell them you're done." He told me to hurry home so he could lick a piece of cake from my bare stomach. It was a nice gesture, but I couldn't even begin to compare his idea of romance to yours.

He awakened easily, having the ability to dip his toes into deep sleep without getting waterlogged. If his phone rang at 4:30 in the morning, he'd leap from bed, dress, and be out the door in five minutes. The limo company he worked for was based in Toledo, Ohio. A number of clients asked specifically for him, presumably liking his friendly, unassuming nature and corny jokes. Long distances or late hours never bothered him. He thrived on change. His goal was to start his own company someday, and he spent hours thinking about a catchy business name.

First he wrote a list of all the qualities he wanted to project: *On Time, Privacy Assured, Safety First, Steady, Fast.* Next he listed different categories, such as scenery, royalty, flowers and animals, and then wrote associated nouns under each category: *Meadow, Baron, Magnolia, Stallion.* After all that he combined random words from each list. I was skeptical. "Mountain Rock Reliable?" He went on the defensive, waving his arm. "Don't dismiss anything in the brainstorming process. This is important shit." He was so intense that I had to laugh. Inevitably, he came back to a slogan using his own name: Anywhere, Anytime: Rely on Schirrick's Chauffeur Service. I asked him if he ever considered using just his initials, but his middle name was Alvin, after his father, which spelled *GAS.*

He liked to sketch out logo designs for business cards, and planned to print notepads and pencils to leave in the back of the car for clients. I told him he should put his logo on packages of condoms, too. I should tell you that I was only joking, but he thought it was a brilliant idea: "We could be a great team. You'd be the brains."

Gavin seldom picked up his phone until the answering machine kicked in, just in case his boss was calling with a job he didn't want to take. A woman named Dixie called at least once a week, asking him to fix a leak in her ceiling, repair a broken stair, hook up her VCR, light her cigarette, whatever. A man with a deep, sloshing voice called one evening to say what I swear sounded like "Pay up or we'll twist your nuts off." I learned Gavin played billiards and had tried to hustle a few hustlers. His mother, who sounded as batty as hell, called six times in one day to ask if his brother Owen was there. Supposedly, Owen had totaled his car while driving drunk, and his wife kicked him out of the house.

Strange people occasionally showed up at Gavin's door, too. He and I were lying in bed late one evening watching *Saturday Night Live* when we heard the apartment door bang open, followed by a woman's voice calling out his name.

"Jesus, it's Blossom," he said, looking as if he'd swallowed a cockroach. A strapping woman with dirty-blond hair and dark roots was standing in the bedroom doorway with her hands on her hips. I thought he'd said "It's Possum," so when I first saw her, I was as repulsed as if she actually was a possum. Her body bulged from stretch jeans and a tight sleeveless tank, and her heavy breasts were in bad need of underwire support.

"What's this?" she asked, pointing at me. The muddy circles beneath her eyes deepened.

"What's this? *What's this?* What the fuck you doing here?" he said, indignant. He leaped up, wearing nothing but his tighty-whiteys, and shoved her out of the room with a strength I didn't know he had. He told me to stay put and shut me in the bedroom. I stared at the TV, listening to the murmur of canned voices. The thought of Blossom being a former lover of his alarmed me. The first night I'd slept with him, it had been Terry on the phone and now this oily marsupial—how many women was he stringing along? I asked myself if it mattered. Sure, we were cohabitating, but neither of us had talked about commitment. To tell you the truth, if he were to have sworn off other women for me, I didn't know if I'd be happy or terrified.

While they worked out whatever the issue was, I wondered what you would have thought of Gavin. I imagined you studying him with that contemplative look, the one you'd get when Skip sang your lyrics.

Their voices grew louder. "Your fucking Johnson is bigger 'n your brain," she said. I guess she knew a thing or two about him, Johnson-wise. I felt a strange sense of disconnect.

"You saying I'm stupid?" he asked.

"Figure it out, Einstein."

I drew a deep breath. Gavin recoiled at any insinuation that he was lacking intelligence. I could only assume that was exactly what his mother or father had told him when he was a boy. The thought angered me—stupid or dumb is a hurtful label for a child, the kind of thing that sticks. I remembered that your father had called you stupid, among other nasty things fathers should never call their sons. I'd never made any kind of connection between you and Gavin before, and it threw me, not that it held any importance other than making me feel melancholy about his childhood. Yours, too. I reached for the bottle of tequila on the nightstand and took a slow sip, feeling sorry for the little boy in Gavin.

Excusing behavior in him that I shouldn't have would be my downfall. The liquor burned all the way to my stomach.

The sound of something hitting the wall was followed by more of Blossom's histrionics. The person in the apartment below us banged on their ceiling and hollered, "Shut up." This tiff had gone on long enough. I slipped into one of Gavin's t-shirts and marched out of the bedroom to announce that I was calling the cops if they didn't stop fighting.

The aberration with the flowery name glared at me, her eyes red with rancor. Sweat shone in the hair above her lip, and her shirt had stains under her arms. My scalp tingled. Maybe inserting myself into their problem wasn't such a good move. She lunged and her open hand hit the side of my face. Stunned, it took me a few seconds to process what had happened. I charged at her, having no idea what I would do. Despite the fact that her thigh alone weighed more than all of me, I was so hopping mad I was confident I could have wrestled her to the ground in a minute flat. Luckily for me, Gavin got between us. She made a noise that sounded like a bark, and I landed on my rump. He hustled her toward the door, saying, "Leave me the fuck alone. I'm clean."

She laughed, as if it had all been a joke, holding up her hands, playing possum, as it were. "Okay. All right. You two make a great pair. Two assholes blowing smoke," she said on her way out. Gavin slammed and locked the door. I slowly stood and rubbed my backside.

"I had everything under control, baby doll. You didn't need to do that," he said, opening and closing his fists.

"Oh yeah, right. I could see that. Who is she?" My knees started to shake as if my body finally realized fear was the appropriate reaction.

"One crazy bitch, that's who. She could've killed you." He examined the side of my face, touching gently. "This might bruise. I didn't know you had so much fight in you. What a little ball breaker," he said, as if proud of me.

I scowled as I jerked away my head. "You told her you're clean. What does that mean?"

"Just that. She's looking for what I don't have. Forget it. She won't come back."

He led me into the bedroom and sat me on the bed, as if disruptions of this sort were common in his life, then got a wet washrag from the bathroom and held it to my face. The concern in his eyes was genuine. The stinging pain slid from my cheek down into the sorely beating muscle in my chest when I realized I cared about this man more than I should. I wanted to kiss him as badly as I wanted to clobber him.

I asked him how tight he and this Blossom person had been, and he said, "Like Scotch tape on cement." The cool rag was soothing. I liked the way he held it to my face. Weighted by vague allegations and indecisiveness, I felt like the wrong answer in an essay test.

"Don't be mad. You're the best thing that ever happened to me," he said as we lay down. His skin felt hot and dry when he rolled on top of me. I took a quick breath, struck by the unexpected burden of his body moving on top of mine, as if he were ironing years of his mistakes onto me. He kissed my face where it hurt, as if to make it all better, like a daddy.

Who was I to question him? A model of truthfulness? So what if he had a few untidy relationships or loose ends? I wasn't going to have his babies, for crying out loud.

◂▴▸

CHAPTER THIRTEEN

I hugged the toilet. Every time I flushed, I had to shut my eyes, because the swirling water made me sicker. If only I could disappear down the white chute. I sat back on the cold tiles and pushed my hair out of my face. Gavin stood with his hip against the sink, holding a mug of steaming coffee. He brewed it strong, and the bitter smell filled the bathroom like something poisonous.

"Ugh. Get that fucking coffee away from me," I told him.

"You probably drank too much last night, partying with Thia," he said, and took a sip, ignoring my request, as if it served me right for going out while he had to drive a client to Hopkins Airport. At least he turned on the vent.

"I had one beer." I couldn't have stomached more than that. I was too worried to drink, anyway, sure I was pregnant and afraid I'd mess up the baby by getting it drunk. The poor thing already had one count against it with me for a mother. I wasn't ready for this, wasn't sure I ever would be. Thia said I was making myself sick with worry, and stress can cause your periods to go missing. I hadn't been stressed until I began to suspect I might be pregnant. "Nice try," I'd told her, but I was never late; Auntie Flow visited me every twenty-eight days without fail. Plus, I used birth control. Most of the time. Apparently Gavin had ferociously obstinate sperm, capable of hanging out in a vagina for a full week, waiting for that lone unsuspecting egg to glide down the fallopian staircase.

He said it might be something I ate. I told him, "No," and he huffed as if I were being insolent on purpose when he was only trying to help. Typically, I'm not a crier, but that's what I did. I wondered if I was going to get really bitchy, and fat, and cry a lot. I wondered how he'd deal with that, if he'd even want to hang around. I hate to admit that I had no idea if he liked or wanted children. It was past time for me to do some serious thinking about my boyfriend and where our relationship was going. "I'm telling you it's not what I ate."

"You don't have to shout at me." He shifted around. His coffee mug clinked as he set it on the edge of the sink. "Okay. How late are you?" He tapped his fingers on the side of his leg.

"Two weeks and three days."

"Jesus. How many hours?"

"I'm never late."

"Never?"

"I'm pregnant. I know it."

His silence ran up my back like a cold hand. I wasn't expecting hurrahs, a marching band, or confetti; but I thought he'd be supportive, or at least get the coffee out of my space. "Great. That's fucking great," he said, and walked out of the bathroom. Hearing the jangle of his car keys, I asked where he was going. "To slam my head in the door," he shouted back.

If he kept this up, he was going to make a really shitty father. It dawned on me that none of the guys I'd slept with would have made a good father, except maybe you. Of course, that was based solely on what I knew of you when I was practically still a baby myself. I don't think I would have recognized good-father fabric if I saw it.

Seconds later Gavin came back into the bathroom to fetch his cup. "Hope you feel better," he said, but it sounded more like he hoped I'd flush myself down the toilet. Groaning, I dragged the bed blanket into the living room, curled up on the couch, and tried to find something distracting on television, glad that it was Saturday and I didn't have to work.

I'd recently got an office job at the Allison House, a rehab center downtown. Fortunately, no one commented on my sudden, frequent trips to the restroom, or the fact that my head hit the desk every afternoon around two. I'd always assumed morning sickness meant this dizzy-gagging feeling would be gone by the afternoon.

Not wanting to starve the baby, I managed to force down two pieces of dry toast. I wanted Gavin here so I could wring his neck, and his big Johnson, too. I didn't know which one of us to blame. Sure, I'd skipped wearing my diaphragm on occasion, but never when I had been midcycle. Gavin said he could feel it "up there." I envisioned his cock bouncing on a trampoline, but he didn't like the idea of hitting a barrier. He wouldn't wear a condom either. He wanted me to go on the pill, but I refused after hearing most women put on at least ten to fifteen pounds on the pill. At my height, ten pounds would look like twenty. There was no way I was going on the pill.

Did you know that half the pregnancies in the United States are unplanned, and most women have only a 25 percent chance of getting pregnant each month? It's a miracle that babies are conceived at the astounding rate they are. I suppose this little bit of data indicated that *my* conception was an unparalleled event. You might think this revelation would have made me feel special, as if some guiding factor had determined that I was destined to be, but it didn't. That was a dangerous thought. I preferred to think I had free will to screw things up on my own.

Sometime past midnight, the thump of something heavy hitting the floor awakened me. A rip-snorting laugh followed, and then Gavin flopped onto the bed and started kissing my face. He rubbed his hand on my belly. "I put a baby in you. I can't believe it," he said, his voice lilting with drunken joy. He tried to wedge his hand between my thighs.

"Now you're happy?" I rolled over and pushed his hand away.

"A course I'm happy. It's fuckin' amazing. A baby. Our baby.

Yours and mine." In the light from the window, his wet grin looked as loopy as a racetrack. He'd probably downed an entire fifth himself.

"You weren't happy this afternoon," I said.

"I sorry, baby doll. See I had to… you know, think on it." He made an indecipherable gesture with his hand. "I was at Pomeroy's, and my best buds, Alex and Hoover, came in." I'd never once heard him mention these two names before. "And they say, 'Wha's shaking man,' and it hits me I'm gonna be a father. So I tell 'em I'm gonna be a father, and the whole damn place goes up in cheers, buying me drinks and slapping me on the back and saying congratulations and all that shit. I never thought I'd be a father. It's—" He belched, his shoulders hitching up. "Amazing."

"What are you saying? You want this baby?"

"Yeah. A course I do." He stood to wrestle off his t-shirt, then stepped out of his jeans. As he backed up to sit on the edge of the bed, he missed and momentarily disappeared from my sight.

"Someone patted you on the back for knocking up your girlfriend, said 'You're the man,' and now you feel all warm and fuzzy? Babies are for life, Gavin. You think you can listen to crying all night long when you have to work at four in the morning? How do you feel about spit-up on your tie? Changing diapers? And where are we going to put a crib in this stinking apartment? Can we even afford one? No. No! We can't have this baby." The more I thought about it, the harder I wanted to cry. I swiped my nose with the back of my hand.

He flopped down on the bed. He stank like smoked salmon. "Wha? Jesus. You think I'm stupid? You don't, I don't, you think I don't know what a baby is? I'm ready, I'm ready as ever. As I ever. As ever—"

"You're fucking drunk." As soon as I said that, it dawned on me that I would have to clean up my language if I had a baby.

I would have to clean up a lot of things.

"No tha's not it. Marry me. Please, please, please, I'll do right by you." His eyes were glassy with tears. "I wanna marry you. I wanna do the right thing for once."

My stomach backed up like a cornered animal against my spine. I was seriously thinking about how I could take care of this, and what it would cost me, monetarily and emotionally. Now I had Gavin blubbering in my lap, begging me to marry him and have his baby. What was I supposed to do? I didn't want to crush him by taking this away from him, if this was what he really wanted. If only he'd reacted like this when I'd first told him. Tomorrow when he sobered up, he might be snarling or accusing me of entrapment. A baby should be wanted, not resented. I thought of Mom not wanting me and the heartache I brought into her life. There were no balloons or cigars for a single mom in the fifties, nor in the seventies, either, for that matter. "The right thing isn't always the best thing."

He moaned. "No don't say that." He wrapped his arms around me, his body stoked like a furnace, full of fervor and hot air. "You'll be the best mama ever. For the first time in my life I got something to live for. I love you. I do. Marry me and you'll see. You'll see." He clung to me like a child as we rocked together, both of us crying.

The next morning I let him sleep. I made coffee, ran to the bathroom to puke, made some toast, gagged into the sink, ate half a piece out of guilt, and then tried to straighten the living room before I started gagging again. He emerged from the bedroom some time after eleven, announced himself with a groan, and fixed a bowl of cereal. Dressed in underwear and socks, he leaned against the counter with the bowl held up to his face, alternately slurping and crunching.

"Do you remember anything about last night?" I asked. He pulled back and gave me a grim look that said he did. I sank onto the couch and stared at the apartment door, wanting to bolt for the free clinic. "Okay. We have to decide what we're going to do, and do it fast, because I'll just take care of this myself before I have this baby alone. It scares the crap out of me."

"You aren't alone. Jesus H. Christ. What kind of man you think I am?"

"Then wipe that smug look off your face," I said. He looked confused, as if I'd read him all wrong. When I got teary, he put his bowl in the sink and sat next to me. I smelled Rice Krispies when he sighed. "Why did this have to happen now?" I asked.

"We got time. I'll get a loan and do what I wanted to do since forever: start my own chauffeur company. How many months afore you pop the kid?"

"Nine. No, eight. I don't know."

"Yeah, so, we got time."

"How can you say that?" It made my head spin.

"Don't get excited. We get married. That's all there is to it. I'll take care of everything. You just eat and get fat or whatever it is you're supposed to do when you have a baby." He sat back and picked his front teeth with his fingernail. "I knew it'd happen sooner or later."

"What?"

"Yeah. You don't always wear your thingy. What'd you think would happen?"

"Are you saying this is my fault?"

"No. It's my kid, too. Get your act together." One leg started bouncing nervously, his bony white knee working like a piston. "Think positive. It'll be fine."

"It will not be fine. I'm going to have to give birth."

"Yeah. Glad it's not me." He threw back his head and laughed, and then stopped to take a deep breath, eyes big, one hand on his chest. "Oh, shit. Shit, shit, shit."

Not wanting to tell Mom face-to-face that I got married,

I called her on the phone. "You're kidding," she said. Her voice dropped deep enough to dredge the Great Lakes, and my stomach dropped along with it. I pictured her with that stricken look on her face, her lips making a blurry line, fingers pinching her neck. "Please tell me you're kidding."

Ever since I was a girl, she'd talked about sewing a wedding dress for me. It would have been the most beautiful, most extravagant gown ever, too, in glossy white satin, handmade French lace, miniature pearls and bows, a ten-foot-long train, whatever I asked for, fitted to my petite measurements. She'd wanted me to have the wedding she never had, and I was sorry to be letting her down. I'd once had that white-wedding dream, too, but you were the man who waited for me at the end of the aisle.

"Gavin and I don't want to make a big production. Both of us are working. We don't have the time or money." I imagined how stressful planning a wedding might have been with Mom, further complicated by her and Dad's separation.

"His name is Gavin? Gavin what? How long have you known him?"

I stopped to think. "Almost a year." Was it possible? The smoke from the barbeque on the deck of the apartment below drifted in the screen door, making me queasy. Stretching the phone cord, I walked over to slide the door shut. In the parking lot below, my car glinted like a little green beetle in the sun. I tried to picture an infant seat strapped in the back. A good car seat probably cost a bundle. "His last name is Schirrick."

"Oh. That sounds Germanic," she said, sounding a bit more hopeful.

"It is." I guessed, but hoped it would help. "We really love each other. I mean, we're perfect together. Wait till you meet him. When he asked me to marry him, he said, 'Let's just do it,' and I was swept away in the excitement."

It went like this: We had our blood tests, got a marriage license, and three days later we went through the indignity of being checked at the door of the courthouse for weapons, along with the good and the not-so-good citizens of Lorain County. I munched on peanut butter crackers, having learned it was better not to let my stomach get completely empty. The air-conditioning made the place an icebox; Gavin gave me his suit jacket, but I still shivered. Our witnesses were Thia and her current boyfriend, Jack, who'd moved into her apartment to help with the rent. They had an arm-waving, finger-pointing argument over the electric bill while we waited. When we stood in front of Judge Alabaster and declared our intentions, it was a moment unlike any other. I almost threw up, but otherwise it was a kick. Gavin was high on happiness. He knew exactly which motel in Niagara Falls he wanted to stay at—The Starburst—with a mirrored ceiling, vibrating bed, refrigerator, and cable TV. The fact that I was carrying a baby didn't deter his sexual appetite. He rather liked not having to worry about me getting pregnant.

I told Mom, "I hope you understand. You'll love him, too."

I heard her sigh. She asked if I'd met his parents and if they approved. From what Gavin told me, they didn't care what he did with his life as long as it didn't cost them money, but I didn't tell her that. She continued to pelt me with questions until my head hurt: "Where is he from? How did you meet? What does he do for a living?" as if she didn't think I knew a good man from a telephone pole; but I let it go. I lied, lied, and lied.

"I don't know what your father will think," she said, the only thing left to reprimand me with.

"Why do you care what he thinks?" Dad hadn't been fazed when I'd phoned him with the news earlier that day. He didn't know what to make of me anymore. Everything he thought he knew about me had changed too quickly to absorb.

It was quiet on her end of the phone. This is it, I figured—she was either going to accept that I was married or fight it, skin and teeth, to the bitter end. I gave her a moment to think.

"Well, if he's the light of your life, I want to meet him."

"Of course. Yes. Right away," I said, my heart sailing, even though her tone told me she was less than thrilled. Maybe this would work out after all.

Mom studied Gavin with the same shrewd eye she used on you. She stopped short when it came to hugging him, as if no one was shoving a son-in-law down her throat until she was good and ready, but she offered a hospitable smile. He gave her a hug and a squeeze, anyway, saying, "Hey, Marta, how're you doing?" From the look on her face, you'd have thought he had goosed her. Cookie lumbered over from her blanket in the corner to sniff him suspiciously, making a few gruff noises for show. I was glad he didn't knock the old girl back with his knee. He liked dogs as much as he liked gnats flying up his nose.

My aunts nodded and grinned as if their heads were on springs. Aunt Luce had a perm that made her look like a creamy-blond poodle. Aunt Janey was selling makeup door-to-door and had slathered her face with every product she offered. Uncle Tim, who'd gained a dozen doughnuts worth of weight, pressed a cold brew in Gavin's hand and pulled him into the backyard so they could discuss NASCAR or baseball.

Out back, my rusted swing set was still in the corner of the yard. I wondered where Gavin and I were going to put a swing set. I wanted our baby to have all the nice things I had growing up, with no ghastly surprises. From the breezeway, I waved hello to my cousins, whom I hadn't seen in years. The girls were standing by the picnic table, catching some sun in their flirty summer dresses and sandals. Their stick-like figures had morphed into something shapely and stylish. I wanted to be shapely and stylish, aware that my hips would widen, my boobs would get even huger, and my ankles and fingers would swell. Carl Junior, the youngest at eleven, dribbled a soccer ball across the lawn and kicked it smack into his sister's rump. Erica squealed.

I went into the kitchen for a drink of water, wishing I hadn't agreed to this little cookout for the entire family to meet my husband. Hiding my pregnancy seemed dishonest, even though my tummy was still flat. Mom reached out to brush a stray strand of hair from my face and sighed. "Your hair looks different every time I see you, but I like this longer style. The color looks good. More like you."

"Thanks." When she asked if I felt all right, I told her was still carsick from the drive to Nopiming. The mix of smells in the kitchen were getting to me, too—rigatoni and meatballs, sauerkraut and pork, and baked chicken.

"You used to get carsick when you were a child," Mom said as she lunged after a fly, whapping the windowsill and then the edge of the table with a rolled magazine. She clicked her tongue as the fly zipped crazily off. We both waited, watching. When it didn't reappear, she set down the magazine and fussed with the table setting. "Gavin has a nice smile. He's not bad looking. It's too bad his family couldn't come. I just can't believe you're married. Never in a million years did I expect—"

I couldn't believe I was married either. I excused myself to the bathroom and locked the door behind me. I didn't know it was possible to cry so many tears. I splashed water on my face and took deep breaths to settle my seesaw emotions. Gavin said it would all work out, and I guess I believed him. I had to.

When I returned to the kitchen, Mom was washing her hands and Aunt Luce was setting out a stack of flowered napkins that matched the paper plates. "Oh, there you are," Aunt Luce said when she saw me. "Tell us how you found your hubby."

"I met him through a friend, Rufus, at college. The two of us just clicked." What else could I have said? That we met in a bar, got smashed out of our skulls, and spent the next forty-eight hours sexing up each other? I put my hand over my mouth and turned my head, feeling a sour burp rise. Mom glanced at me as she opened a bag of Styrofoam cups, then her hands froze and her eyes got big. I could have bet money that she was adding up things—a hasty marriage, upset tummy, tears, pallor—Mrs. Lowsley might have been a lot of things, but dumb wasn't one of them. Her brows rutted at the center of her forehead.

Just then Aunt Luce said, "Should I make an announcement?"

Mom swung around, alarmed, as if she thought Luce was going to blab the news that I was in a family way. "What?" she gasped, hand to throat, ready to pull skin, but caught herself.

"We're all here, and everything is ready," Aunt Luce said.

"Oh! Yes. Let's tell them to come in," Mom said, shifting back into hostess mode.

Aunt Luce opened the door and hollered into the back like a camp cook, "Food's ready, guys."

As the kitchen grew crowded with family, Mom fired looks at me that alternated between disapproving and worrisome. For the rest of the afternoon I tried to avoid her. Dad stopped by to meet Gavin, and ended up drinking too much and talking too loudly. Everyone seemed genuinely happy for us. Was I expecting they'd be disappointed? Disapproving?

Twitching, one foot tapping, Gavin looked like an actor in a low-budget movie, the guy who always got second billing because he was handsome, but not enough to overshadow the hero. He could play good or bad, like a friend with a chain saw and a jug of bleach in the trunk his car. Gavin said something, and Dad's expression was one of amused bewilderment as polite chortles erupted from my uncles. I prayed Gavin hadn't told them anything off-color, some lurid tale about a rendezvous in the backseat of his Cadillac. I imagine his profession hadn't impressed my father, but if Gavin put his mind to it, he could do anything. He was only twenty-six. Who knew what he'd be doing five or ten years from now?

Who knew?

Later, Dad caught me at the top of the stairs when I came out of the bathroom. He blocked the hall, as if about to accuse me of scribbling naughty words on the walls with a crayon, and asked if I married Gavin because I was "expectant."

I was so rattled I almost fell over. "Dad! What makes you think—"

He spoke in a hurry, his beer breath in my face. "Never mind. It's not important. He said he's starting his own business. How are his finances?"

I groaned. Mom had issues with Gavin's appearance, and now Dad wanted to know his portfolio. "He works hard and saves every penny. The bank preapproved us for a mortgage. We're looking for a house," I said, hoping to assuage his worries.

"A house." He shut his eyes as if invoking a hidden reserve of patience he kept in the back of his big podiatrist brain. "I don't see or talk to you in ages, and you turn up married. I'm going to have a heart attack worrying about you."

"You sound like Mom," I said, but I was pleased to know he worried about me.

"Oh God, don't even. I bet she'd love to give me an earful over this. She probably blames me. I've been staying clear of her all afternoon. I'll never figure out either of you. I didn't get you a card, but, here, take this. Congratulations, cupcake." He pushed something into my hand—a wad of money, as soft as a rabbit's foot. Several hundred-dollar bills, warm in my palm, smelling like an old-man's pocket.

"How much is this?"

He closed his hand over mine. "Don't count it now. I'm ducking out. Keep in touch?" He smiled uncomfortably, gave me a pat on the arm, and hurried out. I was glad he didn't have far to drive.

I kept the handful of money pressed against my thigh like contraband as I walked through the kitchen and then furtively tucked it into my purse, setting it aside for the baby.

Carl Junior was on his knees to pet Cookie, who lay as still as a shag carpet. He lifted her upper lip to look at her long teeth and speckled gums. She sneezed. "If she's twelve in dog years, that means she's eighty-four in people years. That's really, really old. When are you going to put her to sleep?"

Everyone pretended not to have heard him.

I told him, "She's fine, Carl. No need for that yet." I grunted as I pulled the liner from the wastebasket to carry the trash outside to the can behind the garage. Late afternoon was sleepy-time for me.

"Angie, this is your party. Don't bother cleaning up. Besides, you need your rest," Mom said. I held the bag in my hand while trying to discern her tone. Did she know? I took the bag out to the trash can in the garage, anyway. If she suspected I was pregnant, I figured she'd wait until we were alone before she started an inquisition, so I was safe for now.

Back in the kitchen, I cut myself a second piece of homemade wedding cake, the only thing I had an appetite for, and glanced over to see her watching me. Her page boy was limp from perspiration and kitchen heat.

"You *had* to get married," she blurted. It seemed she'd startled even herself as she stepped back with her hand on her chest.

My aunts stopped jabbering and stared at her as if flash-bulbs popped in their faces, then all eyes turned to me.

I swallowed and thought quickly. "No. Gavin asked me to marry him. I didn't *have* to."

"But you're pregnant."

"Barely." How lame. Either you are or you aren't. "We were going to get married, anyway."

"Oh, Angelica." Her mouth twitched and her hands fell to her sides. "Why didn't you tell me?" Her voice was a sad bleat, and she looked as though I'd shaken her out like dirt from a rug.

I'd never considered she might have been excited for me,

or hurt that I hadn't confided in her. I couldn't bear to see her so dejected. "Oh, Mom, I wasn't hiding anything. I just haven't even seen a doctor yet. I wanted to wait until I was sure everything's okay." I remembered a discussion among her knitting friends about miscarriages, and whipped it out as an excuse. "It's bad luck to announce a pregnancy before the third month." I looked to my aunts for moral support.

"Oh, that's just an old wives' tale," Aunt Luce said, with a curt wave. "But a baby is a happy announcement at any time. Congratulations."

Mom smiled, but disappointment still showed in her eyes. "Yes. It is." Then her expression lifted. "Oh my gosh, I'm going to be a grandmother." She looked enthralled, undoubtedly envisioning all the baby booties and blankets she could knit.

"Drink lots of whole milk. And when you get bigger, be sure to sleep on your left side so the baby doesn't get strangled by the cord," Aunt Janey said, coming to hug me.

"Now that's an old wives' tale, if I ever heard one. What's next? If she sleeps on her stomach, she'll crush the baby?" Aunt Luce asked.

I hadn't thought about any of these things. I knew nothing about pregnancy or childbirth, what ghastly horrors would be inflicted upon my body besides fifty or sixty extra pounds, disrupted internal organs, stretch marks, hemorrhoids, and varicose veins. Never mind the fact that eight months later I would have a squalling baby to care for.

◄▲►

CHAPTER FOURTEEN

Gavin's parents chose Jimmy's Famous Rib House in Barnstown, two hours south of us, as the place to meet their new daughter-in-law, after apologetically explaining that they were doing renovations at the house and weren't receiving guests. Gavin said, "That's a laugh. They never receive guests, and they couldn't renovate a doghouse." He wasn't looking forward to this visit. It was my idea. I wanted to meet his folks.

We joined his family at a gingham-covered picnic table at Jimmy's and were handed sticky menus by a waitress who looked as if she'd been stiffed so many times that she loathed anyone who could afford to eat out. Gavin's brother Owen, the youngest of the three brothers, had noticeably glazed eyes. I sat next to his wife, Lynette Marie, and her overblown hair. Gavin slid in next to me; his parents were across from us. Gavin had told me that his father, Alvin, had retired from the service and now sold outdoor garden accessories such as benches, birdbaths, frogs, and elves. He had a broad forehead and hazel eyes, like Gavin's, and told me to call him Al. His mother's name was Trudy, but she said everyone called her Toodles, which I quickly learned was due to her peculiar voice, not unlike a kazoo.

Everyone had drinks. The taste of alcohol made me gag, so it hadn't been hard for me to quit drinking. It had been a good time to ditch the cigarettes, too. My due date was mid-March, just five months away. I was taking my prenatal vitamins and eating bushels of carrots and apples. Gavin expected me to start whinnying any day. I started to read *Childbirth without*

Fear, until I got to the part where the author claimed modern obstetrics made it possible for women to replace fear of death with joy. Frankly, I'd never even thought to fear death in childbirth before then and immediately ran outside to hurl the unfinished book into the apartment dumpster.

"Too bad your brother Larry couldn't be here," Toodles said to Gavin with a lament-laden sigh after the waitress took our orders. Larry was the eldest of the three sons. A pouch of fat under her jaw quivered when she turned her head or spoke. Lips pursed, she patted her silver hair and said to me, "He sends his congratulations. That dear boy is always so busy. I hardly see him these days. Him and his wifey live in Suwannee, and they got four of the cutest little girls you ever set eyes on." She buffed her dinnerware with a paper napkin, huffing to moisten it.

At the table behind us, a toddler in a high chair had a screaming fit. I decided I'd never allow a child of mine to scream in a restaurant. Isn't that what everyone who hasn't had a child thinks?

"Four females. No one to carry on the family name. What I wouldn't give for a couple of hearty grandsons," Al said, which was followed by meaningful throat clearing. Owen snorted and said something to Lynette Marie.

I felt a little flutter inside my belly, like a flipping curlicue, a human-amphibian testing out the amniotic waters. I was about to grab Gavin's hand to place it on my stomach, but the baby stopped moving.

I was learning many new things about my husband. For example, once he latched on to an idea, he would refuse to let it go for no other reason than it was his. He was intent on finding a name for our baby based on a Beatles song and was absolutely gobsmacked when I told him I did not want our child named Penny Lane or Billy Shears.

"You didn't come to the last two baptisms," Toodles said, needling Gavin with a harsh stare.

"I didn't know I was invited," he said.

"Of course you were, you nincompoop, but we can't send you an invitation if we don't have your address. I left a message on your answering machine. Don't you listen to your messages?" She turned to me and said, "This boy's a rolling stone. I hope you can keep up with him."

I told her, "I have a good pair of running shoes."

Gavin said, "You're just sore because I roll in the opposite direction."

"You don't call home near enough. It's been two whole years since I last set eyes on you, and now you got a wife in tow." She squinted at me, and then her eyes softened as she turned to him again. I wondered if she was manic. "Larry's in housing. You know, if you want, he could set you up in real estate. There's good money to be made in rental property. You wouldn't have to travel—" Her voice reeked with syrup.

"If he wants to fall flat on his face, it's his life," Al said, then turned to Gavin. "Just give me a grandson before you do it."

Owen said, "Larry's not in housing, Ma. He's a slum lord."

Toodles said, "He is not. Why would you say such a thing? Just because your gun shoots blanks?"

I shifted on the hard plank seat and focused on a cigarette spot on the checkered tablecloth. Owen grumbled something I couldn't understand.

Al made a fist and said, "It's those tight Levi's you wear, Owen. I read about it in *The Star*. Your balls are constricted." Something about him reminded me of your father.

I wanted to hug our nasty waitress when she trucked out of the kitchen with our food, even when she held the plates high and hollered, "Who gits ribs? Who gits steak with fries?" then set everything in front of us, seemingly at random, and left us to sort it out among ourselves. At least it gave us something constructive to do. Gavin ordered another drink as we passed around dishes.

Lynette Marie poked at her steak with a fork, then asked

Owen, who had the same dinner, "Is yours dripping blood like this?" He shrugged, and they switched plates.

Toodles vigorously salted her food before tasting it. "Where'd you say you're from?" she asked me.

I told her I grew up south of Cleveland in Nopiming, and she looked at me as if I'd said I crawled out of a swamp. Did she think Barnstown was more cosmopolitan? Fidgety as ever, Gavin doused his steak and fries with catsup. The rubbery shrimp on my kabob tasted as if they'd been harvested from a swimming pool. Owen's knife flipped onto the floor. Grunting, he struggled to reach under the bench for it, dragging the tablecloth with him.

When Toodles asked me if I worked, I told her, "Yes, at a rehabilitation center, The Allison House." As she licked her fingers, a confused expression crossed her face as if I'd said I was in rehab.

Al asked what kind of name "Lousy" was.

"It's Lowsley. English and Irish."

Toodles and Al nodded like Tweedle Dee and Tweedle Dum.

"You come from a big family?" she asked. When I told her I was an only child, she smiled wanly.

"People tell me I look like Harrison Ford. What d'you think, Angelica?" Owen drawled.

"You look like fermented white trash," Lynette Marie said, and moved his beer out of reach. He stood to stretch clumsily across the table for the bottle and then plopped back down, making the table jump. Lynette tried to snatch it away from him again. I feared they might actually spar for it, but he leaned back and finished it in one gulp.

He flashed a wet smile at me. "Well? What'd you think?"

Gavin said, "Can't any of you act normal?"

Trying to stay neutral, I told Owen, "There's some resemblance in your smile."

"Leer, you mean," Gavin said.

Lynette Marie warned me not to encourage "the boys." I got the impression she and Owen had been married for some time, and she knew Gavin well enough. Toodles and Al were discussing whether his recent bout with food poisoning was from the Grecian Urn or House of Won Ton.

"Did you tell her about the legendary wrestling match, Gaver?" Owen asked, twiddling his fork in the air like a potential weapon but looking at me as if I were the means he intended to strike with.

Gavin said, "No, because it never happened. Least, not how you say it." He took a long drink and set down the glass hard on the table. The tension between the two brothers tightened like a guitar string and vibrated hotly. I was seeing a different side of my husband.

"It was a dark and drunken night. A crowd from the bar gathered behind Tweety's," Owen said to me with exaggerated drama and wide eyes.

"Owe, no one gives a shit," Gavin said, to which Owen grinned broader, A.1. Sauce in the corner of his mouth.

"I keep thinking Angelica looks like somebody I know. Who's that girl that sings with her brother? They have a variety show?" Toodles said in a loud rush, as if to keep the boys from detonating. "Sunday nights? That sweet, pie-faced girl?"

"The Gaver tried to gut-wrench some guy for wearing a bad leisure suit, but he got kneed in the junk," Owen said as he leaned across the table. "So he dropped the guy on his head and—"

Gavin's nostrils widened.

"You mean Marie Osmond?" Al said to Toodles, his caterpillar brows huddled together as he peered lopsidedly at me. Other people have said I resemble Marie Osmond, that tiny country Western singer. I don't know about you, but I don't see it. Besides, she's Mormon and straight laced as a church pew.

"Then the polyester bronco put the Gaver in a rear-naked

choke hold," Owen said.

"From The Donny and Marie Show? Are you kidding?" Al asked Toodles with a snort.

"That's the one," Toodles said with a snap of her fingers. "Itty-bitty and cute as a doll, but her face is more puffy."

"There's something weird going on between them two. They're too close for kin. Ain't natural," Al said.

"Whose face is puffy?" Gavin asked, apparently reaching a saturation point. "Jesus H. Christ, Ma, in case you can't tell, Angelica's pregnant."

Toodles gasped, Al let out an extended hum, and Owen stared, openmouthed, as if slapped in the chops. A piece of green pepper caught in my throat, making me cough. I presumed Gavin had told them and had been stewing all this time because no one had mentioned it or congratulated us.

Lynette Marie thumped me on the back. "Take it easy. We didn't know if you were fat or what."

"I'm glad you're finally getting down to business, Gavin," Toodles said with a slick smile. "A pea in the pod. This is wonderful. You know what? You two should move out this way. You'll need a babysitter if you go back to work, Angelica, and I know you will. You modern girls are all work, work, work. I don't want my grandbaby in day care where some numb-nut shakes them till their brains bleed."

"We're putting an offer on a house in Vermilion," Gavin said.

"Oh, I know you. You can pick up and plop down anywhere. There's a lovely house for sale at the end of our cul-dee-sac," Toodles said.

Gavin was breathing heavy. "There's no way."

Al said, "I hope to God it's a boy."

Toodles pouted and said, "I never see Larry's kids anymore. That wife of his doesn't think her you-know-what stinks. I miss those little girls so bad. She doesn't even let me stop by the house, not since that last time. I'd love to get my hands on a baby. Stand up, Angelica. Let's see how you're carrying that little Schirrick. I can tell if it's a boy or a girl. Come now, don't be shy." She gestured for me to stand.

I did not want to stand. I would not stand. Gavin did, though, and threw his napkin on his plate and started to pull me up. I resisted until it dawned on me that he wanted to leave. I was never so relieved. "Got to run. We'll let you know when she pops the kid. Take it easy, Owe," he said, tossing money for our portion of the bill on the table.

Toodles said, "Gavin, where are you going? Gavin? Don't go!"

He squeezed my arm and walked faster. "Come on, baby doll. You don't need this."

He had just started the car when I heard what sounded like a rock hitting my window. Heart clamoring, I nearly peed in relief to see Owen at the window, holding a cardboard box with a white bow. He yelled louder than he needed to. "Wedding gift from all of us."

Gavin rolled down the window so I could take it; it was so heavy I almost dropped it. Owen winked at me and reminded me to ask the Gaver about the famous wrestling match.

In the box was a ceramic garden frog.

Hospitals made Gavin nervous. He didn't like that fact that a nurse whisked me away in a wheelchair, leaving him to finish up at the registration desk while I was in labor. He feared he wouldn't be able to find me, and an intern would dope him up and amputate his right leg before he could tell them they had the wrong guy, and he'd never be able to drive again.

He was annoyed when the nurse closed the curtain on him to check my cervix; he whisked it back open as if hoping to catch her doing something indecent. He complained about the antiseptic odor in the room. The vinyl chair was too hard. The bars on the bed "creeped" him out. It was taking too long. There was never anything good on TV in the middle of the night. When the nurse started snapping the back of my hand with her finger to find a vein for an IV, his eyes bugged, and he said he was going to duck out for a quick drink. I hollered there was no way in hell that he was going anywhere until this baby was born.

I shoved the nurse away when she said she had to check my cervix for the twentieth time and growled at her offer of ice chips. Getting one tablespoon of frozen water every half hour when you're parched is condescending, and not being able to eat is just as bad. Whenever anyone left the room, Gavin gave me cups of water. Several times, my obstetrician offered me a "spinal," but I didn't want to be in an altered state of mind. Maybe I was trying to punish myself. During contractions, I yelled at Gavin to "get the fuck away from me"; and in the brief moments of rest between them, I cried for him to hold my hand. I called him a demon and swore I'd never, ever let him do this to me again. He yelled back that it hadn't been his idea in the first place: "Don't blame me! You're the one slipped up." If I hadn't been busy, I might have leaped off the table to strangle him.

The focus changed when they wheeled me into the delivery room and told me to push. At last, instead of fighting the contractions, I could direct the pain toward something productive. Gavin kept saying, "Keep it up, keep it up." I bore down, grunting and groaning until I was sure the blood vessels in my eyeballs had popped. It was surreal: the bright lights, everyone cheering me on. I felt like the first woman in the world to give birth. When the baby began to crown, Gavin's face paled and I feared he'd end up flat on the floor, but then the baby slipped out in one big gush. "We got us a girl!" he whooped.

Our baby. The doctor laid her across my chest. She was perfectly calm and as slippery as a seal, just breathing and staring at me, unseeing but already world-wise. I was sure she knew who I was. Gavin was hysterical, jabbering about how perfect she was. "I can't believe it. I'm a father. Holy Mother of God, it's real." His hand was shaking so hard when the doctor gave him the scissors to cut the umbilical cord that he could hardly hold them. Suddenly he stopped talking and stood still, the L-shaped scissors in his trembling hand, looking at the baby, at me, the afterbirth and all the blood, inhaling the strange, earthy, animal smells. His face was sheet white. The nurse made him sit down, and someone got him some apple juice and crackers.

When I was finally settled in a room, he told me he never wanted to see anything like that again. I laughed. That was fine with me, because I never wanted to do it again. He sat in the chair with a blue hospital gown over his shirt and held our teeny girl close to his chest, his head craned down to stare at her. She was no longer than his forearm. He kissed the top of her head like a doting daddy.

I dreamed Gavin and I were standing in the center of a fountain with our baby held high. The water was washing me clean, and people were throwing lucky pennies at our feet. It had been so long since something had gone right in my life. I wanted Michelle with me every minute of the day, and all night, and, yes, you're right, that is a Beatles-inspired name. It's also a beautiful name that made her daddy happy and proud. I loved holding her against my bare skin and smelling her sweet baby scent. I marveled at the strength of her tiny pink mouth when she suckled. Gavin must have been jealous of us, because he warned me that I was spoiling her by nursing her whenever she cried and that my breasts would stretch out of shape. "They don't just snap back," he said. Stretching had already done its damage, and after I told him how much formula cost and that he'd have to help me heat bottles in the middle of the night, he kept his yap shut.

Her tiny fist curled around my pinkie and held on tight. I prayed she would be strong. I prayed she would be brave.

I was the one who needed to be brave. After I became a mother, I finally decided to ask Mom about her pregnancy and the circumstances of my birth.

◂▴▸

CHAPTER FIFTEEN

Mom squeaked with enthusiasm when I handed Michelle to her. I poured myself a glass of orange juice while Mom gently stroked her plump, silken cheek. "I don't want to wake her, but do I wish she'd open those little peepers. Sweet little thing. Have Gavin's parents come by to see her yet?" she asked.

"They did. And then they wouldn't leave."

It had been an exhausting afternoon. Gavin and his father went to get beer, leaving me alone with his mother. After an hour had passed, I began to think the two of them had gone to a bar instead of the store. Toodles talked nonstop about how much trouble her boys were to raise, groused that Al was a disinterested father, and then asked when Gavin was going to buy me a *real* wedding ring, apparently one with a massive diamond like her own. Feigning confusion over her question, I looked at the slim band on my finger and told her it was real gold. I said it with such pride that she didn't respond.

Not wanting Gavin's parents to reflect badly on him, I added, "But it was a nice visit. They brought Michelle a fifty-dollar savings bond and a silver piggy bank." I sat with my feet curled up on the recliner and rubbed my neck. Michelle whinnied like a goat and stretched, then sleepily opened her eyes and blinked at Mom.

"Hello, sweet pea," Mom said. "I still remember when the midwife handed me my red-faced little tempest. Oh, you came out hopping mad. Aunt Harriet was beside herself with joy, praising me for the good job I'd done, like I'd grown a prize pumpkin."

I was too young to remember meeting Aunt Harriet. She was a spinster by choice and a little peculiar, I'd heard, and passed away when I was seven. Her picture, a framed sepia vignette of a short-haired, round-faced woman, sits on Mom's dresser. Grandma once swore Harriet was crackers because she replaced the missing buttons on her shirts and jackets with ones that didn't match. She would often sneak into Mom's room and turn Harriet's picture upside down. I don't have to tell you which one of the sisters was really crackers.

"What made Aunt Harriet so peculiar, besides mismatched buttons?" I asked, eager to know more about the circumstances of my birth.

Mom looked up at the ceiling. "Let's see. She fought with the city when they were encroaching on her rights. By that I mean she marched into city hall with a hatchet because they wanted to pave the road by her farm. And she did the same thing when they wanted to put an electric tower near her property line. When she heard her neighbor sold some of his land to a developer, she tried to sabotage the deal by letting her horses roam onto the property. I guess she spread manure all over, too. But she was good to me. The crazy quilt she made for me is still in the cedar chest." Mom looked happy, but sad, as if far from home. "She was alone on the farm with her goats, cows, horses, and chickens for a long time, you know, since Cecilia passed on. She worked for Harriet. Cecil was a hard worker, too, stayed with Harriet for over twenty years."

"I wish I had known her."

"She was happy to have me stay. Good Lord, she talked nonstop like she'd been saving it all up for someone."

Mom stood to rock Michelle when she began to fuss. Sometimes she had crying jags late in the evening that left me frazzled. Her tiny legs kicked, her body stiffened, and she wailed so hard I feared her lungs would pop. I despaired at not being able to soothe her. Gavin often came home to find both of us sweaty and in tears. He'd take her from me and walk around the house, singing *"Michelle, ma belle,"* fracturing the French lines—*"Sunday more keep on, tray bean on song, tray bean on song"*—jiggling her until she settled. It must have been the vibrations from the high-speed motor inside him that lulled her.

We were happy those first few years of our marriage.

Mom tried to put a pacifier in Michelle's mouth, but she pushed it back out in protest. When her pink mouth opened in a watery wail, I took the livid package into my arms. She made anxious little grunts and waved her fist as if triumphant, while waiting for me to unclip my bra. I held my breath for the initial pinch when she latched on to my nipple, then relaxed into that lovely, drowsy feeling that washed over me whenever she nursed.

I vaguely remembered Mom saying that Harriet's job was to find someone in her church to adopt me, maybe a childless couple or a large family, and that she had refused. "I bet Grandma was furious at Aunt Harriet when she said you should keep me."

Mom started arranging the magazines on our coffee table into a neat pile. "She was. Harriet believed babies were a gift, maybe because she didn't have children. She didn't think there was anything shameful about me keeping you, whether or not 'some stupid man' stepped up to claim the child as his. I didn't know what to think. Your grandmother had already filled my head with talk about shame. She said I wasn't capable of raising a child alone. But when I felt you kick inside me, I felt such love for you. Things are so different on a farm. Babies are born every day. The new mothers know just how to care for them while the stud just runs off. Why should it be any different for people? Aunt Harriet wrote a letter to your grandma saying their mother would roll over in her grave if she gave this baby to some stranger to raise."

I unlatched Michelle and switched her to the other breast. "What happened then? Fireworks?"

"After you were born, I refused to give you up. I stayed with Aunt Harriet for a few months, and your grandma told everyone that I had gotten married. It wasn't my idea, but I didn't have a say in it. When I finally came home with you, she told people that my husband, your supposed father, had been killed in Korea. We passed you off as being a month or two younger. You were such an itty-bitty thing, anyway. Oh, your grandmother worked overtime to convince people. She was a confounding person sometimes…well, most of the time, but she did love you."

I asked Mom if anyone else in the family knew the real story about me, and she said Grandma had told my uncles the war hero story, too, and they were expected to accept it without question. "Neither of them was living at home, anyway, and your grandmother made it clear the subject wasn't up for discussion because it would only upset me, being I was a poor young widow. And then everyone got on with their lives. That's the way it was then. There was no push to talk about everything like young people do now."

"Too bad you couldn't have stayed with Aunt Harriet."

"No. I was lonely there, and she was getting on my nerves. Not to mention the baby was getting on her nerves." She chuckled. "Believe it or not, your grandmother was helpful. She knew babies. She didn't get ornery until your grandpa died and she started having health issues. She seemed to regress. Maybe she never got over the idea of a scandal in the family."

Ever since Michelle had been born, I was itching to ask Mom about my birth father, what exactly had happened, and how. Did I dare bring it up? There never would be a *good* time to ask, so I figured this was as good a time as any. I brought Michelle to my shoulder and patted her back. "How did it happen, anyway?" When Mom tipped her head at me as if she didn't understand, I swallowed hard and said, "The rape, I mean."

She recoiled at the "*R*" word. Wishing I could take my nosy question back, I apologized.

"It's all right. I understand. I assumed, someday, you'd ask. After I graduated from high school, I'd go roller-skating at Brookpark Skateland on Fridays with my girlfriends. We always had such fun. So one time this boy I'd never seen before asked me to skate a few dances. He said he was Susan's cousin. Real polite. He had dark hair and a mustache. Smiled a lot. We skated a few rounds and then he asked to take me home. Since he was Susan's cousin, I thought it would be okay. I suppose it was a lucky guess on his part that I knew a Susan."

I let this new information sink in—it had started out as innocently as letting the supposed cousin of a friend take her home from the roller rink.

"He said he was on a road trip with his folks, and they'd stopped here to visit family, and he wanted to see me again before they left. I thought he fancied me. I knew Grandpa and Grandma wouldn't allow it, so I told them I was walking to Susan's church for a concert that evening, and I met him at the rink."

She paused, biting her lip. I kept silent, giving her time.

"He drove a big gold-colored car, what they call a street rodder. Stupid me. I didn't even bother to ask where we were going. He drove way out past town into the countryside, and then he pulled off the road. I knew something wasn't right. I got out of his car and tried to run, but he caught me. I begged him to let me go. I cried and screamed. He said he'd kill me if I didn't shut up, and then he said he'd kill me anyway." She stared straight ahead, not at me, and rubbed her hands as if trying to remove a coating, a fine layer of grit, something dirty. "After he did what he wanted, he drove me back to the rink. He said he hoped I'd remember him. Like we'd been on a date. He told me I was real swell. That he had a real swell time. I was just glad to be alive. Would you believe I thanked him? Stupid. Stupid, stupid."

"Oh no, Mom. No. I would have said whatever I thought he wanted to hear, too." My birth father threatened to kill my mother to have his way with her. For so long I'd tried to understand this contradiction—I was here in this world because of his assault. I touched my cheek to Michelle's; she turned her wobbly head and bumped her forehead on my nose. After letting out a little whinny, she drifted off with her mouth open, softly exhaling her sweet milk breath. There had to be some good in my father. After all, he'd let Mom live. You may think judging him by that standard set the bar awfully low, but it was all I had. If it hadn't been for him, I wouldn't be here.

When I asked Mom how she felt about that, she made a noise that sounded surprisingly like a laugh. She said, "No. He's a nonentity as far as your existence goes. A sperm donor doesn't even come close to how I see him. After all, he didn't intend to get me pregnant. Your conception happened of its own accord."

I was astounded that she didn't want to get rid of something that would remind her of the rape, that she saw my birth as something good. Would I have been as brave under the same circumstances? I looked down at Michelle. Heart quickening, I remembered I wasn't sure I'd ever want a baby. I pressed my lips to the top of her head where I could feel her pulse. Maybe the fact that I had a choice allowed me to make the decision I did. I wasn't thrilled to be pregnant, but I hadn't felt trapped either.

Mom said, "I looked at you and saw a miracle. You helped me forget the pain. Not to say any of it was easy." She handed a box of tissues to me.

I blew my nose and wiped my eyes. "Just the same, I hope he's living a really shitty life."

"Anger does you no good. Coffee?" Without waiting for my answer, she went into the kitchen. She probably needed a breather.

Michelle's tiny fingers caught my hair and pulled as if to tell me Mom was right about anger. It can destroy you, yes, and it had wound its long, bony fingers around my confusion. I leaned my head back and stared at the ceiling. I still didn't understand what to think about this. If I believed that I was meant to be here, it would be like saying Mom was supposed to have been raped. Would something that horrible happen for a reason? Or do we simply assign our own reasons to the things we can't understand?

My head felt heavy, and my insides were jumpy, as if a big clock was in my chest, *tick, tick, tick,* and I was on edge, expecting an alarm to ring any moment: Wake up, Angelica. This is not a dream. It's time to live your life. It would take a rude awakening, however, for that to happen.

Gavin started his own business, Angel Limo Service, and we signed a loan on an 863-square-foot, three-bedroom, vinyl-sided ranch with a detached garage and a fenced yard along a four-lane highway southeast of Vermilion. It wasn't an ideal location, but the mortgage was manageable. The rooms seemed no bigger than the cardboard packing boxes, and baby gear quickly filled every one of them. I never thought such a little thing would need so much stuff, including scads of frilly clothes she outgrew by the week. There was hardly room in the house for her parents. I was dog-paddling in a sea of dirty diapers while trying to guess when Gavin would be home so I could have dinner waiting for him, but, just like babies, he was unpredictable. Any notions I had about schedules or having a life of my own vanished. I'd be napping with Michelle in my arms when I'd look up at the clock and remember he'd called to say he would be home in twenty minutes, and he'd be hungry.

I often wondered how your mother coped with six children.

Gavin conveniently "forgot" to give his parents our new address. When we were still living in the apartment, he was table-pounding mad when I told him Toodles had dropped by twice, unannounced, and stayed all afternoon, leaving just before he was due home. He didn't trust her but wouldn't say why, which made me nervous.

Twenty months after Michelle's birth, a squirming, eight-pound baby boy we named Jude was born. I didn't think Gavin could possibly be any more happy, but he was delirious over having a son, belting out the Beatles' "Hey, Jude" so often that I wanted to jump out the window. I used to think people were silly when they said, "Enjoy your children while they're babies because they grow fast," but they're right. One day I was picking out a new refrigerator and the next buckling two toddlers into a station wagon. I don't know where the days went. They ran away over the hill.

It was a seven-foot, artificial pine tree at an after-Christmas sale at Sears, and I wanted it bad. Since Michelle and Jude were allergic to fir trees, dust mites, the slimy mold in sink drains, and spring—something we discovered after endless trips to the pediatrician and extensive testing—we couldn't have a live tree in the house.

Gavin and I had inherited an artificial tree from neighbors when they'd moved, but it was a sad-looking affair, with crimped branches and worn bristles, the color of a waxy green crayon. He didn't care what shape or size tree I put up. I could have wrapped lights around a stepladder, and he'd say it looked terrific just to avoid talking about it, so I figured I might as well get what I wanted. As I stared at the pretty Norway spruce in Sears, I imagined it in our house next year: a dancer, a dazzler, the whole orchestra and stage, dolled up with spinning ornaments and colored lights, boxes with shiny ribbons heaped underneath, and Gavin drawn closer to me by its sparkling beauty.

When I thought about the after-holiday credit card bills we'd soon get and how angry Dad was when Mom bought the silver bottlebrush, I left the store without the tree, dragging two crying toddlers. The automatic doors closed behind us, and I panicked. It was foolish *not* to buy the tree. It was an investment in the future, in a happy family.

I guess it wasn't meant to be. When we went back inside, Jude crumpled to the floor in a whining heap. I picked him up and slung him onto my right hip. Michelle plopped her butt on the floor and started to pull off her snow boots. "No, no, no, don't do that. The floor is filthy," I said. Impatient, I pulled her by the arm. "Put them back on." She stood in her stocking feet with that mule-stubborn expression of hers, knees locked, arms crossed, and said, "No can do." You would have laughed.

But I didn't. I said, "You can't shop in this store without your boots, Miss Sassy Pants. It's a rule."

"But my feet are wetty," she said, sounding as if Jude had sat on her birthday cake. It was past my nap time. I was five decibels away from losing my temper. I thought I'd have armloads of patience with my own kids. Where did it go? With a new appreciation for Mom, I told Michelle, "I've had it. We are leaving. Put your boots on, or you'll be sorry."

Knowing it was not good to be sorry, she scrambled to pull her boots on, and then we tromped back out. The clouds parted, and the sudden sun made gritty January look barren and bleached. I stood in the parking lot, overwhelmed by the vast expanse of cars, seeming acres of them, white with road salt. Where did I park the station wagon? Nothing looked familiar. I felt an approaching headache. I wanted my Christmas dream. I was a bad mother wearing acid-washed jeans and a bomber jacket, with snow falling inside my head, numbing my brain. I was certain the rest of my life would be no better than this: lost in a Sears parking lot.

"You should've bought the damn tree if you wanted it so bad," Gavin said that evening, but I knew he would have groused if I had. He was shoveling my homemade macaroni and cheese down his gullet—three kinds of cheese with a butter crumb topping—and it wasn't staying on his tongue long enough for him to taste it. The table shook because he was jiggling his leg.

"Slow down. Why are you eating so fast? You hardly ever make it home for dinner, and when you do, you eat like all you want to do is get back out on the road," I said, gripping the table. "And stop that."

"Got to make a living if you want to buy nice things," he said, staring at me with blank doll's eyes. "You like this house? 'Cause we could move into an apartment, and then I wouldn't have to work so much. And think of the money we'd save if we sold the station wagon. And why pay for the kid's swim classes at the Y? We got a bathtub."

"Okay, okay. Don't get smart," I said just to appease him. Michelle was singing "The Ants Go Marching" while arranging her peas in a line and smashing them with her thumb. Jude watched her intently.

I suggested to Gavin that he hire a third driver. He said, "Yeah, let's just add to my headaches." His headaches would be so severe, he'd have to shut himself in a room and sleep for twelve hours straight. I'd mistakenly thought they were migraines.

"I could go back to work. Something part-time. Betty McCarty, on Harding Road, babysits Sara Millen's girls. I bet Jude and Michelle would love playing there. Then you wouldn't have to work so hard." When I first had children, I was glad to be home, thinking my time was my own. In reality, it was like working for two tyrants. If you hate your boss, at least you can look for another job. I couldn't quit being a mother.

"You staying home tonight, Daddy?" Michelle asked as she flattened her last pea.

"For a while," he said.

"I want to go with you." She crossed her arms and frowned. All you could see across the table were her scrunched shoulders, her big brown eyes, and a head full of curls. Gavin and I glanced at each other, trying not to grin outright.

He pouted back. "I wish you could, but you need your beauty rest. I'll be home tomorrow morning. I'll take you and your brother to the play park inside the mall. How's that?"

"Yes!" She bounced up and down like a wind-up rabbit. I wanted to bounce up and down, too, at the happy thought of getting some alone-time.

"I come too, I come too," Jude said, and started chugging like a train, rocking in his booster seat. "All done. Out." He launched his spoon across the table; it missed his sister and clattered to the floor.

"Close shot," Gavin said. "Keep practicing, my man."

"Don't make promises you can't keep. Michelle's old enough to remember what you say. If you tell her you're going to take her, you better do it."

I quickly unbuckled Jude's safety belt to let him out before he launched himself.

"Think I'm an idiot? And no, you don't need to get a job. We're fine, doll. Just watch your spending."

He swooped up Jude and carried him into the living room, saying, "Here. Play the drums for your ol' daddy-o."

Michelle leaped up from the table then, too, deserting what was left of her macaroni. Gavin sang a nonsensical "bam a lam" over and over as they rollicked in the living room like rock stars to Jude's banging while I cleaned up.

Life with Gavin could be as exhilarating as the Tilt-a-Whirl. He wound up the kids with his tickling, hide-and-seek, monster growls, and airplane spins. He took their brains out of their heads and shook them around like bees in a jar until they were dizzy with laughter. Inevitably, one of them would get elbowed in the mouth or bumped in the head, tears would follow, and he would leave, making me the whip-cracking boss as I tried to settle them into bed.

As keyed up as he was, he often handled the pandemonium that came with children better than I ever could. He whisked Jude off to the emergency room for X-rays when he fell off the swing set while I stood there babbling, "It happened so fast," taking the blame. He calmed an hysterical Michelle (and me) when she had to get stitches on her chin after a spill on her roller skates. And he laughed instead of blowing a fuse when she'd stopped up the laundry tub with a stuffed toy and unintentionally flooded the basement. Meanwhile, our three-bedroom house was always in a state of disarray, toys in every corner, couch cushion trampoline in the middle of the living room or a bed sheet fort in the hall, dishes stacked in the sink, oatmeal on the wall, toast crumbs inside my bra. I never had time to organize or clean. By the time the children were lullabied and asleep, it was all I could do to keep my own eyes open. Most nights I had no idea what time Gavin crept in from work.

The next day when I returned to Sears, wouldn't you know, the Christmas tree was gone.

◄▲►

CHAPTER SIXTEEN

I came up behind Gavin while he was brushing his teeth and wrapped my arms around his waist. I enjoyed hearing his raspy voice, lame jokes and all, in the house that evening. He seemed to be in a good mood, so I thought it would be a perfect time to talk to him about the ten-year, high school class reunion at the Southland Holiday Inn. The invitation and questionnaire had come in the mail a week earlier. I wasn't keen on going, but Paige had called me twice already, begging me to join her and her husband. She and I still sent each other cards for birthdays and Christmas. Her husband, Brad, was a gynecologist; she worked part-time as a nurse at the clinic. They lived in the Heights, most likely in a mansion of a house with manicured bushes and an expansive, weed-free lawn, like all the other houses in that area. Unlike our house, there were no highways eighteen feet from their front doors. No chain-link fences. No cracked driveways. If you'd say I was embarrassed to have her over, I wouldn't argue.

"High school? Oh man, who would I know?" Gavin spat into the sink, wiped his mouth on a towel, and then gargled with mouthwash. It sounded as if someone had pulled the plug in Lake Erie. I reminded him that he'd met Paige and her husband at their wedding. "Like I remember," he said as he walked out of the bathroom. He sat on the bed and set his alarm. I followed after him like an obedient pup, looking for a pat on the head or a scrap of meat.

"But I thought we could take the kids to Mom's, and you

and I could spend the night at the hotel. Just the two of us."

"I hated high school," he said. I reminded him this wasn't his reunion. He pointed at me as if I'd guessed the correct answer in a game show. "Exactly. You'll be off gossiping with your girlfriends or flirting with your old boyfriend. What's there for me to do? Drink myself into a stupor? Sit in a corner and pout 'cause I dropped out?"

"My old boyfriend won't be there." It took a second for his last comment to register. "Wait. You dropped out?"

"Uh-oh" registered on his face before he bounced back with "I told you that."

"You did not."

"I did. Long time ago." He lay in bed with his arm draped over his eyes.

"I would have remembered."

"Well, fuck me. I dropped out. Now you know. Don't make a big stink out of it."

"I don't believe this."

"You think you're smarter than me, don't you?"

"What?"

"It's true. You throw your education in my face. You think you can make more money than me? You have an associate's degree. Big whoop."

"Who's making a stink now?" I asked.

He got itchy faster than a flea bite, which made me suspect he was back to taking amphetamines by the handful. When I'd first discovered his stash, prescriptions filled in his and other people's names, I tried to rationalize it. After all, I didn't want him falling asleep on the road. I assumed he knew what he was doing, but it was soon clear he was locked in on a roller coaster, constantly upping the dose to climb the hill again, gulping jolly beans, black betties, lidpoppers, skyrockets—better and faster than coffee for truckers and drivers. He'd feel down, then pop another, and another, and another, until his nervous system was so wired he'd be up for four or five days straight, growing more prickly by the hour, until he crashed. No wonder he got blinding headaches. Then when he awakened from what he called a deadless sleep, he would be chomping to start over.

We had what must have been our most idiotic argument when I told him it was a dead sleep; he flung open the bedroom door and the knob went through the wall. That was the first of many outbursts. Eventually I convinced him that I wasn't trying to be accusatory; I was concerned about his well-being. I bought him vitamins, insisted he take on less work, and begged him to stick to black coffee when driving. He promised he would. He made many promises.

Anyway, his drug usage wasn't something I wanted to bicker about. It was the reunion. "I really want to go." I ran my fingers down his bare chest.

He scowled at me with the intensity of an impacted tooth, causing me to draw back my hand. "Then you should go. I encourage you to go. Have a blast."

I sighed. I'd go alone in a heartbeat if there were a chance you might be there. On the other hand, leaving the kids with Gavin for the weekend might be good for them. Jude was a rambunctious four, and Michelle, nearly six, was full of bright and exhausting questions about the world. Gavin didn't have a clue about what it was like to have the sticky hands of two toddlers in your hair from sunup to sundown. "You'd watch the small fry, then, if I went by myself?"

His eyes opened as wide as if I'd asked him to ride a tricycle down the turnpike. "Oh man. Can't they stay with your mom? You know I can make a killing on the weekend."

"Yeah. I know what else you can make, too. What's her name?" I was thinking about the time he'd called me from Chicago to tell me he was getting a room when I hadn't even known he was that far away. Lately I found myself checking for lipstick on his Jockey shorts or the smell of another woman on his face when he came home, and finding nothing only convinced me that he was an ace at deception.

"Right. Like I got time for that." He turned onto his side, away from me, arms tightly crossed in front.

"You never told me you dropped out," I said. Before I turned off the light, I noticed the hair on the top of his head was thinning. I huddled on the far side of the bed, fighting the urge to whack him on the head with the table lamp or to kick him out of bed with my feet. He'd pushed me off the bed once.

I was way past drunk when I laughed so hard I accidentally spat on Chris Gallo's tie. The skinny, frizzy-haired clarinet player from the marching band now had a tangled gray bush that sat high on a shiny forehead. Chris said he'd harbored a crush on me all through high school: "You look better than ever. Can I call you sometime, Rebecca?"

My intention was to be unrecognizable in a black vinyl number with cutout shoulders and silver gussets at the thighs, and hair that Mom said looked styled with an egg beater. I could have starred in a music video, fawning over the lead guitarist of a heavy-metal band. I only wanted to gain back some of the attitude I'd lost since becoming someone's wife and mother, but it was clear, when I got to the reunion, that I'd gone a bit overboard.

I was reminded of why Paige and I had been such close friends, because she didn't give me a second look. Her husband, though, raised his eyebrows as I climbed into the back of their minivan. On the ride to the hotel, she turned around to face me and yakked the entire way about her work, her two boys and how she and Brad were trying for a girl, and the in-ground pool they'd installed this summer. She was dressed in a glitzy red dress with massive pouf sleeves and chandeliers hanging from her ears.

The Huggs High School, Class of 1975, Ten-Year Reunion was in a hotel banquet room with bad acoustics and red velvet drapes over fake windows. I can't begin to tell you how disappointing it was. The bar was cash, the chicken was smothered in a suspicious yellow sauce, the green beans tasted tinny, and the DJ wore a tie tack with a flashing light. Not only that, but I felt out of sync from having spent the last couple of years conversing mostly with munchkins. I could offer my opinion on the routine circumcision of baby boys and knew the name of every fur-face on Sesame Street, but don't ask me about NASA's newest venture or Reagan's efforts to end the Cold War.

My worries were unfounded. No one bothered with weighty subject matter. Every conversation began with "I remember." There was a lot I didn't remember. "How could you forget that Ray smeared peanut butter on his hand before he shook Greer's at commencement?" Sam Feigenbaum asked me. He had a head like a two by four with a paintbrush mustache. I told him it was hard to remember because I had been mourning the death of my pet rock. He said, "Bullshit. You were busy in a storage closet with Joe."

Seeing the photograph, however, was worse than the inane conversation or disco music.

Propped on an easel alongside a table with pennants, textbooks, and yearbooks was a photo collage of classmates and teachers, taken at sports events, plays, and proms. The snapshot of you and me hit hard. Was that really you? Me? My face glows. There are no circles under my eyes, no disappointment or bitterness dragging down the corners of my mouth. We're standing at my locker, and you're feigning seriousness with puckered brows and crossed arms. The photographer had taken the picture after lunch when I would stop at my locker for my books for afternoon classes. You never carried books. You said you forgot them, and you often forgot your jacket or lunch money, too. You laughed it off, but it made me wonder. One time, in the cafeteria, you poked your finger into my brown bag, and I asked, "Aren't you eating lunch?" You told me you were broke, so I offered you half of my bologna-and-mustard sandwich, wondering why your folks didn't provide for you. I thought food, along with shelter, was a given. I never said anything. You probably didn't notice that I started packing bigger lunches after that. We'd both wanted our families to appear normal, and from all indications in the photograph, we pulled it off.

I wandered away from the collage, feeling as if I'd been pushed from a bus into a strange city, holding a suitcase full of rain. Glassy-eyed, I watched my old classmates gyrate under a mirrored ball to the bleating trumpets of Chicago. Paige waved me over to join her as I walked to the restroom. I waved to let her know I'd be back in a minute.

I sat in a stall on the toilet with my underpants bunched at my knees, head spinning from too much wine. I dropped my hoop earrings in the box for pads and tampon tubes; it looked like a good place for them. I let my head hang and drifted off. I was a dream my mother once had. I was created at random when a comet collided with a minor planet in the sky, like an asteroid assault, and then I plummeted down to Gavin.

I was still falling when I heard the bathroom door open, followed by heels clacking across the tile floor and into the stall next to me. I immediately straightened up. My knee was wet. I'd drooled onto my knee in a bathroom in Nopiming, Ohio.

The splash of someone's relief echoed as I tottered out to the sink to wash my hands.

"Angelica, I remember you. You were always so nice," I heard from behind me as I wiped the smudged makeup under my eyes. It was a slender woman in a sexy red sheath with LAURA SPOON on her nametag. The Laura I'd known was a shy, pigeon-toed waif with thick eyeglasses that slid down her hatchet nose. She was teased mercilessly for using a sports band to keep them in place.

I held on to the edge of the sink so the room wouldn't slide out from under me and slurred, "Hi, Laura. I didn't know you.

I mean, recognize you. Cute nose."

She gave me what was probably the first genuine smile of the evening. "Thank you. You look terrific." I almost laughed, sure she was joking.

I asked what she was up to, and she said, "I work for Hewlett Packard in the industrial engineering department. It paid for the nose job. How about you?"

I gawked. "Wow. Oh, I got married. My husband has his own company. Angel Limo Service," I said, smiling as I blathered on. "We have a boy and a girl. I never thought I'd be a mom. You could say I work in the mom department." I glanced away, unexpectedly nervous.

Laura giggled, most likely because I sounded as drunk as I was. She said, "That's wonderful. I always thought I'd be married with kids by now."

A toilet flushed, and Bella, the school gossip, emerged from the end stall. You used to call her a bully with boobs. Her shoulder pads were the size of mattresses. Sharp perfume assaulted my senses. "Hey, Angelica, whatever happened to Blue Bus? You and Skip were real tight, weren't you?" She stared boldly at me, one brow raised. Ten years had passed, and some people still talked trash.

"The bus broke down, I guess. And no, Skip and I were *not* real tight." None of the band members were here. Maybe they'd overdosed. Bella jabbed at her massive hair with a pick from her clutch purse and then slicked sparkly copper lipstick back and forth across her lips. I panicked, having forgotten where I'd put my own purse. I rushed back into the stall and found it dangling from the hook on the door.

Bella said, "That's not what I heard. I also heard you didn't go to the university because you were into some pretty heavy stuff. That's what Seth said, anyway. I didn't believe him. Oh, guess who I saw around town? Your old boyfriend."

My heart leaped like a goldfish out of its bowl. "Joe? Here?"

Brows arched, she leaned toward me with a probing smile.

"Yeah, Joe. I almost fell over," she said dramatically, then returned to gazing at herself the mirror. "At a leather store in Great Lakes Mall. He looked good."

"When was this? Do you know what he's doing?" I asked. Watching her pat her face filled me with disgust. "You really should wash your hands." It had to be said.

With a prissy-sounding *tsk*, she dribbled water over the fingertips of her right hand. "It was last year. I think he's married. Say, did you see our class president out there on the dance floor? Still thinks he's a stud. Those pleated pants make him look like an old fart." Her laugh bounced off the slick white tiles to slap me.

Why did I feel crushed? After all, I was married—why wouldn't you be? I banged out of the bathroom to look for Paige.

"I wish you had never asked me to come," I said when I collided with her in the middle of the crowded dance floor. "What a terrible thing to do to your best friend."

It was impossible to converse over the music. She shouted, "Yeah! Best friends forever," and nodded with a thumbs-up. Brad was shuffling while jabbing the air with his index fingers.

"No, that's not what—" I felt an insistent tap on my arm and turned to see someone imploring me to join him in looking like a fool. His tie was around his head, and a small paunch strained his shirt buttons. Name tag: RICHARD CZERWINSKI. Who was that? He was fair haired and heavy, the kind of man who broke out in a rash when he shaved. I shook my head and waved him away, and he did the same, as if I'd invented a new dance step. Bella strutted by, smiling as if she were my new best friend. I gave her an evil look, one that I wished shot poison arrows. I was willing to wager she hadn't seen you. She'd made it up to get under my skin. Someone laughed, and I thought it was at me.

I wished you were there. We could have sat in a corner and

picked apart the sad psyches of our classmates, or made up limericks like we used to:

> There once was a girl named Bella
> Who slandered every good fella
> When she dropped her pants
> At the reunion dance
> They toasted her ass like marshmella

"Hey hot stuff, you win the prize for the juiciest transformation," Czerwinski gushed in my ear. "You never looked like this in school. Va-va-voom." When I burst into tears, he was kind enough to remove the tie from his head and escort me outside. I blubbered pitifully as we sat in his car. Leave it to an old photograph, spiteful gossip, and too much booze to set me back a decade. He apologized, swearing what he'd said was a compliment. I told him I didn't know what was wrong with me, other than my husband was a speed freak, my real father was a filthy pig, I was still in love with you, and my life was a lie. Who knows what else I confessed between sobs.

Evidently, confession turned Czerwinski on. He made a show out of how bighearted and sensitive he was, cooing, "It's all right. You can tell me everything. I won't judge." His fawning seemed impersonal and contrived. I felt humiliated. I wanted to pummel him. I kissed him instead. He tasted like an overripe melon. We pawed each other in the front seat of his car until he suggested we get a room. He said it jokingly, in case I might be offended, but his hands were serious. I answered him by sucking his tongue into my mouth.

He put his arm around my shoulder, I held his soft waist, and we staggered through the parking lot back into the Holiday Inn. Outside it was sweltering, and the air-conditioning in the lobby made my skin prick up in goose bumps while I waited for him to get a room. I didn't think about how I'd feel if any of our classmates saw us together or the fact that he and I were married, and not to each other. I saw his ring, but in my head

I denied it. I suppose I wanted to prove something to Gavin. Or maybe to you. Or maybe it came down to the simple fact that someone wanted to make love to me. I'm sure that isn't much of a shock.

The room smelled like damp cardboard, the bedspread was stained, and the TV mirrored a stranger's face, not mine. When Czerwinski turned on the AC, it felt like a blast of chicken feathers across my bare arms. I remember lying flat on my back on the bed, fully dressed, staring at the halo of white light around the bathroom door, wondering if I'd feel better if I sat up. I had the druggy sensation of being on a Ferris wheel. Whatever he was doing in the bathroom, it was taking him a long time. I thought I heard an alarm ringing somewhere, but my arm was too heavy to reach the nightstand to slap it off.

Czerwinski must have undressed me. I was like a plastic doll whose eyes clicked open and shut by someone else's accord. He was tender, though, so different from Gavin, and so much like you. It had been a long time since anyone had asked me if something felt good. I probably could have convinced myself that picking a tender lover was an accomplishment, if I hadn't been committing adultery. I didn't remember much about him from school other than he staged inventive ruses in chemistry class. He was heavier than he looked, and when he crawled on top of me, I thought it might be my last night on Earth, that they'd find my small body pressed into the mattress, like a flower between the pages of a dictionary.

I tiptoed into Mom's house around five AM, my hair damp from showering with someone I still called by his last name. Trying to find comfort in my old twin bed, I twisted in the sheets. Your face floated above me, large and disembodied, like a moon that slipped in through the window. You held a silk rose from your mother's table arrangement between your teeth. You grabbed my knee where it tickled. You traced the whorl of my ear with your tongue.

Finally, I rolled out of bed and threw open my closet door as if you were inside, calling me. There, on the top shelf, was the striped hatbox with my yearbooks and other memorabilia. I heaved it down and staggered for a moment, caught off guard by its weight, before I dropped it to the floor. At the bottom was the notebook you had left at Skip's. The chain to the heart locket you'd given me was snarled in the spiral binding. It took me half an hour to untangle it and put it on.

Flipping through the pages of your sketches and rants, I found my favorite poem:

> Angelica, you are a dream
> a window just opened
> a butterfly that lights my life—
> you write love all over my heart.
> I have no voice if I cannot hear you
> I have no hands if I cannot touch you

It was strange to see myself through your eyes, again, like a portrait you painted with words.

Then, I read something I'd missed: *A man who cannot touch without bringing pain is not a father. A father who refuses to hear his son cry is not a man.* Years ago I'd focused on the love poems, but so much of your writing was about your own sorrows, a way of peeling back your heart, licking your wounds, and soothing yourself. My heart was seized with fresh pain for you. I packed the notebook in my bag to take home with me.

What do you remember most about growing up? Was it your mother's kindness, or your father's anger? It isn't easy to look at the past without seeing the hurt, but is it a falsehood if you choose to remember only is what is good? What if you don't want to remember?

The next morning I was surprised to see Dad on the couch reading the Sunday comics to Michelle. He glanced up and said hello with a quick smile, then rustled the paper and returned to reading aloud, "Beetle Bailey says 'Hey Sarge, what time is it now?'" Michelle giggled as if flirting, not yet old enough to understand the humor. Mom was in the kitchen making toast for Jude while he fiddled with a miniflashlight on her key ring. I rumpled his soft hair and poured myself a coffee.

"Why is Dad here?" I asked Mom. Jude leaned over to shine the light directly in my eyes. I pushed his hand away. "Please don't." My hangover felt like a wet leather belt strapped around my skull, slowly tightening as it dried.

Mom said, "I knew he'd want to see the kids. We do talk, you know."

I never know what to think of them. Were they together, or not? Maybe they couldn't completely sever the bond. Maybe Dad would move back home one day. Maybe monkeys would fly out of my butt. Mom asked how the reunion was. I shrugged and said it was all right. "I don't know why the committee picked the Holiday Inn. It was probably a nice place when it was new but not anymore."

"It makes sense to have it at a hotel. People come from out of town, they drink, and, you know...." Her arched-brow look hinted that she knew what condition and what time I'd fallen into the house, or was I feeling like a guilty teenager again? I avoided her eyes as I handed her the *What We're Doing Now* book, containing updates from the classmates who'd returned the questionnaire. I was disappointed, but not surprised, that you weren't in it.

Dad popped his head in to say he was taking Michelle for a walk to the park to see the duck pond. In an instant Jude was in motion, scrambling after them.

"Can I have bread for the ducks?" Jude asked.

"Say please."

He said "Please," then started hopping from foot to foot while squeezing the front of his shorts. "I gotta take a whiz," he said, before scampering to the bathroom. Mom looked as shocked as if he'd cussed.

"Gavin taught him that," I told her. She hadn't heard the worst of the wonderful words he had taught them. Then again, she never heard your family cuss either. She busied herself looking for ends of bread and crusts from breakfast to bag up for Jude. Moments later he came flying back, pulling up his shorts along the way. I asked if he'd washed his hands, and he vigorously nodded his head, unaware it was obvious he hadn't. He'd get better at deceiving me in a few years. It was too late for washing, though, because Mom handed him the bag, and he dashed out to the backyard, where Michelle was demonstrating cartwheels for Dad.

I drank my coffee and skimmed the *Plain Dealer*, thankful there weren't any articles about the police busting a Class of '75 orgy. I couldn't shake Czerwinski out of my head. I wondered if anyone else ended up in bed with a classmate. Mom pointed at the book, and said, "Oh, look. Josephine Schuler is a professor. I didn't think that ninny had a brain in her head. Her mother gave permanent waves in her basement. She scorched Mrs. Tresconi's scalp. And look, that nice boy Douglas Papp, he's a dentist." She droned on, while I flipped through the newspaper to the Living section.

I was sure I'd pay for fucking Czerwinski. Every time I thought about him I felt a buzz, like a shaver up the back of my head. I felt trashy in a thrilling sort of way. I'd earned the right to do something wild, but there are consequences for certain behaviors, and, for the life of me, I couldn't remember if Czerwinski had used a condom. The other unfortunate reality: I had to pack up the kids and go home to a man I did not love.

Mom asked what was new with Gavin. I said, "Working like a dog, as usual." I didn't mention he was addicted to amphetamines and probably snorting coke like a bloodhound, too.

Dad burst into the kitchen, carrying a sobbing Michelle. "She ran ahead of me and fell," he said as he sat her down on the kitchen counter. The pinkness of her skinned knee screamed of fresh pain. Blood oozed out in little specks from the scrape. "Mommy will fix you up. I'm sorry, Angie," he said.

"It's all right, Dad. You can't possibly keep her from doing everything. She'll be okay."

Mom flew into action, wetting a towel and blotting the scrape. Michelle blubbered, her eyes as big as Frisbees. "Mishie falled down," Jude said. I dug a Snoopy Band-Aid—the only kind she would wear—from my purse. My stomach flip-flopped when I spotted Czerwinski's business card at the bottom.

Michelle kicked her heels against the cupboards with shocking strength. "No! I don't want that kind," she said, and smeared a dirty hand through the tears on her cheeks. "I want Grammy's Band-Aids." Mom quickly fetched a box of her store-brand bandages from above the sink.

Michelle insisted Poppy put it on. His fat fingers fumbled with the wrapper before he handed it to me. "Here, sweetie, you open it."

Michelle screamed bloody murder. I hurriedly unwrapped the bandage and gave it to him. "I'll be your assistant today, Doc, but if this keeps up, I want a raise."

Feeling neglected, Jude leaned against me and pushed his fists into my belly with a demanding whine. Dad picked him up, sat him on the counter next to Michelle, and said, "Show me your boo-boo, little man." Soon they were laughing, their arms and legs decorated with bandages like flesh-toned medals of valor. He called Michelle "cupcake." I got teary eyed watching them play. The next thing I knew, I was bawling.

He looked at me, puzzled, then he and Mom exchanged curious glances. "It's just a skinned knee, Angie, honey."

Wiping my eyes, I nodded. "I know, Dad. I know. She'll be okay."

◄▲▶

CHAPTER SEVENTEEN

Spring dragged its feet with blustery winds and slush, and strep throat was being passed around Jude's kindergarten class like a tray of chocolate cream-filled cupcakes. While we waited for the pharmacist to fill his prescription, Jude lethargically scanned the toy aisle at Gray's drugstore. I had promised him something for being a good boy and letting the doctor swab his throat; he sat so still with his mouth open wide, a wild stare fixed on me while tears rushed to my eyes as if I were the one having my throat scraped. "This?" he asked, and pointed to a plastic gun that shot suction cup darts. "No weapons," I said. "This?" He pointed to a miniature camouflage army tank. "Fine," I said.

On the way out of the drugstore, a flyer on the bulletin board from the crisis center caught my eye. I slowed to take a closer look, thinking *That's me, always in crisis.* I reached for Jude's hand to stop him so I could read more. The center was part of the new YMCA, and they offered support services to victims of rape and domestic abuse. They were looking for volunteers for general office work and manning their twenty-four-hour hotline. "The center needs caring and compassionate people like you." Immediately I thought of Mom, and how she needed someone who understood and believed her. The center only asked for eight hours a week. A volunteer. I liked the sound of it. Gavin wouldn't even have to know.

I was already keeping plenty from him. One sunless, Thursday afternoon shortly after the reunion, I impulsively called Czerwinski. We met for lunch at The Stagecoach Inn.

He told me his wife had chronic fatigue syndrome and balked at everything the doctors suggested. "I'm not looking for a shoulder to cry on. I just want something else, someone else, to think about for a while. Looks like you could use a little of that, too?" he asked.

Whether or not his story was true, he was right about what I could use. Gavin's carnivorous lust now came at me like suppressed rage, if it came at all. Against the tiles during a morning shower. From behind when he came to bed late at night. I once fed off that aggression, but without love or trust, it now felt repulsive and crude. I longed for something slow and gentle. Thursday afternoons with Czerwinski at The Bluebird Motel was, for a time, the highlight of my week. His damp body sliding over mine helped me realize how parched I was, how my insides had twisted dry like an old root. It also gave me a sense of power to have something over Gavin.

You know these things don't last. There was no future with Czerwinski beyond stained motel sheets. What troubled me most, though, was that I never felt I was cheating anyone, not my husband, my children, or even myself. Eventually Czerwinski said the guilt was eating away at him and asked that we stop seeing each other. I ached for him almost as badly as I'd once ached for you. Maybe it was transference, but I thought I'd go mental. I wanted to curse the moon and scratch at the window screens like a caged cat. Instead, I turned to an old friend and started drinking in the evening after the children were tucked in and Gavin was gone. By midnight I'd have numbed the hunger and emptiness enough so I could lay in bed and hear nothing but the dull drone of my brain, like a thousand crickets in the dark, not a single logical thought skittering among them.

Crisis intervention was definitely what I needed.

Ten other women took the training course in support services with me, among them a retired elementary school principal looking for meaningful work, a mail carrier who'd stumbled on an assault while walking her delivery route, and a policeman's wife. We sat in a room on mismatched chairs at tables caked with dried glue, glitter, and paint. Construction paper cutouts of children's hands, with first names written on them, were taped on a wall, and *Hands Are Not for Hitting* was painted above them. On another wall was a large sheet of butcher paper with a list of positive thoughts: Make someone smile. I have choices. Stand tall. Knowledge is power.

The volunteer coordinator, Kathy Ahee, had a floaty, little-girl's voice and an annoying habit of smacking her lips, but I liked her because she was a short, muscular mesomorphic, like me. She told us the crisis center recently made their hotline available twenty-four hours a day, and they had plans for a domestic violence shelter that would temporarily house women and their children. After the three-week training, they placed me in the office. My job was to file case folders and cover the business phones during the agency staff meetings, which ran from two to three hours on Tuesday mornings. It wasn't quite the challenge I'd craved, but it was more constructive than getting laid or soused in my free time.

Apparently there was no office manager at the center. Paperwork, stacks of forms, registries, and case folders were heaped on a table along the wall. The wheels on the chairs stuck, the computers were cranky, and the copy machine spat out everything in shades of gray. The carpet showed wear from a previous arrangement. I told the staff director, Charnell, that I would be willing to organize the office.

"Organize? Don't waste your time," she said. She sat me down at one of the computers and asked me to help her create a database of anyone who had provided past funding, and to add any other businesses that I thought might do so in the future. I wasn't sure what she meant when she said, "Think crazy."

Charnell was a woman with sizable heft who wasn't afraid

to put her weight in the way of anyone who disagreed with her, like a bulldozer in perfume and polyester pants. She told me that a National Crime Victims' Survey reported that the majority of sex crimes are committed by someone who knows the victim. "That discovery," she'd said to me one morning, jabbing her finger on the desk, "means we have to change the way society views rape, because it's not just when a woman is dragged off the street or assaulted with a gun in her mouth. Education is vital."

The words left my mouth before I could stop them: "My mother was raped." I felt heat spread across my face and chest, as if I'd betrayed Mom.

"I'm sorry," Charnell said, her voice switching from strident to squishy. She reached out to touch my hand, as if she hoped her shining offer of compassion would entice me to reveal more. The gesture unsettled me. "How is she?"

I eased my hand away. "Fine. It happened before I was born. She doesn't talk much about it."

Charnell took a chocolate Kiss from a glass bowl on the reception counter and unwrapped it. The office staff took turns filling the bowl; every week there were different candies. I tried not to indulge, afraid I wouldn't be able to stop once I started. "That's not surprising," she said, popping the chocolate into her mouth and rolling the foil into a ball between her finger and thumb. The candy made a lump in her cheek while she talked. "Most women bottle their feelings. They think no one wants to hear horror stories. Their voices need to be heard."

"Talking isn't the only way for a person to get over something. It's just as important to respect people's need for privacy," I said.

"Well, yes, what's right for one person isn't right for another. Or, I should say, what helps the majority of people doesn't help everyone. Personally, I don't understand how someone can get past the shame without talking openly about it, though." She took another candy and pulled the paper slip to unwrap the foil. "I wish they wouldn't put chocolates here. Things have changed since your mother's generation, but we still have a long way to go." She took three more Kisses and walked into her office.

I stared at the bowl, then started taking candies, one at a time, ripping them open and popping them into my mouth, every last one, at least fifteen. Then I went home and took a nap.

In the summer of 1988, The Crisis Center received a major funding pledge from the Cleveland Cavaliers. The center separated from the Y to become a private non-profit agency and was renamed Safe Harbor. Charnell asked me to work part-time as her assistant in raising money to purchase their first permanent shelter. I was thrilled.

When Gavin protested, I told him I wasn't asking for his approval. It marked a turning point in our relationship. He decided he didn't need my approval to do whatever he wanted to do, either.

There were times I thought I loved him, and times I wanted to throttle him. Using his brainstorming methodology, I listed reasons to leave him and reasons to stay. The reasons-to-leave column turned out to be longer. If you wonder why I stuck around, having a two-parent household for Jude and Michelle was at the top of my reasons-to-stay list, as if a bad father was better than no father. If there was any chance that he and I could salvage things, I'd put in the extra effort, for their sakes. The question then became: did he want to salvage our marriage? Hesitant to ask him outright, I sought tangible evidence that he loved me and was committed to our family. I got my answer without asking.

◄▲►

CHAPTER EIGHTEEN

Taking the children to Cedar Point for the day was my idea, the closest thing to a family vacation we'd have that year, and I suspect Gavin agreed only because I made him feel guilty over the insane hours that kept him on the road. We sat at a picnic table in the shade by the Midway for a lunch of corn dogs on a stick and limp fries. It was humid, at least ninety degrees. My shoulders felt raked by the sun. The park was packed, and the scent of overripe humans was as pungent as the livestock barns at the county fair. Jude accidentally splurted ketchup on the crotch of his shorts, and Michelle dumped her frozen cola. They gobbled their food like animals and then pestered us to hurry so we could take them river rafting on the Thunder Canyon.

"I hear it's a soaker," I told Gavin. "Maybe they could go without us? I'm not keen on getting drenched. Twelve people fit on a raft, so it's not like they'll be all alone." Michelle was nine and Jude was seven.

His scorn for me sharpened his hazel eyes, as if I were the spoilsport. I noticed a fly on his corn dog. He said, "I don't want a bunch of strangers rubbing against them. Who knows what kind of creeps hang out here, waiting to sit next to some kids. I'll take them."

I hid my surprise at his generosity.

He swallowed the rest of his lunch. "Okay, bugaboos. Let's go rafting."

They cheered as they yanked off their socks and shoes and threw them at me. I offered to hold Gavin's sandals so they wouldn't get wet, but like a martyr, he insisted he'd be fine.

I shrugged. It was fine with me, too, as I sat back on a bench and sucked down another lemonade while they waited in line. Like his father, Jude was lanky, and, in shorts, his legs were like twigs with knots in the middle, but he was as tall as his sister. With their toothy smiles, long eyelashes, and russet hair, they could have passed for twins. They looked immersed in their own private joke, making silly gestures and faces, while Gavin scratched absently at his arms. Thinner than ever, he seemed particularly keyed up that day, like bones shaking in a paper bag. The fear that a strong wind might blow him away gave me the urge to weigh him down by stuffing him with funnel cakes, fritters, cheese steaks, and Italian sausages.

I had no doubt he was bingeing, again, like a speedball down a one-way highway. Whenever he was home, which wasn't often, he was in constant motion: charging in and out of rooms, sitting down in front of the TV then hopping up again, opening and closing windows and slamming doors, as if he couldn't stand being inside. Dealing with his paranoia, twitchy moods, and unaccounted absences exhausted me.

The three of them were inside the Thunder Canyon loading area, which meant it wouldn't be long before they'd come to the waterfall finale, so I headed in that direction. Jude made me promise I'd watch.

A jolt to the heart stopped me. Not more than twenty-five feet away from me was a man who looked just like you. Frozen, I gaped like a stunned dog spun off the road by a car. You walked as if looking for someone. Your hair was short but just as dark, the build was heavier, and the height seemed about right; but with those aviator shades, how could I be sure? What were the chances of us bumping into each other, here, now? I told myself it was the heat. You were a mirage, an iridescent look-alike. Yet that languid walk was so familiar.

You looked in my direction. I couldn't breathe, and my ears

were ringing. I wondered if you recognized me. I hardly resembled the girl you once knew, but then you smiled. At least I thought you smiled. Someone bumped into me from behind—just a jostle—but it knocked the wind out of me, and my bag slipped from my hands. I fumbled clumsily for it, dropping the kids' shoes in the process. Then the camera fell and hit the pavement with an awful-sounding crack. I winced as I bent down for it.

I gathered everything and straightened to see the man who could have been you lift his shades and wave at someone behind me. I was mistaken—he was definitely not you. I combed my hand through my sweat-damp hair, disappointed, yet relieved. I looked like a troll. My roots showed. I was wearing cutoffs that did little for my short legs, flat tennies, and a ribbed tank top with a mustard stain. What extra money we had went into the children's clothing, not mine.

I walked on rubbery legs to the Canyon ride. The air was punctuated with screams and laughter as the rafts bumped along in the churning water. I wondered what I meant to you, how you'd framed our brief time together, after all these years. Did you blot me from your memory as if I had never existed? The thought sank in my stomach like a brick.

The next thing I knew, Michelle and Jude were running in my direction, shedding water, looking like someone else's children, surely not mine. Jude was eager to share his great adventure. "Mommy! Mommy! Did you see us go down? Look at me. I'm all wet. Did you see? Did you? It was awesome." He plucked at his Ninja Turtle t-shirt.

Michelle, her shirt stuck unashamedly to her flat chest, was just as exuberant, talking loudly to steal my attention from her pesky brother. "It was excellent. The raft was bobbing all over the place, and it spun all around when we went down the falls."

"I thought we were dead meat," Jude said.

"We had life jackets, dope," Michelle said. "The other guys in the raft with us hardly got wet at all, but we got pounded. We were so lucky. It was the best." She took my hand and pulled. "Daddy says you should take us on the Sky Ride to dry off."

"Oh, did he? Stop pulling at me, please." I wondered where Daddy was and what he planned to do in the meantime. He finally caught up to us, looking as scrawny as a carnie. I was embarrassed to claim him as mine. Why couldn't it have been you? My gut tightened to a thick knot when it occurred to me these were the children I'd wanted to have with you someday. Then I felt horrible. This was my husband, these were our children, this was my life.

Gavin stood next to me in squishy sandals, noticeably distant, his eyes cast down as he shook water from his sunglasses. Trying to appease him, I reached out to dry them for him, but he jerked them away, latent hostility apparent in his clenched jaw. The tips of my ears burned, as if he knew I was thinking about another man.

I was crumbling inside, despairing over the mess I'd made of my life. I had been gearing up to give him an ultimatum, and then I felt as if I'd wronged him because, for the rest of the day, everywhere I turned, I saw flashes of you and me together: the Deep Purple concert at the racetrack when pouring rain turned the field into a mud pit that swallowed one of my shoes. You hooting at bloody *Viva Chiba! The Bodyguard* at the Cloverleaf drive-in while I screamed in terror. You reciting Firesign Theatre's "I Was a Cock-Tease for Roosterama!" routine to Paige and me as we sat in your car in the school parking lot one morning—she laughed so hard she started hiccupping, and I nearly peed my pants. How the inside of your Bel Air smelled like damp carpet, rust, and Brut cologne. Your smooth silvery kiss, your hands on my body, the newness of sex.

The Earthquake ride jerked my family through a dark,

smoky maze of burning, falling buildings to a sound track of cartoonish screams and crashes. The kids sat in the front seat, unaware of my inner crashing, and I sat next to a husband who had a hornets' nest buzzing inside him. I shrieked when our car swung around a corner and a plummeting building stopped inches from my face. Gavin didn't flinch, too stubborn to acknowledge me or the peril we were in.

I couldn't recover. I told myself pining after you was futile. I told myself I didn't know who you were anymore, that you might have a shrew for a wife and seven squirmy kids with rashes around their mouths. You might be an unemployed machinist who drank a twelve-pack of Schlitz every night and a bottle of milk of magnesia every morning. Who knew what you'd think about me. I'd look like a washout to you, a little brown wren who flitted around in a house built from sticks and rubber bands. I wondered what you'd say if you knew the ugly story I'd learned after you disappeared: the truth about my father. I feared you'd find me as repulsive as I found myself.

Yet that was preferable to the awful thought that you were no longer on this earth. I hated not knowing.

Our family closed the day with our favorite ride, always saved for last: the Antique Cars. Gavin and Jude were in the Model T in front of Michelle and me. I barked at her until I was hoarse, "Give it gas, turn this way, not that way, hit the brakes," as if I could teach a nine-year-old how to drive. Gavin let Jude do it all on his own, unconcerned with driving skills as their car jerked and bumped along, grinding into the guardrail while both of them howled, Gavin the loudest.

We were on a collision course.

In Ohio, tornadoes can machete houses and trees into piles of matchsticks in seconds. Your life can be changed in one swoop. I awakened one day knowing the wind had shifted.

Gavin was pacing in the kitchen, turning in circles, head snapping, while flicking a pencil between two fingers so fast it was a blur. "You know what I'm doing. Working! That's all I ever do," he said so loudly I cringed. He came home late yesterday after being AWOL for three days, supposedly driving. All night, he was restless, anxiously jumping out of bed and then coming back to root around, as if he'd wanted to give me the impression of domesticity by sleeping with me, but he couldn't keep it together. Something was always crawling under his skin. It wasn't me, I knew that much, even though he tried to blame me. "You're like a noose, always nagging: 'Where you going? Why do you work so much?' Jesus! I don't always know when I'll be home."

"I just wondered if you'd be here for dinner, or if it'll be days before your family sees your face again," I said as I set down my coffee.

The pencil flipped from his fingers. "What the fuck's that mean?"

Jude's head jerked up. He was in the kitchen, eating a bowl of Lucky Charms cereal at the table, where he could view the television in the living room. *The Flintstones*, a modern, stone age family, was on.

"Don't talk like that. I wanted to make a stuffed chicken for dinner," I said, resentful of having to let go of my dream of a normal life with this man. He no longer wore a tie and had managed to misplace his best jacket. I didn't know who of any importance he could be driving anymore, which explained the bounced checks, even though he always seemed to have cash. I took a quick breath. If I acted as if whatever he did was fine with me, maybe he'd leave. "All I meant was it would be nice to see more of you at home," I said.

"What's nice would be you off my fucking back."

"Fine. Just go then. Don't come back unless you really want to be here," I said.

Michelle came in from the living room and motioned for Jude to get out of the kitchen. Both children knew their father could get testy when he was "stressed from working long hours," as I'd often explained, and learned to stay out of his way.

He whirled around to face them. "What're you doing? You going somewhere?" My heart seized to think his paranoia now included them, too. "I've seen the two of you whispering and telling secrets. What's going on?"

He grabbed Michelle's arm and put his face in hers, his jaw muscles chewing like a machine press. She cringed at his harsh voice.

"Gavin! Let her be. They whisper because they know everything annoys you."

When he let Michelle go, she and Jude went to her room, and she shut the door like a good girl.

"What'd you say?" he asked me, his fist held tight.

I backed away, uneasy. "Nothing. Please—"

"You're a lousy liar. Know how I know?" He opened the refrigerator and pushed around things, then yanked out a package of ground beef, a head of lettuce, a carton of sour cream. He cleared all the shelves onto the floor while I watched, stunned. "There's no chicken in here. 'I thought I'd make a stuffed chicken' my ass. What else you lying about?"

"Don't get worked up. The kids'll hear you. Just calm—"

"What're you trying to pull? Don't think you can hide it from me. You got plans, don't you? You're going to take everything from me, and then you'll turn around and say it's all my fault."

He was breathing fast, and his eyes were black as he rushed at me. Blank eyes. Two holes. A double-barreled shotgun. With his face in mine, his breath fearsome, he thumped his chest. "You're my wife. This is my house. These are my kids. Mine. All mine. Don't think you can get away with anything."

"I'm not. I don't."

He grabbed a handful of hair at the back of my neck and held tight. "No one's ripping the Gaver off. I want you right here when I come home, and I will come home. Stay in the house. No one comes over. You go anywhere, you do anything, and I'll take the kids. I'll take them away from you, and you'll never see them again." His voice was deep and cold, like something crawling out of the river, dark and thick with silt.

"What's wrong with you?" I tried to worm away, but he kept me off balance, twisting me around by my hair. My feet scrambled to find footing. "Stop it!" I dug my fingernails into his arm.

"*Gaaa*...you bitch! You fucking bitch." He let go of my hair, looked at his arm, then clamped his hands around my throat and pushed me back against the counter with his forearms. He had me. He was capable of crushing my windpipe like a cardboard tube. I held still, praying. "You stay here. The kids, too. Say it. Say you'll be here when I come home. Look at me, damn it."

I nodded, hoping he couldn't read the terror in my eyes. I wished I knew what cutlery might be on the counter, or in the sink, anything I could grab and use against him, but I didn't dare look away from him. His grip eased. I gulped air. "Yeah, yeah. The fuck you will. How dumb you think I am? You're planning something. I know it. You're going to leave me, aren't you?" I'd never said anything to him about leaving. Was it something I projected? That he might be able to read my mind terrified me, as irrational as it was. "It's gonna stop, right here, right now. No more bullshit. I'll fix it so you can't go anywhere." He started to laugh, a cruel cackle.

I was afraid he'd snap me in half, like a stick on the edge of the counter, but he pushed me aside and flew outside without a coat or jacket. He ran down the cracked driveway to the Taurus, parked in the open garage.

I quickly locked the door. Fear kicked like a boot in my chest. From the window in the door, I watched him smash the headlights of my car with a wooden baseball bat, then bash at the windshield, over and again, until it was shattered. Bat in hand, he came storming back up the driveway, looking tormented by a white-hot fire raging inside. His hands were nicked and bleeding. I ran for the phone while he beat on the door, calling me names. "You hear me, bitch? You stay here. Right here!" With a crash, the bat flew through the door window, and glass sprayed into the kitchen.

Hiding behind the counter, I heard him get into his car and tear backward out of the driveway. Anticipating he'd crash into the stream of traffic, I cowered, but heard only honking and squealing tires. I dropped the phone and ran to the children, not about to wait for the police to come to me, or worse, for him to return. I burst into Michelle's room. She was frantically trying to work a doll t-shirt onto her stuffed Pound Puppy. Jude sat on her bed, holding his knees and rocking.

I spoke slowly, trying to stay calm for their sakes. "We have to go. Let's get your boots and coats. Right now," I said. My throat hurt when I talked.

They scrambled to their feet. I helped them with their things at the back door, wishing I could blindfold them from seeing the food on the floor, the shattered window, the fear that must have been leaping in my eyes.

"Is Daddy gone?" Michelle asked as she wiggled her feet into her snow boots. Cold air was rushing in. "Jesus H. Christ, what happened to the window?"

"Don't talk like that," I said.

"What happened?"

"I slammed the door and it broke."

"Where are we going?"

"To the Stones'. We'll call Grandma, and she'll come get us." The Stones' house was at the end of the block. I'd met Christine just once; her son was in Jude's fourth-grade class. That was good enough.

"Why? I don't want to go there." Michelle scrunched her face in disgust. I wanted to slap her, then hated myself for it.

"Daddy said to stay home," Jude said as he yanked the stubborn zipper on his jacket. I tried to help, but my hands were shaking uncontrollably. They must have heard everything Gavin said.

"We can't. We have to leave."

Jude's eyes raced around the room, as if he panicked at the thought of disobeying his father. Michelle said, "I hate him. He's mean." She pulled her hand from mine. "I want Squeaky."

"No, we have to go now."

"I need him," she screeched, and before I could stop her, she raced back to her room for her stuffed pup. I watched her run into Jude's room, too, my heart beating twice for every wasted second, until she came tearing back with her brother's Pound Puppy, too. I helped them step carefully over the broken glass. Out of habit, I turned the knob to lock the door as I shut it behind us, even though anyone could reach through the broken window and open it. Let the thieves gut it. I took nothing but my purse. My children's small, soft hands and mine were locked tightly together as we crunched across the crusted snow under a puff-cloud sky, zigzagging through the backyards because I didn't dare run out in the open. Neither of them asked why we didn't just drive the car to their grandmother's—I imagine the circumstances were too bizarre for them to suppose anything ordinary. It was like a nightmare, the one where something is chasing me, and I stumble in the brush and brambles, and my feet turn into fish that slip out from under me as I run.

◂▴▸

◀▼▶

CHAPTER NINETEEN

I filed an Assault and a Malicious Destruction of Property report with the Vermilion police. I also took out an emergency Personal Protection Order with the Third District Court to bar Gavin from entering our house or coming after me, although there was no way to serve it unless the police knew where he was. I wouldn't stay at home until I was sure it was safe.

The next morning Mom took the children to school. After I called Dick's Towing to take the car to a collision shop to have the glass and headlights replaced, Dad drove me to the house to get what we needed to stay with Mom. Gavin hadn't been back—everything was just as I'd left it: the window broken, food on the floor, Jude's half-eaten cereal turned to a sugary paste in the bowl, and a transparent sheen of spilled coffee on the counter. When Dad saw the sorry state of the kitchen, he said, "Mother of God," which was an unimaginable profanity coming from a man who rarely invoked the Lord. I'd told my parents that Gavin "lost it" when we had an argument, but apparently Dad didn't expect this.

I threw out the food, washed the dishes, and wiped up while he solemnly swept the broken glass into a trash can by the back door. "What's wrong with a man that he'd do this kind of thing?" he asked as he dumped the dustpan contents into the metal can.

I sighed as I rinsed a rag in the sink. "I don't know, Dad."

He glared at me as if he could see through to what I was hiding, and he wanted it out. "How can you not know? What did you two fight about? It had to be something major."

"What does anyone ever fight about? Anything and everything."

He thought for a moment, conceding, then fired up again. "Does he always do this kind of thing when he gets mad?"

"No. Never like this," I said. I wanted to let loose and cry. "Things have been going downhill for some time. I didn't want to worry you."

Quietly, Dad swept the floor for a second time, then said, "Mom said she thought...." He stopped to scratch his ear.

"Thought what?"

"That there was something going on. That things weren't going well. You know how she gets, though. I told her to mind her own beeswax." He carried the trash can outside.

Apparently, my parents were communicating just fine, and about my marriage, no less. I stuffed underclothes, a few shirts, slacks, and a skirt into an oversize duffel bag while mulling over a vision of the two of them, sitting at the kitchen table, voicing opinions on what they thought was wrong with my life. Mom had never asked how Gavin and I were getting along, at least not directly, but I wouldn't have been truthful with her, anyway. Maybe it was time we quit tiptoeing around each other.

Dad began to nail a sheet of plywood over the open window. My heart jolted every time the hammer struck. It seemed like he was hammering with deliberate fury, as if knocking some sense into Gavin. How many nails did it take to secure a door? Each bang echoed. A deal gone bad. Shot dead in an alley. Ten bullets in the head. I put my hands over my ears until the pounding stopped.

I lugged our packed bags into the kitchen. "I want to get out of here. I have what I need." I was shaking. My voice sounded like a frog croak. He stared blankly at me, his lips in a broken line, uncertainty in his eyes. I touched the welt on my throat, wondering if he knew it came from Gavin's hands. He opened his mouth to speak, but no sound came out.

One time I had been riding my two-wheeler up and down the driveway while he was walking back and forth on the front lawn, methodically squirting dandelions with weed killer from a metal canister and pump. I was still wobbly, and a wide turn took me into the street just as a car passed. The driver laid on his horn. Frightened, I completely lost control as the car zoomed around me. Dad came running faster than I'd ever seen him move, graceless and uncoordinated, his arms and legs flung in all directions. I'll never forget the look of desperation and helplessness on his face. Bad things will happen in this world, no matter how hard you try to stop them. I thought he'd spank me for riding into the street, but he groaned with relief as he picked me up with one arm and dragged my purple bike from the street with the other. He smelled like sweat, mown grass, and weed spray, but I was never so glad to have his arm around me.

Seeing him now, in my broken house, with the same stricken expression on his face, affected me deeply. After all we'd been through, I was still his little girl, and he only wanted to keep me safe. I dropped the bags and hugged him, wetting his shoulder with my tears. He awkwardly patted me, as if burping a grown-up, but we would work on that. There was no doubt in my mind that he had done everything for me, always, with only the best of intentions.

"Daddy made himself sick," I said as I stirred milk, sugar, and raw eggs into the freshly fallen snow until it turned creamy. I hoped I wouldn't make my children ill with this concoction. Mom used to make snow ice cream for me as a special treat, but acid rain and salmonella wasn't much of a concern years ago.

"Is that why he takes pills?" Jude asked, effectively blowing the idea that it's possible to hide things from your kids.

"No. Well, yes. The amphetamines kept him awake when

he was driving, but then he couldn't stop taking them. He used them whether he wanted to stay awake or not. And then he started using other drugs when those didn't work anymore," I said. Jude touched the tip of his tongue to a spoonful, tasted it, and then put the spoon in his mouth.

"Officer Gledhill taught us that," Michelle said as if this was old news.

"Good. Then you know your body can only handle so much before things go haywire. He wrecked his car. When you get in an accident, you're supposed to stop and call the police, but he didn't. He left the car and ran." Explaining why Gavin was headed for the Madison Correctional Center without demonizing him wasn't easy, but whether whacked out on blow and multicolored mind-rotters or not, he's still their father.

Shortly after I left home with the children, Gavin was involved in a hit-and-run east of Toledo. The woman whose car he'd hit was in critical condition with multiple fractures and internal injuries. Gavin sustained a concussion, shattered nose, and several broken ribs. He was high and had a sizable amount of cocaine in the trunk.

After the police had notified me, I went to the hospital to see him for myself. Heavily sedated, he lay as still as winter on the white sheets. I stood inside the doorway and stared at his bandaged, misshapen face. I'd had two beautiful babies with this man. I wanted to gather his poor, broken soul in my arms and nurse him back to health. I wanted to yank the IV from his arm and shake the sorry son of a bitch until his head flew off.

From the hospital, he went straight to the county jail, where he stayed until charged and sentenced. Besides the drug charges, there were multiple counts against him: Leaving the Scene of an Accident, Reckless Driving, and Evading Arrest. That was in addition to the charges I had brought against him. I wasn't shocked, not anymore. I was tired and disappointed. And I wasn't the only one. No one in his family was willing or able to pay his bond or get him a decent lawyer, not even Toodles, who was living with her sister in Arizona after Al had passed away. She was wheelchair bound with arthritis and hadn't spoken to Gavin after our refusal to buy into her Amway enterprise years ago. She'd preached to him as if the almighty Amway could cleanse our very souls. Gavin told her, "It's soap, Ma."

He pleaded guilty on some charges in order to have others lessened, was sentenced to Madison, and left me to explain his trespasses to our children.

"Gross. You sound like a pig," Michelle said, after which Jude slurped his ice cream even louder. Wanting to be his polar opposite, she scowled down at her bowl. "This is runny and there's, like, strings of egg white in it."

"When will Daddy get out of jail?" Jude asked.

"In four years, when you're twelve." Michelle would be fourteen, bubbling over with hormones, angst, and acne. It was quiet in the kitchen except for the clink of spoons on the bowls. The counselors at Safe Harbor told me, if regular visits were impractical, it would be helpful at some point for the children to at least see where their father was staying, assuming he smartened up and wanted to maintain a relationship with them. I asked if they wanted to visit him.

Michelle's upper lip curled. "What's it like there?"

"Madison? I can find out. In the meantime, you can write him a letter. You can send him pictures, too, if you want. It's fine if you don't want to, too." I hoped they'd send him rants. It would do him good to see how he'd hurt them.

"I don't want you to get divorced." She sucked her bottom lip, eyes getting bright with tears. "Carly's parents are divorced. She has a stepbrother and stepsisters, and she says they're stupid and mean. Her stepfather bosses her around like he owns her."

I sat down at the table with them. "You don't have to worry. I won't ever do anything like that. Daddy is in jail, and I know you're upset, but nothing bad will happen to us." I was relieved it was over. I no longer had to worry about where he was, or when and how things would fall apart. He'd gutted our family and strung it up to bleed out like a pig. I had an entirely new set of worries now.

"He's a stupid butthead." She went into the living room and flopped facedown on the couch, with her arms at her sides as if they were useless. Jude quietly watched as I took her bowl from the table and rinsed it in the sink.

"Can I go to Nate's now?" he asked as if ready to get back to daily life, but something in his eyes told me he'd lost his best friend.

◄▲►

CHAPTER TWENTY

If their father could run afoul of the law and be jailed, Michelle and Jude wondered what crimes might land me behind bars. Forgetting to sign a permission slip for school or letting a "shit" slip out when I stubbed my toe on the dresser were minor infractions, but Michelle screamed at me when I hurried through a yellow stoplight, screeching, "You might get caught!" She reprimanded Jude for not wearing a seat belt because it's a state law, and, if he didn't comply, the police might come after me. Since when does a ten-year-old care about state laws?

Then there was the time I forgot to bring the cashier's attention to the case of Pepsi in the bottom of a shopping cart before I paid and left the store. The children exchanged glances with each other as I loaded the groceries and the soda into the back of the station wagon. I didn't think anything of it. They often give each other strange looks. When we pulled into the driveway, Michelle burst into tears, and Jude cried, "You'll get arrested for stealing!" After I had figured out what had happened, I tried to convince them it was an honest mistake, explaining that I once worked in a supermarket, and things like this happen. I told them I'd pay for it the next time we went to Giant Eagle, but they wouldn't settle down until I went back, right then and there, to pay for it.

Both of them cried over the simplest things: broken rings in a notebook binder, a friend being unable to sleep over, all the cheese sliding off a piece of pizza with the first bite. Michelle became obsessed with our mail. Every afternoon she sifted through the junk, opening everything and anything so that we didn't miss a cash prize or Disneyland vacation. No opportunity would pass us by. One morning I found a rubber-banded stack of credit cards in her book bag when I opened it to pack her lunch inside. Fearing she'd been pilfering cards from somewhere, I nearly collapsed in relief when I saw they were only the nameless samples that banks enclose with their mail solicitations. I tucked them back inside without saying anything to her. I figured I'd let her think she could support herself and Jude if anything happened to me.

He played "prison breakout" with his G.I. Joes and Ninja Turtles. Using cardboard, pencils, and Scotch tape, he built miniature jail cells under his desk and in his closet, criss-crossing kite string from the bedposts to his dresser knobs and desk for his action figures to hang from. I couldn't walk to his bed to hug him good night without getting tangled, stepping on a bent paper clip, or having him yell at me for detonating a land mine.

Safe Harbor renovated a vacant house into a fully staffed, organized office. In the summer they added an advocacy program and child abuse services. When the marketing and community service director stepped down, I was asked to join the staff full-time as her replacement. It was the perfect opportunity.

I'd been hearing good things about the Take Back the Night movement. The first women's protest march down San Francisco's pornography strip in 1973 had blossomed into an annual nationwide event where women would gather and talk unashamedly about their experiences with rape and abuse. I proposed that Safe Harbor organize a gathering at Tri-C, Cleveland State, or one of the other college campuses. It would help the community, and make our services known to the public, but I also had a private agenda that included Mom.

My other plan was to organize a group of women at the center whose lives had been positively impacted and have them speak at the Elks, the Shriners, Ladies Auxiliary, and other civic organizations. This would give faces to our cause of ending domestic violence and assault, and, hopefully, increase donations. I began attending an abuse-survivor support group to listen to their stories.

The women there struggled with seemingly insurmountable obstacles on an everyday basis. Sondra was a spindly limbed woman who'd fled from her husband in the middle of the night with three children, one of them disabled. She had no identification, driver's license, money, or credit cards. She had no family to turn to, no way of supporting herself. But she knew if she stayed, her husband of ten years would kill her. He'd crushed several of her fingers, blackened her eyes so badly that her vision was permanently impaired, dislocated her shoulder, broken her left foot, kicked her in the stomach and back, pushed her down a flight of stairs, and smashed her head against the floor and a wall. He told her she was a fat cow, careless, inconsiderate, and undeserving of love.

"And I believed every word of it," she said. "I stayed with him because I thought no one else would want me. I thought he was trying to help me be a better person. I would promise him I'd try harder. It didn't make sense."

I carried their stories home with me to hang like dresses in my closet, trying on each one to see if it fit. At the same time I'd believed my circumstances were different from theirs as if what had happened in my marriage was atypical. It wasn't really abuse. I didn't consider myself a victim. I'm embarrassed to tell you I soon discovered my experience mirrored theirs in many ways. Like the other women, I had a dark cave in my body, I carried secrets in my hips, and I swallowed when I should have spoken out. Like Isabel, I had an affair and drank to cover what was lacking in my marriage, instead of insisting I was worthy of something better. Like Mayetta, I looked the other way when I knew Gavin was coming unhinged. Like Sue Ellen, I didn't consider how my tolerance of his unacceptable behavior might affect our children.

There were times I couldn't help but cry at night. Even though I had left Gavin, I felt stupid for having stayed with him for so long. Why did I beat myself up? One of the things I learned from the group is to take the word *should* out of my vocabulary. There is no point in saying: "I should have left sooner. I should have been stronger." What matters is now.

In a dream, I climbed a spiral staircase, alongside other women and girls, to a platform decorated with ribbons and flags, over a pool of water. It was warm, the sun was shining, and everyone was excited as they took turns jumping into a net, where water splashed on them in some kind of baptism or blessing. I wasn't watching them jump, though. I was fussing with an ill-fitting, neon yellow swimsuit—the bottom kept hiking up, and my breasts spilled from the top, exposing me. As I climbed, I tugged and pulled, until I noticed how close I was to the top. Afraid, I asked the woman in front of me how to jump. It was Sondra. She told me she wasn't sure how to do it, and then she jumped anyway. When the water sprayed her, she was transformed into a shimmering mermaid.

Volunteers set up Safe Harbor's table of pamphlets and newsletters, buttons, bracelets, and t-shirts in the hall outside the meeting room of the community college. Davis General Hospital, Tri-C Student Center, Lighthouse Learning Center, the local police department, and other support facilities had information tables as well. There were armbands—white if you were a rape survivor and red if you were a supporter—for those who wanted to wear them. Red band on my arm, I waited anxiously as the six o'clock hour approached, hoping for at least a modest gathering to attend the first Take Back the Night rally. Mom passed on wearing an armband altogether and wandered along the outskirts of the tables, scanning the material. When I first asked her to attend the rally with me, she said it sounded radical. I told her it was supposed to be reaffirming. My reason for wanting her to attend was partly selfish because I wanted her to see what I'd accomplished. This was my first big project as marketing director.

College students in jeans, sandals, and t-shirts straggled in. Then middle-aged women in pantsuits, teenagers, and a few men, too, some holding their spouse's or girlfriend's hands, began to arrive. Within a half hour, the hall was full.

Mom sat with me in the front, near the center aisle of the auditorium, when it came time for the presentation. I took the stage to welcome everyone and introduce the tall, dark-haired detective. She rattled off the National Crime Victims Survey results while Mom stared at her, her hands clutched in her lap, blue eyes moving back and forth in frisson. "We can no longer isolate victims of violence or compound the injury by denying them their story," the speaker concluded, and everyone applauded. After a symbolic march around the campus, an activity Mom declined, the participants filed into another room to sit at tables, set with white tablecloths and candles. Smooth rocks painted with words—*destiny, courage, strength*— were in the center of each table, painted by the women in the support group. I counted roughly a hundred people.

The lights were dimmed. One after another, women walked to the podium to tell their stories. Just when it seemed as if everyone who'd wanted to speak had done so, another brave soul found her way to the microphone, and another story was told. As the evening rolled into its second hour, I worried that Mom might become catatonic, uncomfortable with the frankness of these testaments. I felt guilty for urging her to come against her inclinations. Then her chair scraped the floor as she pushed it back to stand. My stomach pitched. She was going to make a break for it.

She walked up to the podium instead. I held my breath and stared, wide-eyed. In her fifties, she was the oldest woman to take the microphone. My mother, dressed in pleated slacks and a cardigan with embroidered flowers, spoke to a group of strangers about the life-shattering experience she survived as a young woman. It was an electric moment. She didn't give details or even say the word *rape*, but I could see the blunted sorrow in her face and hear the tremble in her halting voice when she said, "It's a horrible thing to feel so alone, even when you're surrounded by people."

She bowed her head for a moment to wet her lips, then looked up at all the different faces in the room. I was afraid she'd look at me; I didn't want to be exposed. I'm part of her story, but this wasn't my story. Her voice grew steady as she thanked everyone for sharing their experiences, and told them they were brave and strong. She never looked so beautiful or radiant. I wish you could have seen her. As she walked back, several women held out their hands to clasp hers. A few even stood to hug her. When she reached our table, I stood, took her hand, and pulled her close. She felt somehow lighter.

When we speak out, Charnell had told me, we let go of the burden of holding our memories outside the story of our lives. All I know is it happened on a cloudless summer night. The moon may have been shining like a silver coin in the sky, but my mother was in darkness, her eyes shut tight. It was her only defense when my father raped her and left his trace inside her body. Neither she nor I consented.

Her eyes were watery, yet bright, as she sat and stared straight ahead, processing everything. I hope she saw what community can do and felt validated. I settled into my seat, crossed my legs and smoothed my jacket, feeling like an outsider at my own party. Why did I feel shame? Because it was my father who terrorized her? Was that my burden to carry?

The repair list on the house kept growing. The cracked driveway was sinking. The storm windows leaked. The furnace thumped erratically. The front door stuck, and some evenings I would find it wide-open when I swore I'd shut and locked it.

I feared that, after a long day, I'd come home to find a stray cat giving birth under my couch, or that our television, stereo, and microwave (the few luxuries we could afford) had been stolen. The three-bedrooom ranch was a good handyman's special for an ambitious couple, but for a divorcée with two kids, it was nothing but a headache. The worst part, however, was that I kept bumping into memories of my failed marriage. Nothing could repair that.

I priced the ranch as a fixer-upper. It sold in three weeks.

I wasn't looking for a house in the town where you and I grew up, but that's where I was drawn. The word *Nopiming* means "in a forest" in Algonquian, and I suppose it once was all forest. When I was a girl, there hadn't been much here to speak of besides a few tool and die shops, warehouses, and small businesses. Now there's a town square, a meeting house, and a main street with boutiques, specialty shops, and restaurants, like The Spotty Dog and Firewater's. The old Maple Theater, where you and I had our first date, now has three screens.

I found a cute brick bungalow along Willow Creek Drive with azaleas in the front yard, dogwood in the back, and, instead of an unfinished basement with mildew, this one had a tile floor and wood paneling. With Dad's help on a down payment, National Title approved the mortgage.

Within five minutes of racing through the house, Jude picked which of the three bedrooms he wanted and how to arrange his bed, desk, dresser, and Transformer collection. He flushed both toilets and ran water in the tub, peered into cupboards, thudded down the wooden stairs to the basement, and climbed into the stifling hot attic with Dad. He was an explorer at age ten, a conqueror in a Super Mario Brothers' baseball cap as he struggled hard to open the sliding glass door in the family room, unwilling to believe he didn't have the muscle.

"It has a pin lock...up here. See?" Dad said, reaching high

to pull the pin. The door grudgingly slid open with a grating sound, and Jude bounded outside.

"It smells gross," Michelle said. I hated to say it, but I agreed. When Dad and I had first looked at the house, neither of us noticed the strong odor. We smelled cookies, and now I understood why the homeowner just happened to be baking them at the time. It covered the wretched cat pee odor.

"Paint should kill the smell. If not, your olfactory nerves will be so overwhelmed that you won't notice it anymore," Dad said.

"Get real, Poppy." She snapped her gum.

"Take another look at the basement. You can put your stereo and video game system down there. You and Jude can have your friends over," I told her.

"Ping-Pong!" Jude said, bounding back in

"I don't have any friends here, remember? And just because you can't see them doesn't mean there aren't earwigs, spiders, and silverfish down there," she said.

"Since you're an insect-eating troll, you should feel right at home," Jude said.

"Suck the big one." She took my car keys from the table and huffed out the kitchen door to the open garage, where the car was parked. I heard the car door slam. Concerned, Dad started to follow after her. I suppose he thought she'd drive off and smash the car into a pine tree. I told him not to worry. She just wanted to be alone, probably to listen to the car radio. Seconds later I heard "I'm Too Sexy" by Right Said Fred defiantly blaring out. Jude started to hop, ducking his head and crossing his arms in front.

Dad cocked his head. "What is that? You let her listen to that stuff? She's only thirteen."

"It's supposed to be ironic," I said.

"Oh, is that what it is?" Lips pursed, he stood in the open doorway and flipped the light switches on the wall. Except for the ones in the garage, no lights that we could see went on.

He kept flicking, up and down, up and down, *click, click, click,*
like the hammer of a toy pistol. Jude was doing the moonwalk
across the kitchen. Dad said, "If she cranks the radio up any
louder, she'll blow the speakers. I don't know how you manage
raising two kids alone. One was enough for me."

I told him, "One of you was enough for me. Two kids, no
problem."

I don't mean to make him sound cranky. You probably
remember him as being an okay guy. Edgar has softened into
an obliging grandpa, having retired after handing over his
podiatry business to a younger doctor. He would have worked
until he was eighty-eight had it not been for my divorce.
He stepped up to help with his grandchildren, and I'm glad.
Seeing him do things with them that he didn't have the time
or inclination to do with me gives me pleasure. In the winter
he took them to the Polar Toboggan Run and brought them
home with chapped cheeks, and hair and clothes that smelled
of wood smoke. He and Jude built a remote-control car
together. He helped Michelle with a science project on contact
electrification. On career day he went into their classrooms
and talked about the twenty-six bones, thirty-three joints, and
one-hundred muscles, tendons, and ligaments in the human
foot, then had the students make lists of everything we expect
of our feet, from being shock absorbers to propulsion engines.
They were in awe. The teacher gave him an A+.

What Dad will do, if and when Gavin shows up here for
the children after his release, is anybody's guess. He never was
fond of Gavin to begin with. Sometimes I wonder if he would
have preferred you as my husband.

What do you think he'd say about you now?

◄▲►

CHAPTER TWENTY-ONE

I thought the move might give the kids and me a common goal, and insisted they help me strip the faded, cabbage rose kitchen wallpaper. Maybe it was overreaching, but I had this notion of us working together to make the house look nice. I thought it would instill them with pride, but Jude didn't care if he lived in a moldy army tent, and Michelle would rather lick wallpaper paste than help with what she saw as a lost cause.

She examined her ragged fingernails and clicked her tongue in disgust. "I quit. This is the United States of America, you know. Child labor was outlawed after the industrial revolution."

"I told you not to use your nails. Here's the scraper," I said, handing it to her. The paper was peeling off in stubborn shreds despite using a puncture roller and gallons of steam. The walls would need sanding once they were stripped.

"Why don't we just paint over it? That's what Dad did in the other house."

"I'm not Dad."

She picked under her nails with the edge of the scraper. After a few moments of peaceful silence, she said, "You should write to him. He misses us. He misses home."

I scowled. "I have nothing to tell him." How could he miss home when he was hardly ever in it? Who knew what other nonsense he wrote to them?

I admit, though, I often wonder if he asked about me, and what they told him. As Michelle sailed like a dart into adolescence, she probably told him that I made her eat boiled newspapers for dinner and beat her at night with a rubber hose, and I bet he gave her all the sympathy she craved. In absence, he had become the perfect parent: patient, sympathetic, never raising his voice in anger or forcing chores on them. He was in jail, and I was the bad guy.

I moved the heavy steamer over the last section of paper. Sweat rolled down between my breasts. Even my hands, inside rubber gloves, were sweating. Jude took a break and sat cross-legged on the floor, lifted his baseball cap, scratched his head, and put it back on. He looked bushed. I felt like a mean mom, a slave driver, a bitch; but I didn't want them to think quitting was an option.

Her voice rose in frustration. "He's sorry. He says he wishes he had done things differently."

I said, "Good. That's what's supposed to happen when you're in jail. Here now, this should be ready to strip."

"I don't get why you're still mad at him. You should practice forgiveness. It's a zen thing." The childlike whine in her voice set me on edge. She halfheartedly jabbed the wall with the scraper. "This isn't even loose."

"For your information, I forgave him a long time ago. Meditate on that. After all, he did give me two wonderful children." I held up the steamer again, and my hand began to shake.

Jude snorted. "*Two* wonderful children?"

She gave him a narrow-eyed sneer, then looked at me. "He'll be getting out soon. Maybe he could stay with us. You sold our house. He has no place to go. I bet you didn't even think about that, did you? It's not fair. It's like you're punishing him more."

"There's nothing unfair about what happened. He brought this on himself, Michelle. Your father—" I stopped myself from going into a tirade, put the steamer in the tray, and grabbed the scraper from her hand. "Never mind. Here. Let me do it."

"Ow! You scratched me with your fingernail."

"I did not. Anyway, fair is a fantasy. Consequences are what's real."

"My fantasy is Michelle runs away from home," Jude said.

"Dickhead," she said.

"That's a dollar in the swear jar," I said.

"I didn't swear." She glared stubbornly at me.

I blinked at her in utter astonishment. "Don't you dare give me that look! That's my look. And *dickhead* is a swear word."

"Not if it isn't in the dictionary." Head high, she strolled out of the kitchen into the living room. I heard the TV turn on, too loud.

I shouted. "It's a swear word in my book, and that's what counts. And we aren't done here."

"Dude, she needs to chill." Jude got up, tripped on his untied shoelaces, and fell onto one knee. "Fuck."

"Hey! That's a dollar for you now." I positioned the scraper under the paper, gave it a hard, angry push, and a muscle in my shoulder knotted up in mutiny.

"Can I be done, too? I did a lot. More than she did, anyway. Freak." He nosed around in the cupboards for a snack, stepping on the discarded paper rather than taking the time to put it in the trash bag. I was more than ready to be done. Painting over the paper with some fancy faux flourish that would make the walls look purposely textured began to sound like a good idea. I yanked the steamer plug from the wall by the cord.

I was curious if Jude also wanted his supposedly repentant father to move in with us, not that I would even consider it. Maybe he dreamed about camping or building model cars with him. I imagined them together, laughing and having fun, as they once had. Then I saw Gavin getting high on glue when no one was looking, or drinking a six-pack while telling Jude he doesn't have to do his fucking homework if he doesn't want to, that he doesn't need a diploma. I have no idea what to expect from the man. Or from Jude either.

Boys are more apt to slam the door, emotionally speaking,

on their mothers, don't you think? When Jude was four, he used to talk in his sleep. He'd sit upright in his bed and cry and babble. Sometimes he kicked his legs while his hands turned invisible doorknobs. I couldn't imagine what was upsetting him. What does a four-year-old have to worry about? Bogeymen? It was disturbing when I first realized that my children are more than just an extension of me, and there are aspects of their lives I will never be privy to. If I don't know what's wrong, I can't make it right.

Jude shut the cupboard and said, "There's no more cookies. The abnormal hormonal freak ate them all."

Michelle called out, "What did you call me?"

"No one said it was you." I shut my eyes and rubbed my forehead. Dealing with the children's rivalry is an ongoing challenge for me, having no siblings to compare their squabbling to. Gavin clashed bitterly with his brothers when growing up, and he'd likely assure me that tattling and name-calling are typical. You and your brothers might have been feisty scrappers, but I remember the good-natured ribbing and what seemed like a genuine fondness for one another.

She came roaring back into the room. "He's always calling me names and telling lies about me, and you suck it up like he's so perfect. I heard you tell him I *lost* my Nirvana CD. I didn't lose it. He stole it."

"You lie! You lie so bad. You lose everything, dim bulb."

"That's enough," I said. "You know, Michelle, that CD *did* turn up in your room."

"Doh! That's because he put it there. He gets away with everything. You don't know half the crap he does. Want to know how the garage door really broke?"

He hissed at her. I was too shaken to call her on swearing. I said, "If he broke the door panel, I'd rather hear about it from him."

Her cheeks reddened, and tears turned her eyes glassy and bright. "Yeah, because you don't want to hear the truth. I hate

you both. When Daddy gets out, I'm going to live with him."
My heart locked. Did she really mean that? She snatched
Jude's hat from his head and threw it into the trash before
blustering off to her room.

"Bitch," he muttered as he walked over to pick up his hat.

"Two dollars now!" I said, furious at them, Gavin, myself,
and the entire rotten situation. Evidently, fining them for
swearing wasn't having any effect. Evidently, none of my
disciplinary actions were working. I feared I had become the
nightmare parent whose children were out of control. "Is there
something you want to tell me about the garage door?" I asked
Jude.

"Don't listen to her. She makes stuff up just to get me in
trouble," he said as he headed for her room.

"Wait. Don't you go anywhere. Tell me what happened," I
said. I started after him, determined to get it all out in the open.

He banged on his sister's door. "I got news for you—if
anyone gets to live with Dad, it's going to be me."

His words stopped me cold in my tracks. Something must
have escaped from me, a whimper or yelp, because his ears
instantly turned scarlet.

"I didn't mean it. I said it to make her mad."

I didn't know if I could believe him.

Gavin's incarceration hit Jude the hardest in his eleventh
year. Apparently, he talked his friend Emir into sneaking into
CinemaTown with him to see *Lethal Weapon 3*. Emir's mother
gave me an earful when this fact slipped out of her son's mouth,
along with: "It was Jude Schirrick's idea." The police brought
him home at three AM after he was caught swimming in a
neighbor's pool. He used another boy's name to rent "Legend
of Zelda," a pricey Nintendo game, with no intentions of
ever returning it—a store surveillance camera had recorded
the entire transaction, and one of the clerks recognized him. I
began to think Jude aspired to be his father's cellmate.

Last spring he wanted me to buy him the newest athletic shoes that evidently every boy in America coveted, whether or not they played basketball. I scrutinized the shoe in MC Sporting Goods. Whatever the pump in the tongue did, it wasn't worth such a big bite of my weekly paycheck, but I'd failed to consider the status they would give a boy whose father is different from everyone else's, something I should have been able to relate to. I told him I'd pay for the right shoe, but he had to earn the left one. To my surprise, he was soon cutting grass and scooping dog poop from several neighbors' yards. He earned those coveted shoes. This also earned him the admiration of his friends, which, in turn, helped refocus his energy toward something positive: being an entrepreneur. I suppose his drive may be the one good thing he inherited from his father. Jude's next venture is to build a skateboarding ramp and give lessons to the neighborhood kids after he masters the skateboard himself.

Michelle alternately loves and hates her father, but the fact that he's in prison causes her to keep her girlfriends at a distance. She compulsively bites her fingernails until they're bleeding, and picks at her eyelashes and brows. For a while she made house rules that included: Don't sing along with the radio. Don't scrape your knife across the plate. Don't ask me if I'm wearing "that" to school. Don't clear your throat around me unless you're really sick. If you're sick, don't come near me. There were additional rules for Jude, such as Don't suck your teeth. Don't spit on the faucet when you brush your teeth. Don't imitate voices on the phone when my friends call. He tried to break them as often as possible.

Somehow I had believed that my daughter and I would have a more open relationship than I had with my mother. I don't know if you can relate to this, but my hopes vanished the day I opened the bottom cupboard in our bathroom and spotted a box of tampons. It hit me like a cold-water balloon: Michelle had started her period and didn't tell me. After the disappointment had sunk in, I had to ask myself, Really, what did I expect? A trumpeted proclamation? I hadn't told my mother either.

I often catch myself sounding like a watered-down version of Mom. Michelle and I enjoy shopping together, but when she models jeans or skirts in the dressing room for me, I ask her, "Isn't that too tight/short/revealing for comfort?" as if being comfortable is ever important to a teenager. I try to have a dialogue with her rather than grill her about her friends, or what they're up to. At fourteen, she's "going out" with Ian, a boy who wears a dog chain and lock around his neck, carries a sketchbook and crumbled Conté crayons in his pockets. I'm not naive about what going out involves in the nineties, or how some girls believe giving sexual favors to boys is a requirement, or that it will gain them popularity. Some things never change, though, and a girl who does these things is still labeled a slut. I impress on Michelle that her obligation is to no one but herself. "Wait for that special one. You'll know it when you find him," I tell her. I can't help but think of you.

Since my divorce I've dated only two men. Matt was a soft-spoken detective who responded when the window of my car had been smashed in for a lousy case of CDs. I was drawn to Matt's reassurances. He had a dimpled chin and golden-brown hair that looked like an aura around his head when he stood in my driveway late in the day, the sun at his back. He filled out his report with one shiny shoe propped assertively on the bumper of the squad car. His thighs and ass were well-rounded, like a baseball player's. We went to dinner twice, and to a Dwight Yoakam concert, but it became apparent that, of all the stressful things he'd dealt with, from chasing crack heads to investigating murders, children made him nervous. Late one evening at my house when he'd started to get overly affectionate with me, there was a loud crash from upstairs. He leaped off the couch and said, "God! They always like that?" I half expected him to draw his weapon.

I think Michelle and Jude were looking out for me.

I had a brief relationship with a clown I met at a party given by the parents of one of Michelle's softball teammates. I was dressed as Columbia from *The Rocky Horror Picture Show*. The red hair, sparkly top, striped shorts, and top hat didn't stray far from my old look. The partygoers, being incognito, were extremely salacious. On my first date with Frank, it was a novelty to see each other in street clothes, but the attraction wasn't the same. At least, it wasn't for me. Frank felt differently. We usually split the bill whenever we went to the movies or had dinner at the new Chinese restaurant, where waitresses in kimonos serve loud, sizzling rice dishes. On the few occasions that he tried to kiss me, I turned my head so his lips met my cheek. "Oh, I get it. Friends," he'd say, laughing. The last time I saw him, however, he held my chin so I couldn't reject his kiss. When he asked if he could come inside, I told him I didn't want to bring a parade of men through my children's lives. Huffy, he said, "You can't shelter them from everything. I want to be friends with your kids, too. I want to help you." When I told him I didn't need his help, he said, "You're not being honest. You're afraid to have a relationship."

I'm not sure, but one thing is true: I don't want anyone telling me what I am or am not afraid of. As much as I long to feel weight on the other side of the bed, to have someone to hurry home to or who hurries home for me, I keep focused on my job and raising sane children. There are rewards in being single, such as wearing flannels to bed, watching Leno with an egg mask on my face, and hearing my children crash around the house late at night. I'm content with fond memories of sex.

Unless, of course, the sex would involve you.

◄▲►

CHAPTER TWENTY-TWO

I'm sure it was an accident, not fate, or serendipity, as you would say. I was cursing to myself as I trotted down the hall in my heels toward Charnell's office for a 9 AM meeting. I checked my watch, but before how late I was could register in my brain, I tripped on something and landed on my hands and knees. The long-legged boy whose feet caught mine hopped from the bench to help me up while he mumbled an apology. A gum-chewing girl next to him covered her grin with her hand. It seemed he'd stretched his legs as I ran past, intentionally or not, throwing his feet in my path. From my vantage point on the floor, I noticed he was wearing Vans, flat skateboarding shoes with lots of rubber, the same brand Jude wore but much larger. Gaping holes in his jeans exposed his bony knees.

His apology accepted, I brushed myself off and stepped into Charnell's office just as our volunteer coordinator, Lucia, was walking out. She handles the steady flow of adolescents and young adults sentenced by the courts to perform community service for alcohol or drug offenses. Her head was turned as she told Charnell, "I need to escort these volunteers down to the Clothes Closet first," and then stopped herself short of walking into me. Unflappable, clipboard in hand, Lucia laughed and said hello.

I overheard her talk to the teens in the hall: "You must be my new appointees. Meghan Liberty? Mick Vadas? Come with me. I'll show you where you'll be working."

I leaned out of Charnell's doorway for another look at the boy. He was tucking his collar-length hair behind his ears when he noticed me. He winced, perhaps assuming I gaped at him because he was a slacker. Of course, that wasn't it. It was the Vadas name that compelled me to watch him walk down the hall. He glanced back in my direction. I looked away, feeling obvious and silly.

I don't have to tell you that Vadas is a common name in Ohio. I only know because I've looked it up in different directories over the years. In the Nopiming area, the name fills a page and a half of residential listings, but there is no Jozsef, Joe, or J. So I don't know what I thought I'd find there other than the reassurance that, with scores of people having the same last name, this young man was not related to you. Besides, he was likely too old to be your son. The phone book thudded, like the closing of a chapter, when I tossed it into my bottom desk drawer. Forget it, I told myself.

I kept seeing Mick's face morph into yours, wearing a different set of clothes from another era. I saw you standing in your kitchen, raising a glass with your brother, your family all around you. The name Mick kept prodding me to think harder, but I came up blank.

After a week of disrupted sleep, I walked down to the Clothes Closet, located in a storefront on the same block as the business offices. If Mick Vadas was given twenty hours of service, I figured it would take him three Saturdays to complete his sentence. Battered by a brisk wind, I pulled my sweater coat around me.

The floor manager directed me to the back storeroom where he was sorting clothing. Safe Harbor receives generous donations of children's and adults' clothes, sometimes more than we can handle, but we don't accept anything that's stained, torn, or covered with animal hair.

His back was to me as he picked through stacks of boxes and bagged clothes. Two rollaway racks with empty hangers were to his left, and a rumpled pile of discarded clothing was on the right. When I said his name, he quickly turned, his sharp eyes wary, as if he'd been caught. I told him my name and then mentioned that I'd seen him in the main office last Saturday. "I hope you don't mind if I ask, are you related to Joe Vadas?"

He brushed his hands on the thighs of loose jeans that hung at his hips, this pair having intact knees, before he said, "He's my uncle."

His unexpected answer sucked the air from my lungs. I grabbed a chair, afraid I might pass out. My strong physical reaction baffled me. My mind was flooded with questions, but I didn't want your nephew to think I was obsessed or crazy. He called me ma'am when he asked if I was okay. I felt so uncool with my head at my knees.

"Blood sugar. I need to eat something, that's all," I managed to say when I sat up.

"Oh." He hid his yawn with the back of his hand. The room was stuffy, with little ventilation.

I concentrated on breathing normally, trying to sound offhand. "They're not working you too hard, are they?"

He shrugged. "No. I can't complain. I could have been sent to clean up the city dump." He grabbed the neck of a large black bag and dragged it along the dusty floor toward a rack. Sweat dotted his upper lip. "It's a pain to find sizes on everything. Do the people who donate this crap really think someone will wear it? A lot of it stinks. I mean, it smells nasty."

"You'd be surprised what some people think. Don't worry about sizes. Just weed out the worst and get the rest onto hangers. Lucia is glad to have you here."

Chatting him up felt artificial. I cleared my throat, wanting to get to the point. "So, do you see much of your uncle Joe?"

He told me he was working with you. The fact that you were here felt like another blow, this one hitting me square in the chest. I swallowed hard. Before I could say anything, he said he planned to start classes at the Art Institute for the winter semester. His hair fell into his eyes as he knelt on the tile floor over an open bag. I was saddened to hear him say that his father—one of your brothers—died two years ago. Mick became a real person then, not a subject or interviewee, and I felt out of line. When I told him I was sorry, he simply said, "Yeah. Well. Thanks." He pulled out a black sweater with shoulder pads and sequined flowers in fuchsia and hot pink, held it up by the shoulders, and squinted. "What do you think?"

"Someone will like it."

With a doubting smirk he pulled the sweater onto a hanger, where it drooped unhappily. "How do you know my uncle?"

"Knew. We were in high school together. Class of '75."

"Hey, I was born in '74." He smoothed the front of a silky blouse with his hand in a tender gesture that reminded me of you. An image of you affectionately touching a young child came to mind. Suddenly, it clicked. He was the "monster" baby in the arms of your sister-in-law, in your mother's kitchen on her birthday.

"Oh! Your father was...Laz, right? And your mom's name is...is..." As if someone waved a snapshot in my face, I could see her but couldn't recall her name.

"Doreen."

"That's it. And she was holding you." I remembered your mother, the decorative plates on the wall, the deliciously rummy *dobos torta* drummer's cake, drinking Schlitz beer, your father, oh God, your father.

"She was what?" Mick squinted, evidently puzzled, as he cracked his knuckles in loud pops.

"Holding you. I was at your grandmother's house. You were just a baby when I met your mom and dad, your uncles, cousins. What a coincidence." I started to laugh, light-headed, nearly giddy with joy. My emotions were disturbingly out of control.

With a quick nod of acknowledgment, he said, "Oh."

I watched him return to pulling tangled shirts out of the bag, lips pursed in annoyance. He wasn't interested in reminiscing. Who would be, except for me? I didn't know what to do. As much as I wanted to, I couldn't sit there gabbing with your nephew all day.

As I said good-bye, I added, without much forethought, "Tell your uncle Joe that Angelica says hello."

Mick said he would as he held up a sweater. The furry collar was the same ripe orange as your rabbit's paw key chain, smooth and soft. When I had pressed it between my fingers, I could feel the tiny bones, toe pads, and claws. An amputated foot, swinging from your key ring, clawing through the air trying to get back home.

◂▴▸

Chapter Twenty-three

Most days Jude bounds out of the school building with a flushed face and damp hair, bringing a wild-grass, salty-ocean smell into the car with a *whoosh* and a *slam*. Gym, his last class of the day, invigorates him. Although a new addition cheers the straight-faced, two-story building of the same middle school I used to walk to as a girl, seeing it puts me in another era. I remember select moments of my adolescence there, like the after-school dances where the girls wore pleated skirts and jumpers, and danced with each other because the boys were shy.

Michelle moves as if burdened when I pick her up from high school, scowling as she sloughs off her heavy backpack before she slides in. The pine-antiseptic smell in the halls and the clamor of the cafeteria come to mind. I remember you carrying your lunch tray as you passed behind me. I think of all the hidden corners and private places you and I found. The images are colorless and flat, like a scratchy newsreel, the film as thin as cellophane. It's like watching the movie of someone else's past. I hear your voice in my head but wonder if I've scrambled the words or dubbed over them so I hear what I want to, not what was really said. Did you love me?

For so many years you were a memory circling my bed at night. I talked to you as if you were there with me, nodding in approval, understanding, never judging. You were a benevolent bird, a wise owl perched on one shoulder as if my brain insisted you stay in my life, even though I cursed you for leaving without a good-bye.

Nopiming rezoned the area where your house had been and built a shopping plaza. The razing of that side of town had neatly ended my compulsion to drive past your house in hopes that I'd see your Bel Air parked out front. The first time I'd ventured into the shiny new store, I stood in the spot closest to where I guessed your bedroom had been. I saw us playing cards, and rolling around in your wrinkled, dirty sheets. Then I opened my eyes to be accosted by glinting, stainless steel cookware, toaster ovens, fondue pots, slow cookers, waffle irons, and rows of fluorescent lights. I feared it would fall in on me, that I'd be buried under a mountain of clattering houseware.

Our old haunts have been excised like plantar warts, leaving nothing but rubble under the graffiti-strewn bridges. Manners' drive-in restaurant is gone. The Flats were cleaned up for suburbanites, and the new hot spots have valet parking and bouncers dressed in suits. Men with chain wallets and motorcycle jackets don't go there. No more Mickey's with pinball machines, no folkies, no working-man blues.

It's no surprise that I felt out of sorts when I returned to my desk after my lunch break to find a misspelled message scrawled on a while-you-were-out pad: *Joe Waddis called. Said old friend. Please call back earliest convenience,* followed by a phone number. I had assumed Mick would forget about my message. I stared at the seven symbols that would connect me with you. It was no imaginary bird or owl—you had called and had given these numbers to Lucille at the main desk, and now they were in my hand, burning brightly. Alive. Here. You.

I tried to convince myself it would go like this: We'd meet for coffee at the Java House, chat stiffly, and I'd go home with stomach cramps and a headache. There would be no sparks, no desire to reheat the leftovers from the Styrofoam carton left by the side of the road. You would think I'm portly, my hair too short, my demeanor hardened—certainly not the good-natured girl you remembered. You'd be different, too.

Half the man I'd built you up to be. And I could be just as cold
to you as you were to me when you left.

In my dreams, something else took place. We were joyriding
in your Bel Air again. We were mashing lips in the basement
of the rec center during the Battle of the Bands. We were in
the backseat of your car, your tongue in my mouth and your
hand between my legs while I squirmed in your lap. We were
delirious, naked and sweaty in your bed. My body felt it all as
if it had happened yesterday.

I awakened breathless, aching, and wet. I wasn't sure if my
heart could take the strain.

That's why it took me nine days of emotional hand-wringing
before I finally returned your call. I suppose it's human nature
to want closure, to pick the old scab open, just to see if it
bleeds.

The greeting threw me more than the polished female voice
that answered the phone in such practiced cheerfulness:
"Hello. JV Custom Concrete Floors. This is Nicole. How may
I help you?"

Concrete? I pictured you alongside a mixer, wearing a hard
hat and overalls, waving a tanned arm to the driver. Nicole
had to repeat herself, "Hello? Hello?" before I answered her.
I stuttered. She informed me you'd left for the day and did I
want to leave a message? Of course I did, but what? I took my
time, aware that she was getting irritated. She could wait. I'd
certainly waited long enough. I figured I'd put the ball back in
your court and left my home number, but no message.

A ribbon of dust floated in a stab of sunlight from my office
window as I sat and thought. Then I grabbed the Yellow Pages
and thumbed through cleaners, clinics, clocks, and computers
until I found a half-page ad for JV Custom Concrete Floors.
*Highly Experienced Designer Specializing in Everything You
Need for Beautiful Concrete Interior Flooring. Options available
include polished concrete, acid stains, stamps, dyes, stenciling, and*

hybrid polymer overlays. We also specialize in the beautification and restoration of existing concrete surfaces. Commercial and Residential Applications. Call to see what we can do for you!

Michelle could be an Olympic hopeful if telephone lunging were a sport. As we finished dinner—chicken stir-fry with whole-wheat noodles—she bolted from her chair to answer the ring, then stretched across the table to hand me the phone with a murderous look on her face, as if it were my fault the caller wasn't her soul mate, or her father, who has called from prison on rare occasions. When I asked who it was, she sighed dramatically. "Joe Vegas." Funny, isn't it? It's not like your name is hard to get right.

I swallowed, took the phone, and tried to sound relaxed. Did I? You sounded delighted when I said, "Yes, it really is me." I was thankful you did most of the talking, telling me how you'd offered to keep your nephew, Mick, busy until he decided what he wanted to do with his life, but it hadn't been going as well as you'd hoped. Obviously. "But what are the odds that he would end up volunteering where you work? And that you'd run into him?" you asked.

Your voice was like a hallucination as it slipped into my ear, sounding just as it had when we were teenagers, but it was hard for me to concentrate with the kids bantering as they cleaned up the table. When you asked about my marital status, I didn't want to elaborate in front of Jude and Michelle, but your "Oh, really? I'm sorry" sounded hopeful when I said I was divorced. I didn't want to ask if you were married, or if you had children, or what the hell you'd been doing and why you were here, now. I told myself I didn't care. I wasn't supposed to care. I should be indifferent. You didn't care when you left me.

My heart was overriding my mind, though. You wouldn't have called me if you didn't care.

Jude shook a package of Oreos two inches from my nose, asking for my approval. I held up three fingers and watched him take a stack of six from the bag. Michelle interrupted to ask if I picked up her fuchsia sweater from Speedy Dry Cleaning. I had forgotten, and later I would be accused of sabotaging her school picture. Then the doorbell rang. Most likely it was Em, who was coming over to deliberate hairstyles and makeup for picture day with Michelle. I hoped Em would help her pick out an alternative outfit, too.

You said, "I'm glad to know you're doing well." I nearly dropped the phone, wondering how you could say such a thing. Were you glad? What did *glad* even mean, after all this time? Glad? That was all? Indignant, I struggled to keep my voice even. It was good you weren't able to see my scowl. The best I could manage was, "Gee. How nice." Someone behind me coughed, and I turned to see Dad in the kitchen doorway. He'd stopped by to look at Jude's remote-control car, which was swerving when it shouldn't. I nodded hello, wondering how much he'd overheard. Looking nonplussed, he said hello as Jude pulled him through the kitchen to the garage.

You cleared your throat and said, "I'm sorry if I said something wrong." More throat clearing—were you nervous? "Listen, I'd love to see you. Can I buy you dinner? Remember I once told you I'd save my money and buy you dinner at the Spanish Tavern one day?"

I didn't remember. I squeezed my eyes shut, knowing I was going to give in. I had no good reason to end the conversation on a sour note. I didn't like feeling so horribly conflicted. Old friends getting together to reminisce—that's all it would be. I wanted to get it over with and put it behind me. I figured we would rehash things, say our piece, clear the air, air our dirty laundry, and then, washed up, we'd wonder what we ever saw in each other.

The moment I hung up the phone, Michelle clicked on the TV in the living room to a *Saved by the Bell* rerun. Obviously, she was eavesdropping. I asked her if her schoolwork was done. As if drained of life's essence by the demands imposed on her, she lifted the remote with a limp hand and flicked off the TV but stayed put, stubbornly staring at the blank screen.

Jude and Dad came back from the garage. "I can take it to the hobby shop tomorrow morning," Dad told him, holding the controller in his hand. He studied me for a moment. I must have looked anxious, upset, or confused. I felt all of the above. "Who were you talking to on the phone?"

"No one. How's the shoulder?" I asked, trying to get a grip on myself. He'd aggravated his bursitis by playing a late-season game of golf.

"No one named Joe Vegas," Michelle sang loud and clear.

"Joe Vadas?" Dad said too quickly. When I told him yes, his eyes zinged back and forth under pressed brows. "What's he want?"

I considered ignoring his impertinent question, but I couldn't help myself. "I thought I'd have the basement tile ripped up and the floor redone. He installs concrete floors, you know."

To my surprise, he said, "I know what he does."

"She's meeting him for dinner," Michelle said, delighted to stir up trouble.

"You are?" Dad asked me.

"How do you know what he does, anyway?"

"From a TV commercial."

"And Joe is in it?"

"Yes," he said as if I ought to know. I was disappointed. I felt trumped. I never once saw a JV Custom Concrete Floors commercial. I guess I didn't watch enough television. "Well. Is it all right with you if I have dinner with him? You seem a little put out or something."

"Me? Not at all. Do whatever you want. I'm just surprised, I mean, after all this time." He coughed into his fist. "I'll be on my way, I guess." He walked to the front door and, in his haste to escape, nearly hit himself in the face with it when he pulled it open. After a bit of fumbling, he stepped out and shut the door. Two beats later he opened it to fetch the car remote from the hall table. He seemed as rattled as I did. "Almost forgot this. See you later, Jude. Bye."

"You and Poppy are freaking weird," Michelle said after he was gone. "What's the big deal with this guy?"

"It's a long story. And you—" I started to reprimand her for being a smart aleck, but she interrupted me.

"He installs floors? I bet he's one of those guys whose butt crack shows when he bends over. Gross." She snickered.

Jude thought this was hysterical.

I felt a peculiar tightening in my stomach, believing the reason Dad had asked to meet me for coffee in the middle of a workday had something to do with you, and I suspected it wasn't going to be good. Why else would he have wanted to talk to me somewhere other than my house, away from young, impressionable ears? He was already inside The Java Hut, sitting at a little round table along the wall, reading the paper, his fingers tapping the handle of a coffee mug. I got myself a large black hazelnut and joined him.

"So, you're really going to have dinner with Joe Vadas?" He was never one for wasting time.

I told him I was and asked why he wanted to know.

He said, "Then there's something I should probably tell you." I tried to read his expression, but couldn't pick up anything other than a nervous lick of his lower lip. Was he going to give me a warning, tell me the Better Business Bureau listed complaints about you for shoddy work?

His voice was surprisingly uncertain. "Remember that incident in school, when you were suspended? Well, I was… your mother was…we were pretty upset, so I decided to have a chat with Joe's father. You know, make a few things clear. So that's what I did." He brushed the side of his nose. "I, um, told him to keep his son away from you."

"What?" Skeptical, I sat back and studied him, but nothing

told me he was kidding. It was hard to picture him going to your parents' house, knocking on the door, stepping into that strange land, and having a chat with a madman. The coffee shop buzzed with a peculiar energy that agitated me. Two men bustled in and barked their orders at the barista. "Where? At his house?"

"No. I tracked him down at Rendell's Tavern."

"Tracked him down" created an image of Dad as an investigator, sleuthing through the neighborhood bars in Cuyahoga County.

"It was kind of odd. He didn't believe me when I told him both of you were suspended. Then I thought he was going to slug me. Two of his sons were with him. I mean, that's who I assumed they were, and they looked ready to scrap."

I could not fathom the gawky, mule-faced Dr. Lowsley marching into some bar to face off with a man who had a reputation as a pugilist. Not only that, your father had been flanked by two of his Big-Time Wrestler boys, liquored up and keen to fight. What was it Mom had called them? Hungarian thugs? What could have made mild-mannered Dad do such a thing? Then I remembered the sick look on his face in Greers' office when he realized that his daughter, the one he'd sworn to protect and love when he'd adopted her, had been deflowered by the very boy Mom swore would do it.

Evidently, he had to redeem himself by shaming your father. Shaken, I took a sip of coffee, but my nerves made me overshoot, and Columbian blend splashed down my chin.

"Whoops." Dad handed me a napkin from the dispenser.

"Crap." I blotted my chin and blouse. I hoped I wouldn't do something stupid like this when I had dinner with you. "What exactly did you tell his father?"

"That he better keep his bastard son away from you, or I'd castrate him."

"Dad! You didn't! What did Mr. Vadas say?"

"Something I won't repeat."

I can't tell you how shocked I was. I was certain your father would have spit bricks after having his nose rubbed in the dirt by someone he likely called "a self-entitled American with the devil's cock up his ass." He couldn't have been pleased with his youngest son when he learned you'd been suspended either for messing around with a *dilis* girl.

I asked if he knew what had happened to you.

Dad fiddled with his spoon. "Well, that's what I wanted to tell you. His father came by my office a couple days later and told me I didn't have to worry about you anymore."

Alarm ran through me like ice water. "Why? Why did he say that?"

"He said Joe was out of the picture. That's all I know."

Something pushed its way up my throat as I was spun back through years of angst over being in the dark, feeling deserted. I was obviously mistaken. I felt sick. What did "out of the picture" mean? Your father yanked you out of school and sent you away? I couldn't imagine.

Evidently, I looked as distraught as I felt because Dad's face looked stitched with regret. "I'm sorry, cupcake. I thought it was for the best. You were so determined." He reached across the table for my hand. "Sometimes parents do things that aren't always right."

What could I say? I couldn't be angry with him, not anymore. It had been difficult for him to tell me this. Poor Dad. He'd only wanted to appease Mom, and protect me. We'd been through so much as a family, and here he was, setting the record straight. I turned my hand so my palm met his and squeezed his warm, cushiony hand. "It's okay. Thank you for telling me. And thank you for being my dad. I love you."

◂▴▸

CHAPTER TWENTY-FOUR

Walking into the dimly lit, castle-like Spanish Tavern, with its beamed ceilings, stucco walls, and bloodred carpet, was like stepping into the past. The gas fireplace still licked flames. The armored knight stood guard in the lobby in need of a dusting and polish. Silver swords and crests hung with implied menace on the walls. I imagine the place looks horrifically ugly in daylight. When the hostess led me to the table, you smiled, promptly stood, and pulled my chair out for me. I tried to breathe normally. It was really you, after so long. I was a little disappointed that you didn't hug or kiss me, but maybe my testiness on the phone had something to do with your formality?

I tried not to stare outright as I sat across the table from you. For someone I never expected to see again, you looked amazingly real. Your hair was clipped, and I wondered if the soul patch below your bottom lip was all that remained of your rebellious streak. When you smiled, crow's feet fanned out from the corners of your eyes. Your red-and-silver tie, in a perfect Windsor knot, complemented your stone-gray shirt and sports coat. It occurred to me you were wearing grown-up clothes, refined and handsome.

You seemed to study me with equal interest. Were you thinking the same thing? What did you think when you saw my short hair? I'd chosen my outfit carefully, aiming for sexy yet sophisticated, in a knit dress and knee-high boots. Earlier, when dressing, I had trouble holding my hand steady to apply lipstick—it fell from my fingers and smashed softly onto the bathroom tile. I hoped it wasn't an omen.

So often it seems, in relationships, one person loves more than the other. Up to this point I had always assumed I loved you more than you had ever loved me. Vanished or banished, it still bothered me that you never once called or wrote me. You never bothered to let me know you were all right. Soon I would have the opportunity to look you in the eye and ask why.

The waiter had come by for our orders before we had a chance to say much. It was interesting how our eyes locked when I asked for club soda with lemon and you ordered a Perrier. When we dated so long ago, we both sucked down anything alcoholic. "So, here's to Mick," you said when we had our waters, and we toasted him.

Before I could ask even one of a dozen questions I'd saved up for so long, you asked me what my job entailed. Nervousness made me talkative, as if I had to fill the air between us with something substantial enough to keep you at a distance. I didn't want to be swept away like a schoolgirl again. I had to guard my heart. You smiled when I told you I'm the marketing and community service director at Safe Harbor. After I described my newest funding project for the new women's shelter, Adopt-a-Room—I love that name, and the concept of financing the furnishings—you did everything but stand on the table and applaud. I had to laugh.

"I'm in awe. I always knew you'd be doing something altruistic," you said. At first I was embarrassed, but I got over that. I'm proud to be supporting myself and my children, pleased that I can afford to pay for braces on Jude's wild-pony teeth, that I own a house with central air, and stopped the wasps from coming in through the upstairs windows on my own.

Our small talk was interrupted when our dinners arrived. My nervousness began to settle. My palms stopped sweating. Was it familiarity? Feeling a bit reckless, I dumped both tubs of sour cream and butter on my baked potato.

I tried to figure out your agenda. Was it curiosity, or something more, that made you want to see me? I had so many questions, yet I was afraid to ask. That's why I stuck to safe subjects, such as how you ended up in concrete. You said you apprenticed with your uncle. "I learned how to stamp and engrave concrete, and then I discovered concrete staining. Interior work is more practical since you can work year round." As you explained more about the artistry end of the business, I realized that's what happens when you cross a creative person with a concrete contractor. It pleased me.

I didn't know how much to tell you when you asked why I divorced. Should I have said one of my demons is Gavin? I didn't want to admit he was in prison, or soon to be released. All I managed was "We haven't seen him in a few years. He's got some ongoing health and legal issues. I don't want to bore you with the details, but he was a good father. I think he can still be a good father if he can work things out. I'm hopeful."

"That's good. You're still an optimist," you said with a genuine smile that made me feel like a pessimist.

I'm not so sure. "Some days I get tired of looking for the silver lining when I might have better luck looking for aluminum cans along the roadside."

You said, "We all do. You're the same girl I remember." That surprised me, but I didn't argue. Your smile faded as you pushed a piece of your filet into your sauce au poivre and then apologized for getting me suspended from school.

Was that why you wanted to see me? To right your wrongs?

"Getting caught wasn't all your fault. I was just as guilty, remember?" I said, but what you don't know was how horrible the gossip and the sidelong looks were. I was ostracized while I planted worry sticks over you in the hard Ohio clay, and you still didn't know the worst of it. We didn't get to that until later.

The waiter, with his probing grin and shiny face, came

to our table to ask how our meal was, for the second time. When he left, looking dejected by my snappy "Yes, we're fine," I asked you what happened, saying, "I heard your father sent you away."

You shrugged, looking noncommittal, which made me wonder. "Well, my old man found out I was suspended and went ballistic. He told me I had two choices, either the navy or the air force. Did you know he died five years ago? The cops rear-ended him at Fifth and Prospect, chasing some asshole who robbed a Quik Pik, if you can believe it. They had to pry him from his car with the Jaws of Life."

Your voice sounded flat when you told me the details, as if you were giving instructions on grouting tile. I felt a chill when I remembered you once said you understood how Jim Morrison could hate his father so much he'd write a song about wanting to kill him. The more you talked about your father, the more nauseous and unsettled I felt. It sounded as if you took the brunt of your father's rage on a regular basis, being the last child to leave home. I had no idea it had been so bad.

"When I got the car, at least I could leave the house at night before he came home from the bars. I'd sleep in it and go to school in the morning. It was better than letting him wake me up just so he could have someone to pummel," you said, and the bitterness I'd desperately clung to all these years shifted to sadness. To everyone else in school, you looked like a heavy-lidded stoner who stayed up all night listening to rock albums, drinking, smoking cigarettes, and scribbling in a notebook. No wonder you nodded off in the mornings. Who can learn under that kind of stress?

The busboy came by to ask if we were finished; I thought it was obvious. When the waiter came by with a tray of perfectly sculpted desserts, I was thankful you asked for the bill.

I was also thankful when you asked, "Can we go somewhere to talk? Your place, my place, a coffee shop, bookstore cubby—it doesn't matter." More talk sounded good to me.

As we left, you placed your hand on the small of my back. You were always full of gentle gestures: holding my hand, touching my hair, buttoning the top button of my coat, protectively pulling my stocking cap down over my face before plopping me into a snowdrift. The sky was a deep indigo, and the cold, crisp air smelled like burning leaves. Snow was in the forecast. How easy it would be to fall back in love with you. How the heart remembers.

As I followed your pickup truck from the restaurant to your house, my emotions were pushing me in all directions. I was a teenage girl with a crush, a cornered mouse, a sucker. I didn't want to fall in love with you again. I still loved you. I didn't want to end up in bed with you. I was ready to jump in bed with you. I was terrified of being hurt. I didn't trust you. I broke out in a sweat and had to wiggle out of my jacket while driving. At every stop sign, I was tempted to turn around and head in the other direction.

Then I was standing in the kitchen of a two-story Craftsman in the little town of Berea.

"Decaf or regular?" you asked, such a good host. Decaf. It was late. I sat at the wooden table and looked around, curious about what you'd have in a house of your own. It was comfortable and cozy. I liked the rustic, chipped-paint look, the wicker seat chairs, the rooster-themed artwork.

"I've done a lot to this house. Paint, carpet, new doors and windows, roof, paneling in the basement. You know."

Having fixed up my own home, I understood the work involved in making something your own. I nodded, watching with a strange fascination as you whisked off your tie and theatrically flung it behind you, then unbuttoned the top button of your shirt and pulled the tails from your waistband. You abruptly left the room and returned with a framed photograph of two girls. Beautiful girls, looking up at the camera, smiling, standing close together, one in front of the other. Two round faces with pointed chins. They were identical imps with brown eyes and golden-brown locks, the sun in their hair and faces, and bright green grass behind them. I looked at you, curious.

"My girls. They're twins, ten years old in this picture. Miranda and Nanette. Can't believe they're sixteen now." You set the picture on the counter, as if they should be witnesses, and poured two coffees. Resentment pranced in my gut. You were married? You had children? Why hadn't you told me? Some protective instinct, that fight-or-flight thing, got me up on my feet. I admit I didn't want to know anything more. I was done chatting with you. I was on my way out the door.

Of course you tried to stop me. When I turned, you must have seen the fire in my eyes and stepped back. Well, then again, I told you not to touch me in a way that left no doubt. It was true that you hadn't led me to your home with pretenses other than "talk," but you could have told me up front about a wife and children. I had to wonder what else you might be hiding. After hearing and telling lies my whole life, I wanted honesty.

You apologized, saying, "I don't know how to do this. I'm a mess. I've been a mess since I came back to the States," words that made me pause. You asked me to sit down, "Please," and held your arm out to the chair.

Before I was willing to stay, I wanted to know more about the so-called mess you were in. I hope it didn't sound mocking when I asked you to enlighten me. I kept myself from shaking by standing against the wall, near the door, my purse held tight against my side.

You looked troubled, not at all like the confident man I'd had dinner with. "Angelica, when you and I first met, I was angry all the time. I hated my life. I got you into trouble, and then I hated who I was. That night, after my old man found out I was suspended, he lit into me like never before, ranting and throwing his fists, telling me how stupid I was. I'd had enough of his bullying and so I laid him out. I knew he'd kill me if he got up, so I ran."

My mouth went dry as I listened intently. "There was no way I was joining the service. Terrified of my old man, I went to Laz. He said if I left him my car, he'd front me the money for a plane ticket to Hungary. We have a lot of family there: aunts and uncles, and cousins on my mother's side especially. I didn't know what else to do. I didn't want to leave you, but I knew your parents loved you. Maybe they were upset and angry, but they were good parents, so I figured you'd be okay. I figured I'd just mess up your life if I stuck around. I had to get away from my old man or I knew I'd drown. I'd either kill him or myself."

You seemed relieved when I finally sat back down at the table. I couldn't believe what I was hearing. You didn't enlist?

You said, "Hell, no. Laz swore not to tell anyone where I went, and he kept his word. I hoped my parents assumed I'd joined up. Anyway, my uncle Miklos welcomed me. I traveled around with my cousin Sebastian for a while. Spain, Germany, Austria, Italy, Greece. At some point, though, I had to figure out what to do with my life, and so I started working in the concrete business with Uncle Miklos. My aunt knew I had a broken heart because I talked to her a little about you. She kept fixing me up with girls. That's how I met Helena, my wife. Ex-wife."

I loosened the grip on my purse and took a breath. You were divorced, but the reason surprised me.

"It didn't work out. I drank a lot. Cursed a lot. Worked long hours. I was turning into my old man. Obviously I wasn't happy. My wife and I divorced when I came back to the States in '88 after my old man was in the accident."

"Oh, but your girls?" My heart ached for them, wondering how you could have left them.

"That's the worst part. I hate being so far away, but they've been here twice, and I've been back to see them. I hope to bring them to the States this Christmas. It's a long shot, but maybe I can convince them to get their higher education here. That's a long way off, though." You shook your head as if you were disappointed in yourself. "I go to bed each night and get up every morning knowing I've made a horrible mistake, and there isn't anything I can do to fix it."

I tried to digest all this, not knowing what to say. You had been on another continent, living another life. I stared at you as you stared at your hands, and I let my anger go but felt oddly miserable inside. Maybe I was sensing your misery.

You broke my trance when you said there was more to tell. I couldn't imagine what more you'd say unless it concerned me. I suppose that's what I was waiting for. Your eyes never left mine when you told me the first snowfall of every year still reminds you of me. "The way it smells, how it sparkles, how it brightens and hushes everything. It always takes me back to our first date, that blizzard, how we walked out of the theater into all that swirling whiteness, and our first kiss in my car. It was magical. I've never felt anything like that with anyone else. I thought I could forget you as if it had been just a high school thing, but you were always in the back of my mind, everywhere I went. I can't tell you how many times I'd see some girl and think it was you, as if you'd ever be in Hungary. When I came back to the States, the extent of the loss hit me hard. It was devastating. It was like I'd never grieved over losing you until then. Maybe it took me that long to see how deeply I loved you."

I hung tightly on to every word you said as if it were a string, the one I needed to reel me back in.

"I am so sorry, Angelica. I'm sorry I hurt you. I'm sorry I left you the way I did. I'm sorry I never called. I'm sorry I never wrote. There's no excuse. I know that now. I hope you can forgive me. I'll beg on my knees for your forgiveness if you want me to. If I can have that much, I know I'll be okay."

Of course I forgive you.

Then I knew I would tell you everything that happened to me after you'd left—the whole, horrible truth about my birth father and my wretched marriage. I tried so hard to keep my voice from trembling when I said I wanted to tell you something I'd never told anyone else. A look of concern crossed your face as if I had an injury you couldn't see, but you listened with a passive attentiveness that allowed me to talk honestly. You didn't grimace. Your jaw didn't drop. You didn't withdraw. You stayed right there with me. That meant the world to me.

I feared it would be too thorny to revisit the pain of learning about my mother's lie, and her assault, but talking was transforming. Accepting who my birth father is has taught me about the person I want to be. My life is good, not in spite of him, but because it is my life. This is how I defy the violence in which I was conceived. This is the bridge that has allowed me to move past the kind of man he was, and to accept myself for who I am.

It pleased me when you said mine was an amazing story of resilience and strength, and that you were proud of me. "I live with the pain of never having my say with my old man," you said, something I'd never considered. Life has not been easy for either of us. There is an ugly truth that connects us. It gives an extra beat to our hearts—my birth father was a horrible stranger; yours was an unspeakable horror.

Sitting on my feet, having slipped off my boots, I'd rubbed most of the makeup from my face. I felt drained by confession. You seemed energized. When you rolled up your sleeve and I saw my name on the inside of your arm, I felt the same high as when you first showed it to me so many years ago. You never once thought about having it removed? All this time you've been walking around with ANGEL etched on your arm? Your bare skin was warm when I ran my fingertips across the faded letters. Touching your flesh, I felt an ache deep inside, where I hadn't felt anything for a long, long time. Sitting close to you, I noticed the smell of sweat mingling with soap. I breathed deeply, liking it.

"My wife wanted me to have it lasered off, or at least tattooed over, but I couldn't erase you. You're part of my life. If I couldn't have you, at least I have this memory of our love." You seemed suddenly unsure when you asked, "You did love me, didn't you?"

Your question surprised me. Didn't you know? Of course I did.

You swept me away when you recited the poem you'd penned for me years ago. "'You are a dream, a window just opened, a butterfly that lights my life—You write love all over my heart. I have no voice if I cannot hear you. I have no hands if I cannot touch you.'"

I blinked away my tears. You seemed ridiculously happy when I told you I still have the heart charm you gave me, and the notebook of your poems. I pulled the charm out from under my sweater to show you. I love that you've matured into the kind of man who isn't embarrassed to cry.

"There has to be a reason why we kept these things, don't you think?" you asked. So wise.

You actually asked if you could kiss me, which had to be the most tender and respectful gesture ever. Surges of joy and despair washed over me when you did, though your kiss seemed hesitant, gentle, like smooching a child good night. You kissed me again like you meant it, and it was just as I remembered, plush and electric, and it made me curious about the other parts of your body I remember so fondly. It seemed as if a heady rush overcame you, too, as you sat back and took a deep breath. You didn't let go of my hand, though. Your thumb rubbing across the top of mine felt so erotic that my entire body went fluid, in case you couldn't tell.

Despite our mutual yearnings, or should I just say lustings,

I worried we were trying to relive the past. We might fail. Things have changed. I said, "We're completely different people from the ones who were in love so long ago. Aren't we?"

You said, "Maybe. But I believe we belong together. We always did, and it will be this way no matter where our lives take us."

I'm not sure I can believe that. Forever sounds too lofty, too out-there, for a pragmatic like myself. That's why I said, "Maybe you need to convince me."

When you led me to your bed, I realized you're still the same reckless romantic who could convince me of anything. I'm not a cynic. Oh, I still enjoy life. In many ways I guess it's true: I am the same Angelica, at least inside. Thank you for showing me that. And thank you, too, for undressing me in the dark and kissing my body along the way. You seemed to enjoy every bit of clothing as it came off. I enjoyed doing the same, letting you explore my nakedness as I undressed you.

Gone was the adolescent awkwardness when we were trying things we'd only heard about or experimenting with uncomfortable-looking positions we'd seen on a black-light poster in a head shop on Coventry Avenue in Shaker Heights. This time we reveled in every pleasure-giving move we'd honed to perfection with other lovers, moves we would have been embarrassed to think about when we were teens. I bared my throat to your tender bite, felt your skin burn like a brushfire against mine. I surrendered my heart. You gave me yours. I forgave you everything. I forgave myself.

Despite your thickened waist, your coarse hands, and the curled hair on your chest and belly that buffed my bareness, you will always be eighteen to me. And despite the fact that when I lay on my back, my breasts slope from my chest to the sides and my soft belly is marred with silvery streaks from two babies, I felt like your girl again. That's how I would want you to remember me.

I don't know what the future holds, but I wish I could have

straightjacketed the arms on your clock that night to keep them from stealing more time from us than it already had. I wanted to linger in the silence between our words and soak in the warmth of your body while I lay in your bed, breathing the scent of cedar, bergamot, and musk from your skin and sheets as if it were incense.

Dawn taunted us, the early light edging in through the part in your curtains, reminding me I'd better hurry home before Jude and Michelle awakened. They usually sleep late on Saturdays, but I would have bet money this would be the one morning they'd awaken early, and wonder where their mother was.

◄▲►

CHAPTER TWENTY-FIVE

Their sleepy faces were still pressed into their pillows at noon when I opened my front door and stood on the stoop in my jeans and sweatshirt. I felt transformed. Flakes as big as cotton balls were falling from the sky. It looked like January in early November. You and I once built a snowman and snowwoman doing it in the park. I had the urge to dig out a pair of boots, mittens, and a hat from the closet and start sculpting.

We carry our loves with us all our lives. Stamped in our psyche, they become part of us. Maybe it's true: our chance to make it together was stolen from us. If I could return to the days before I lost you and alter what happened so we'd never have parted, I'm not sure I would. Who knows if my life would have been any easier, or better? I could do without Gavin in my story, but I couldn't give up Michelle and Jude.

Last night you said you want to build a six-bedroom, four-bathroom Tudor, big enough for me, Jude and Michelle, and your girls too when they come to stay with us on holidays. And we'd have our own child, the one you said you had always wanted. Why not throw in your mother and Mick, too? I laughed when you told me there's wooded acreage for sale in Brecksville, and as if to tempt me, our house would have the best of everything, because you know contractors you can trade with. You always were practical for a dreamer. It must be the cement man in you, the Schlitz beer, the *dobos torta*, the Mr. Mojo Risin' in you.

The best of everything would be nice, but what I have isn't

so awful. So what if my plates are chipped and I don't have Mikasa crystal or Lenox china? I don't have a dining-room set either. My end tables have water rings, chew marks from toddler's teeth, and dings from Tonka trucks. Dust collects on the same laminate bedroom set Gavin and I bought for our third anniversary. My comforter is not goose down; it's duck feathers. My bed sheets are not Egyptian cotton, and their thread count exfoliates my body while I sleep. I've become as frugal as Grandma, who used jelly jars as drinking glasses. Does any of this matter more than Michelle's sterling silver flute, private lessons, and the perfect prom dress, or Jude's top-of-the-line hockey equipment and the expense of travel baseball? I say no.

All right, I'd be thrilled to live in a *House Beautiful* home filled with Ethan Allen and Pottery Barn, cherry wood cabinets, granite counters, and a sunken bathtub. The fairy tale opens wide with all of us gathered around a blazing fireplace, you and me, and your kin and mine, like one, big, happy family.

Who am I kidding? I imagine Jude grousing that you aren't his father when you set limits after he gets caught running some ridiculous scam. The boy is cocky for twelve. He has to be with a felon for a father and an activist for a mother. Michelle would likely seethe with resentment. Given a choice, she would rather have me remain single forever. She wants to believe her father and I might reunite, and she'd likely blame you for swinging a wrecking ball into her dreams. She had been poking around in our past before our dinner date, asking me what you and I did for kicks when we dated. What she really wants to know is if I spread my legs for you. Don't worry. I didn't tell her you were my first, nor that her grandmother was certain your sole intention was to knock me up.

What would Mom say about us? A framed watercolor of strewn red roses that she painted for me hangs in my living room. After she had mastered the basic techniques, her work took a decisively expressive turn. She is amazing. She once told me she lives knowing every day is a day where unthinkable evil is possible, but "There are other possibilities, too. Life is good for the simple reason that it goes on." You know what? I think she'd be pleased.

I've wasted so much time thinking What if, What if, wishing for a normal life.

There is no such thing.

But there are always possibilities.

Midafternoon, I sent Jude and Michelle outside to shovel with a promise to take them to Video Palace to rent movies later. The ecstasy on your face when we were making love last night suddenly came to mind while I poured steaming water from the saucepan into the mugs for hot cocoa. I nearly scalded my hand. The imprint of your body lingers on mine.

How long will this distraction last? Will it turn into a malady I'll need to purge?

The door flew open, and Michelle hurried in. "Delivery," she said, handing me a paper-wrapped package set in a shallow box from Beacon Hill Flowers. Excitement infused my senses. I've never once had flowers delivered to me before. It's fitting that my first would be from you. As I unwrapped them, Michelle shed her boots, coat, hat, and gloves in a wet pile and then walked over in bare feet to investigate. Jude burst inside and lobbed his soggy mitten across the room at her head. She called him a butt wipe as she ducked, and the mitten splat on the wall. Both children carried the fresh scent of the outside, their cheeks pink, noses bright and shiny.

The yellow roses looked like a dozen pale-velvet suns bobbing from a fluted vase. I read the card aloud.

> Snow like sugar dust, snow like kisses,
> each burns as it melts on bare skin.
> Thank you for last night.
> Love always and always love, Joe.

Pleasure fluttered in my stomach. Jude gave the sentiment

a wise-ass smirk as he plopped mini-marshmallows into his hot cocoa. He quipped that the note "sounds like something written by a sissy." After he had shoved a handful of marsh-mallows into his mouth, he retreated to the basement to play Nintendo.

"Ugh. From the concrete dude," Michelle said with a crumpled brow. Her damp hair curled in baby-like ringlets around her forehead. She stared at the note as if to burn it to ash with her eyes. I tucked the card among the baby's breath and reminded her that the concrete dude has a name. She bit her bottom lip, perhaps thinking about what these flowers might signify, envisioning the turmoil of a wicked stepfamily. Sometimes I wish I could sweep her sky clear of clouds and wrap her in a cozy skein of pink chenille.

I squeezed her shoulder and said, "Relax, will you? Yellow roses signify friendship and freedom, not love." I didn't tell her that, in the context of love, the idea of friendship and freedom speaks deeply.

"Oh, by the way, Poppy called late last night," she said in her singsong troublemaker voice, breaking my momentary illusion of grand romance.

"How late?"

She shrugged. "Maybe two? I don't remember. He said he was checking up on us. I was watching a movie. Jude fell asleep in the basement and didn't come up until three."

Damn. They knew I was out later than I told them I'd be. Dad, too. I wished I could have hidden the slow burn of embarrassment that crept across my face. It's as if I have a curfew again. "Well, Joe and I had a lot to talk about. It's been a long time, you know."

She looked at me through tasseled lashes, not sure if she should believe me, but then her expression softened, shifting toward something like reluctant acceptance. Hopefully, she can understand that, if I move forward with my life, she can do the same. She abruptly turned her back to me, walked to the counter, and dropped marshmallows, one by one, into her mug of steaming cocoa. The silence felt scratchy and raw. What did she want to hear? I feared I'd say something that would only cause her to bristle out of the room, slam a door, hate me even more.

Head tipped, she pushed the bobbing white puffs down with a spoon. "So, when do we meet this concrete, um, this guy Joe?"

◂▴▸

Acknowledgments

I owe a big thank-you to the late Robert Bixby, my poetry editor, for convincing me I could write a novel, and I'm eternally grateful to MaryChris Bradley and Buddhapuss Ink for bringing *In the Context of Love* to fruition.

Many thanks to my mentors Michael C. White, Alan Davis, Lewis Robinson, and Elizabeth Searle, and to my fellow alumni and instructors in the Stonecoast MFA program.

Personal thanks to Chelsea Gilmore and Marcy Dermansky for their keen editing skills, Nancy Pervanje for being willing to read my drafts, Donna Drake-Fyler for early guidance, Mary Ann Wehler and Diana Muñoz Stewart for hand-holding, and Olga Klekner for teaching me how to curse in Hungarian.

Thank you to ML Liebler, John D. Lamb, and all the wonderful Detroit-area poets and writers for their hugs and support.

Lastly, many thanks to my entire family, my husband, and my children for being my anchor.

Linda K. Sienkiewicz is a published poet and fiction writer, cynical optimist, fan of corgis, tea drinker, and wine lover from Michigan. Her poetry, short stories, and art have been published in more than fifty literary journals, including *Prairie Schooner*, *Clackamas Literary Review*, *Spoon River*, and *Permafrost*. She received a poetry chapbook award from Bottom Dog Press, and an MFA from the University of Southern Maine. Linda lives with her husband in southeast Michigan, where they spoil their grandchildren and then send them back home.

In the Context of Love is her debut novel.

A Note from the Author

I hope you enjoyed reading my book. If you did, please feel free to tell a friend about it and post a few kind words on Amazon or Goodreads.

Writing is a solitary pursuit—not that I'm complaining—but knowing a reader liked *In the Context of Love* would mean the world to me.

Thank you,

Linda K. Sienkiewicz

To learn more, or to connect with the author, go to:

Website: lindaksienkiewicz.com
Facebook: linda.k.sienkiewicz
Twitter: LindaKSienkwicz

CPSIA information can be obtained at www.ICGtesting.com
Printed in the USA
LVOW07s1754130815

449953LV00001B/1/P